Linda Sealy Knowles

A Stranger's Love

ISBN: 978-1-0880-4869-6

Dedication

Yvonne Collins Kimbrell

A friend who enjoys the same things I like,
my secret-keeper, traveling companion, and
cousin. Who can ask more from a childhood friendship?
Thank you for your love and support.

Prologue

"Ned, please let me go. You're hurting me." Precious grabbed a clump of his hair. "Please, I need to go back inside before Pa wakes up to get water or go to the outhouse." She'd been as quiet as a mouse as she tiptoed outside and raced to the barn.

"Naw, he's dead to the world. His snoring could wake the dead," Ned huffed. "I could hear him while I was tossing rocks at your window." He kissed and sucked on her neck and lavished a wet tongue over her skin.

Precious was becoming more afraid of Ned's' actions. She should have dressed instead of just throwing on a thin robe over her nightgown. "Please, stop. Let me go back inside, and you come back tomorrow."

His breathing was getting harder. "You know you want me. I saw how you were looking at me in town. I can tell you want me just as much as I want you."

Before Precious could push him away, he swung her away from the barn post he'd pinned her against. Then he shoved her down on a pile of fresh hay, jerking her pantaloons down around her knees.

"Stop! I'm going to scream." Why wouldn't he stop this assault on her body? She didn't know much about him because they had only spoken twice while in the dry goods store.

"Go ahead and scream, and your pa will come out here and kill us both," he said as he continued to grope. With her knees bound together by her underwear, she couldn't kick him. He was holding her two hands over her head while she bucked, but her movements

1

only excited him more. Ned had his way with her, then fell forward covering her body with his. The guy was sweaty and breathing like a giant hog. Though Ned wasn't a big man, he felt like dead weight.

With an angry thrust, Precious shoved him off her petite body. She was hurting and felt so dirty. "Get away from me, Ned. Don't ever come back out here, or I will hurt you."

He winced and held the side of his head. "You don't want to hurt me, baby. You were wonderful, and I'll come tomorrow night. I understand a girl's first time hurts, but I won't hurt you again." Ned stood grinning like a cat who had swallowed a bird.

"I don't want you to come back, and you'll never have your way again. Get away from me before I take a pitchfork to you."

"All right, I'm going." He smiled. "You'd better put on a fresh nightgown. That one is all bloody." Peeking out the barn door, Ned went off into the dark, whistling as if he'd just conquered the world.

A couple of months later, Precious couldn't keep any food down. Whenever she cooked, she had to rush into the bedroom and empty her stomach into the chamber pot. While she placed a soft cool cloth on her face, Pa entered the room and grabbed a handful of her red curls.

"Have you laid down with a dirty dog, gal? You got a child under that apron?" Pa tightened his fists. "Who's responsible for your condition?"

Before Precious could answer, her tall, hawked-face father slapped her across the face. He removed his wide black belt and beat her until she thought this was her time to meet her Heavenly Father.

"Stop, you fool. You're going to kill her." Mama stood between her and the meanest man in the world. "Precious is my baby."

"She's a whore. A jezebel just like you." He placed his belt back in his pants and turned to leave the room. "Put her in the cellar until I find out who is the brat's pa."

Chapter 1

The lovely young woman peered up at the miraculous sun. The blue sky appeared as clear as pure water. Shading her eyes with her palm, she twisted her face to peer at her surroundings. With sharp pebbles embedded into her neck and back, nothing looked familiar, not even the tall trees with dark brown and gold leaves surrounding the area. A broken covered wagon lay over on its side with two long-eared, brown and black mules hitched to the front. A loud braying came from one of the animals, which caused the girl to jump, followed by pain exploding into her head.

Closing her eyes for a minute, she attempted to sit up and get her bearings. Everything was slightly hazy in her sight and mind, but something told her she needed to get up. She rocked her cumbersome body side to side to roll up into a sitting position with more determination than she felt because she ached all over.

Glancing down, she saw that her wrists were bleeding and raw. How in the world did I get hurt? Using the hem of her dress, she wiped the blood off her arms and wrists. She crawled over to the wagon's broken wheel and pulled herself to a standing position. A glance down showed her clothes were dirty, and several buttons were missing. The world was spinning around, so she held tight to the broken wheel until she could focus.

Once the dizziness was gone, she used the side of her long green skirt and patted her wrists again. Something on the ground caught her attention. A woman and a man were sprawled on the ground. They both appeared lifeless. Who were these people, and what on earth had happened here? She crept along the wagon with a death grip on the edge, and finally kneeled and touched the woman.

The woman had seen many years, and her body was cold to the touch. She was wearing a long black dress with a heavy white apron. A black headpiece covered part of her hair that was in a tight bun. The man lying beside the woman looked like he was asleep. He appeared thin and old. He was wearing a long black coat and pants. Lying near his body was a black wide-brimmed hat. His forehead showed a deep gash, and dried blood covered his dead body. She gently turned him to his side. A bullet hole appeared in his back.

The two mules tried to pull the wagon forward, causing her to stagger, but she managed to stand upright. She lifted her dark green dress and saw that she wasn't just dusty but caked with mud. She must have been rolling around on the sandy trail.

Easing herself to the front of the wagon, she tugged on the hinges and straps that held the animals hitched to the wagon. Once the animals were free, she used part of a strap and slapped the rump of one mule, making it walk a few steps away, pulling the other along. At least they could roam freely. As she gazed down again at the dead couple, she wondered why they had spared her.

She continued to lean on the broken wheel, bent forward, and rested her head on her arms. A piece of jewelry dangled from her neck, and she fingered it for comfort. A ring. Shaking her head to clear her mind, she tried to remember where she was and what had happened. An unfortunate accident had taken place here. Where was she going and who were these poor souls whom she was traveling with?

She lumbered to the back of the wagon with heavy footsteps to see if she could find something to cover the two bodies. There was no way she could bury them by herself. After finding the wagon empty except for a box of women items and new baby nappies and blankets, she squinted down the trail. Had a baby been here, too? She needed to search for help and get somebody to come bury them.

With blurred vision and a queasy stomach, she stumbled her first few steps, but slowly trekked down the man-made road. Hopefully, she could find a farmhouse with friendly people who would take care of the old couple.

After thirty minutes of shuffling along, she found a log beside the road and eased down to rest. Leaning forward, she placed her arms on her knees and prayed. "Lord, I have no idea where I am." The wind began to blow, and sand twirled, spraying her body. She covered her face for protection. An ominous sky had replaced the blue one. "Please help me find people or shelter soon."

While she was staring up at the dark clouds, she heard an animal. "Lord, please let the sound be a dog and not a wolf." Surveying her wrinkled, soiled clothes, a glimmer of hope rushed over her. Dogs usually meant people. Muttering, she hurried as fast as her full-figured body would allow toward the animal's sound. Pushing brush and tall weeds away, the sight before her was breathtaking. There, like in a fairy tale, stood a quaint log cabin. A dog that looked like a small bear was barking and pacing back and forth on the porch before he jumped down and raced toward her, growling. The warning sounds of the animal didn't bring anyone out of the house or barn.

"Hello?" the girl called. "Is anyone home?" The dog didn't act like he would harm her, but she prayed there would be a friendly family that could offer her help.

With no answer, she bent forward and motioned the dog to come to her. Suddenly, the furry hound placed big paws on her large belly while wagging a bushy tail. She patted the dog's head, but he only wanted to lick her hand and rub his fur against her stomach.

She thanked the good Lord for His favor when she spotted the outhouse. The big dog trailed her every step and stood guard. When she came out, he jumped around in circles and barked. He wasn't a good guard dog, but he was friendly.

A stiff breeze blew several large drops of cold rain into her face. Again, the girl patted the dog's head and waddled to the front of the cabin. Stepping up on the porch, "Anyone home?" she called as she wiped the raindrops off her face and arms. The dog continued to bark.

She knocked, but no one answered. Easing over to the window, she peeked through it, but there was no movement inside. The doorknob turned easily. The dog rushed in and roamed from one room to the next, looking for someone.

"Hey, fellow. Where's your master?"

The dog barked and put his nose down in a big pan on the floor. He pushed it until it turned upside down. The young girl was sure that the animal hadn't missed many meals, but it must be his dinner time.

With her body still weak and shaken, she sat down in a straight-backed cane chair. Glancing around at the interior of the cabin, she was surprised to find it clean and tidy. Curtains hung on the glass windows, a scarf spread over the mantel, and a checkered oilcloth covered the table. Indeed, a woman lived here, she thought. Before standing, she noticed a shelf beside the fireplace filled with big brown books. She eased over to the rack and removed one. It was an important-looking book with big words that she didn't recognize. Putting the book back in its place, she heard the dog whine.

He was hungry. She glanced around the kitchen area for something to eat. She found a few cans of beans, jars of jams, flour, and sugar. She should cook something if someone didn't come home soon. She pulled back a heavy curtain that led into another room. An open window blew the curtain apart allowing in the fresh air over the four-poster bed that stood in the center of the room. She shut out the rain and latched the window.

Someone lived here for sure, thought the wide-eyed girl. A piece of large glass hung on the wall. She saw her reflection and couldn't believe how awful she looked. Her eyes were hollow with black circles, and her hair was a mass of wild, red curls that spiraled in every direction. Her scalp felt like a bucket of sand had been poured on her head.

She backed up from the looking glass and bumped into the bed. It looked so inviting. Her back hurt something awful. It might help to lie down. She slipped off her shoes, sat down on the side, and lay on her back for just a minute. The bed felt heavenly. She would only rest for a minute and then go back with an old quilt or covering for the two dead bodies. With a sigh, she closed her eyes and slipped off into dreamland.

A big hairy man was in bed with her when she woke up. "Get away from me," she screamed and shoved at the man who smelled like a wet dog.

A tongue lapped her across the mouth and woke her up. She opened her eyes and gasped. Standing in the center of the bed was the dog that had met her when she arrived. "Mercy, dog, you gave me a fright."

The dog leaped down and raced into the kitchen. Hearing a metal pan being tossed across the floor, she walked into the kitchen.

"All right. I'm hungry too." Glancing out the window, it was as black as midnight and still raining. "I must have slept for hours, big boy." She opened the door, and the dog rushed outside. He barked, and before she could close the door, he hurried back inside.

"Give me a minute to go to the outhouse and I'll feed you," she said as she grabbed an old quilt to protect herself from the rain. The dog turned his head as if understanding her. After reentering the kitchen, she was thrilled to find a hand pump in the sink. Finding a bucket of water near the sink, she primed the pump, then filled a large pan and washed her face and hands.

"All right, let me see what I can find for you to eat." She searched the cabinet and found several cans of beans, so she opened one and fed it to the animal.

Realizing it was too dark outside for her to try to go back to the wagon and care for the old couple, she lifted the lid on the stove top, placed several small wooden sticks under it, and put a match to them. Finding a small pot, she opened another can of beans and warmed it for herself. She had no idea how long it had been since she'd eaten last.

She felt so much better with a full stomach, but she was so dirty. Her clothes were filthy, and she needed to wash her hair and get some of the dirt and sand out of it. Filling a large bucket with water, she placed it on the stove. While the water was heating, she went over to the cold fireplace and noticed that someone had laid a fire. She lit a small piece of kindling wood and put it on the logs. The fire blazed up quickly.

She took the pins out of her curls and dipped her head in the wonderfully warm water. With broken fingernails she scrubbed her scalp, frowning at the pain she felt in her head. She rubbed her hand over the back of her skull and felt a large bump. Once her hair was clean, she used a rough towel hanging by the sink and wrapped her mass of red curls. With another small cloth, she washed her face, neck, and raw wrists. "Oh, dog, I feel so much better."

The animal rubbed against her belly. "You are so sweet." She petted his head and walked into the bedroom. A big chest had four drawers. Opening one, she found several large shirts—all plaid, but she didn't care. She removed her dirty dress and shift and put on one of the shirts, which hung down past her knees. The man who wore these shirts must be tall. She rolled up the sleeves.

She must be a sight with her pantaloons peeking out beneath the shirt. Carrying her dress and shift to the kitchen sink, she gave them both a proper washing. She eased open the front door, and feeling safe, hung her things over the porch railing. The rain had stopped so maybe her things would dry. Hopefully, she would have clean clothes to put on in the morning.

A loud bark came from the porch. The dog had run outside. She let him in and laughed. "I'll have to remember when I open this door that you'll run outside."

Yawning, she noticed the lock on the front door was flimsy, so she placed a chair under the doorknob. Feeling more secure, she walked back into the bedroom and climbed into the bed. She fluffed the pillows and pulled the quilt over her body. The dog barked and jumped upon the bed with her. Smiling, she patted the mattress and he lay down. His presence gave her great comfort in this isolated cabin.

Chapter 2

Jack Mills was chilled to the bone, wet and exhausted from riding for miles back to his home in the hills of Gibson, Texas. He'd been in the saddle for two weeks, helping the local sheriff chase two bad men who had held up the stagecoach, shot the guard, and robbed the passengers. After placing them in jail, Jack turned and headed home.

The other men went into The Long Branch Saloon to celebrate, but Jack was sick and tired of bad men and loudmouthed posse members. All he wanted was to return home, take a dip in the cold stream that ran behind his cabin, and climb in his big, soft bed.

By the starlight near his cabin, an overturned wagon appeared on the trail. He searched around the area for survivors and saw two people lying near each other. Even before he got close to them, he knew they were dead. Poor souls, he thought. Looking in the wagon for something to cover their bodies, he didn't find a thing. Jack walked to his horse, took off his bedroll, and covered the wet, dead bodies. He would come back in the morning and bury them properly.

A strange feeling overcame his tired body as he neared his cabin. Bear, his big dog, wasn't on the front porch, and strange items were covering the porch's rail. He noticed that a dress was spread out to dry.

He felt for his gun that hung around his hips as he tried to open the front door. He pushed but someone had placed something under the doorknob. A chair. One of his kitchen chairs. He shoved again and heard growling. "Bear, it's me." The big dog began barking and jumping as his master pushed harder on the door.

***

The girl was suddenly awake. She hurried to the kitchen, peeked out the window, and watched the dog's reaction. He must know the stranger. She had started to remove the chair just as a giant of a man shoved it away. She jumped back and hurried around the kitchen table to put space between herself and the stranger. "Who are you?" the girl demanded. Her bottom lip was quivering.

***

"Who the heck are you? This is my cabin." Large veins popped out the big man's neck. He glanced across the room and noticed that the fire had gone out in the fireplace.

When she tried to run toward the door, the man grabbed her arms.

"I need to go to the outhouse now, or I'm going to make a mess in the middle of your floor."

The giant quickly turned her arm loose and watched as his plaid shirt waddled out the front door with Bear trailing her every step.

Slowly, the girl and Bear made it back to the porch. He watched from the window as she felt her clothing on the railing. Of course, everything was still wet.

"Look, lady," Jack said, stepping in the doorway. "Bring those things inside, and I will build a fire in the fireplace. You can hang your clothes on a couple of chairs in front of it and the things should be dry by morning."

***

The girl suddenly stepped back and peered up into the giant's face. He wore a short beard, dirty brown hair, and had the deepest green eyes she'd seen on a man. He was in need of a bath, too.

He walked back into the cabin and began building a fire. After gathering her clothes, she walked over to the table to carry a chair to place in front of the fireplace as he suggested. He stood and took the chair while she went for another one. She spread the pieces of clothes over the chairs and stepped away from him.

"Look, Lady, my name is Jack Mills," he said, holding up his hand. "What is your name? I can't keep calling you Lady."

She looked to the floor, wringing her hands together. "I don't know my name. I can't seem to remember anything. I woke up on the ground, back on the road, with a bloody knot on the back of my head."

"Were you in that accident back on the road? I saw the wagon and two dead bodies lying on the ground."

"Yes, I woke up and found them dead. I couldn't bury the couple by myself, and there wasn't anything in the wagon to cover them. I had hoped to find someone to help me."

"Let me see the back of your head. It might need medical attention." Touching her shoulder, Jack turned the girl around as she lowered her head and pointed to the area where she was hurt.

"Yep, you sure got an ugly cut. Sit down and I'll put something on it." Jack pushed her into another straight chair.

***

He walked into the bedroom and opened a drawer in the chest and collected a few medical items that he needed. The covers on his big bed were all tumbled. "Great," he mumbled. All he wanted was to come home and climb into that comfortable bed. He ambled into the main room.

"I hope you don't mind, but I used your dry sink and a bucket of water to wash my hair. My hair was covered with dirt and filled with sand and small rocks. I washed the blood out of my hair, but I can still feel a sticky scalp." The girl lowered her head. She was nearly asleep.

"Lift your head so I can part your hair. I have a salve that will stop the bleeding and help it to heal. I'm going to wrap this rag over your hair to keep blood from getting on everything."

"Thank you. I'm so sorry to be using your home without your permission, but no one was here. I will leave when it's daylight."

"If you don't remember anything, how do you know where to go?" He hoped to trick her into telling him the truth about herself.

"I don't know. I need to go back and take care of those poor pitiful souls. Don't know their names. I woke up on the ground and saw the wagon was turned over on its side with two mules hitched to it. I was able to free the animals, but I just started walking, hoping to find someone."

"I will take you to the wagon in the morning. It's very late. My bedroll is covering the bodies for now, but I'll take care of their graves in the morning. Look, I am exhausted. I'll make a pallet in front of the fireplace. You can have my bed since you were already sleeping in it." Jack walked outside and led his horse to the barn. He unsaddled the tired animal, rubbed him down, and fed him a bucket of oats and fresh water. Giving him a pat on the rump, he said goodnight to his faithful steed.

Entering the house, he walked softly over to the curtain that closed off his bedroom from the kitchen and peeked into the room. The girl was snoring softly with Bear lying at her feet. The dog raised his head and flapped his large, bushy tail.

"Traitor," mumbled Jack to the dog.

Once comfortable on the floor, after putting plenty of logs in the fireplace, Jack fell immediately asleep. A scream made him bolt up. He shook his head. Was he dreaming? Maybe, he thought and started to lie back down. Bear came in and barked just as another scream came from the bedroom. Bear's teeth grabbed the blanket and pulled it off of Jack, then the dog raced back to the bedroom.

Jack hurried to the side of his bed and watched the intruder roll from side to side, moaning with tears covering her face. "Lady, wake up. What's wrong?" Jack touched her arm.

"Help me, please. Something is wrong with my stomach. I only ate some beans, but I feel like something is rolling around in my belly." The girl held her stomach and pulled up her knees. "Please." She reached out to Jack. "Help me. I need a doctor."

"I will have to leave you for about an hour while I get the doctor. Bear will stay here with you." Jack didn't wait to hear her answer as he pulled on his boots and grabbed his hat and jacket. He rushed to the barn, saddled his horse, and rode down the trail to town. "Thank goodness the doctor lives on this side of town," he said to his horse.

***

The girl got out of the bed and started pacing the room. If she didn't know better, she would think she was with child. She had never been with a man. It had to be those beans that she ate earlier. It had to be a couple of days without food or water that has made her so sick.

Another sharp pain hit her in the back that nearly made her fall to the floor. She slid down beside the bed and stretched her legs out in front. The cool floor felt soothing to her body. "Oh, Lord, please help me. Help the man bring the doctor," she said, as she bit her bottom lip until it bled.

Bear trotted to the front door and back to the girl. He knew something was wrong. Finally, he settled down beside the bed and laid his head on her knees. The girl rubbed his head and felt comforted by his presence. She laid her head back against the bed frame and closed her eyes. Then she woke up when she felt herself being lifted off the floor by the man called Jack.

"Up you go, little Lady. The doctor is here, so let's get you back on the bed." Jack appeared thrilled to see that she was still alive. "Lady, this is Doc Hays. He is here to take care of you. Don't be afraid." Jack laid her on the bed and left the room.

***

Doc Hays smiled down at the girl and laid his hand on her belly. Suddenly, her belly moved. "Miss, are you with child?" When no answer came, he asked, "How far along do you think you are?"

The girl only stared at the man. "I am not married," she whispered. "I have never been with a man."

"Mercy," the doctor said, as he laid his stethoscope on her swollen belly. "I hear a strong heartbeat." Then he moved the instrument up to her lungs and heart. "You appear to be in good health," he said with a grin. "Miss, you are going to have a baby. You're in labor now, and it shouldn't be long before you meet your new daughter or son. I'm here to help you." He watched the girl turn as white as death. She had no idea that she was in the family way.

"I'll be right back. I need to get a few things prepared for the birthing. You just lie still and try to rest between pains." The doctor smiled sweetly and patted her belly.

"How is she, Doc?" Jack asked, like an anxious husband.

"Well, Jack. She isn't about to die like you said when you came after me. You said she was fat, and she had great belly pains." He smiled at Jack. "She is not fat, son. She's going to have a child in a few hours."

"Child? She's going to have a baby?" His legs became weak. Jack sat down in a straight chair at the table.

"Yes, sir, and she told me that she wasn't married and has never been with a man. It must be a miracle child." The doctor couldn't hold back a chuckle.

"This is not funny, Doc. When I found her here tonight, she told me she had lost her memory. She doesn't even know her name." Jack rubbed his face. "It's possible a lot of things happened to her that she doesn't remember before she came here. She woke up lying in the road with the wagon turned over with mules still hooked up to it. The two people she was traveling with are lying near the wagon dead. She doesn't even remember them. No one else was around, so she walked until she came to my cabin."

"I checked her heart and lungs, and she seems to be strong and in good health. The baby is moving around, which is a good sign that it's healthy, too." A scream broke the two men apart as the doctor rushed back into the bedroom.

Jack stomach growled, so he went out to the smokehouse and pulled down a slab of bacon. He sliced part of it and carried it over to a table. Then he headed into the chicken yard and gathered a couple dozen eggs. After tossing feed, he watched the rooster strut his long legs and flap his wings at some of the hens. Jack took the eggs over to the pump and washed them clean. Gathering up the meat, he went back into the cabin to cook a hearty breakfast for himself and the doctor. The bread was moldy since he'd been gone for a couple of weeks, but he would cook plenty. He filled the coffeepot with water and grounds and placed it on the stove to boil.

"Something sure smells good," the doctor said. "We're going to need some rags and plenty of old quilts to cover your bed. Child birthing is a messy business, and without another woman here to help, we've got to gather things ourselves. Do you have some oilcloth or several old horse blankets?"

"I have an old oilcloth that I used on the table when I first got here. Will that help?"

"Yes, and the horse blankets will pad the bed. We'll put the oil cloth over the blankets. Take one of your sheets and cut it up into squares to fit the baby. A soft blanket needs to be cut into large squares to wrap around the child."

The bacon sizzled and the coffee perked. Jack shook his head and cracked a dozen eggs to scramble. "I'll have to go into town and buy a new supply of bed linens when this event is over." He rolled his eyes at the doctor, and they both smiled.

Jack checked on the girl after the kitchen was cleaned. She seemed to be resting. The doc was sitting beside her while Bear lay at his feet. Jack approached the bedside and spoke softly. "I think I will ride to her wagon and care for those two people. I'll search around the area and hopefully find some of her things. She only had the clothes on her back when she arrived here last night."

"Good idea, son. Maybe she had some things prepared for her

baby." The doc watched as the girl began to move side to side again.

"I'll go now. Be back soon," Jack said as he hurried out the door. Bear raced out beside him and barked.

"All right, you can go with me. You need to get out of the cabin. Maybe you'll catch yourself a rabbit."

Arriving at the damaged wagon, Jack saw a busted wheel on the back. One of the mules was grazing off the road's side while the other one stood watching Bear's every move. Jack opened a box that contained a stack of nappies and a few flannel baby blankets. Another carpet bag had a few personal items for a woman—a hairbrush, comb, a pile of white strips, several pair of pantaloons, two white shifts and one old gown. He pulled the carpet bag out of the wagon and set it on the ground. There were some cooking items—a coffeepot, skillet, spoons and forks, several tin plates and cups. Jack stacked that box on top of the other one. Walking to the wagon's front, he found a box that held a shaving mug and razor. A nasty comb and several stained towels were in the bottom. He didn't bother retrieving those things.

He took a rope off his horse and caught one mule and then the other one. They looked to be in good condition, so the girl could sell them for some money.

After digging a deep grave, he buried the couple together. Later, he would make a cross and return and place it on the grave. He tied the items from the wagon across one of the mule's back.

Once he arrived back at his cabin, the girl was in full labor, as the doc called it. He could hear the doctor's voice over the girl's screams.

"Push, girl, push. I can see the crown!" Doc's voice was firm and demanding to his patient.

"I'm dying," the woman screamed. "You're splitting me in two!"

Jack felt his knees go weak. He slid down into a chair. After another blood-curdling scream, he placed his elbows on his knees, held his face in his large palms, and prayed. "Lord Almighty, please help this beautiful, young girl."

Silence from the bedroom. Oh, my goodness. She has died, he thought.

The doctor peeked through the curtain dividing the two rooms and his eyes widened. "You're as white as a sheet and look like a herd of cattle has run over you." The doctor smiled as Jack looked up at him. "You would think by the way you look that you're the proud papa of that beautiful baby girl." Doc loved to tease.

Jack leaped out of the chair. "Is she all right? I couldn't help but hear all the screaming, but I never heard the baby cry."

"Both are just fine, but I need your help. Warm a little water and test it with your elbow to make sure it isn't too hot. When it's ready, bring it in and bathe the baby. I still have some work to do on the new mama."

"Me? Wash a baby?" Jack glanced toward the door, hoping he could run.

"Do you see anyone else? I need your help, so do as I say. Now." The doctor disappeared behind the curtain.

Jack placed the water on the stove and scrubbed his hands with the lye soap. He poured the water in a shallow pan, warming it to the touch. He'd been at his friend's house when his wife had a baby. Remembered cleanliness was the important thing when handling a baby or helping with the mother.

He carried the water into the bedroom, and Doc passed him the baby girl. She was no bigger than his palm. The little thing stretched her arms over her head and pulled her short legs into her body. Jack held the baby over the pan and splashed warm water over her tiny, pink stomach. The belly button was already taped down. He lowered her closer to the water and took a palmful and rubbed it over her lovely red curls.

This was the most beautiful baby he had ever seen. Heck fire, he thought, I've never been this close to a newborn. After he was sure she was clean, he dried her well and attempted to put a nappy on her bottom. He wrapped a soft cloth around the back and pulled it up between her legs and pinned it. Not bad for his first try. Taking a soft piece of quilt, he used it as a baby blanket. Jack pulled her tiny body up in his arms and swayed her back and forth. He remembered the items he had brought from the wagon, but they would have to be cleaned.

The infant tried to suck her fists. "She's hungry, Doc. How do we feed her?"

"It will be a while before the mama's milk comes in, but we can make a sugar tit for her to suck on. She will soon go back to sleep."

Rocking back and forth in front of the fireplace while the baby sucked on the homemade sugar tit, Jack wondered if others felt the same way he was feeling now. Looking down at the tiny blue veins in the baby's eyelids and touching the fragile, clear fingernails gave him a flutter in his chest that he'd never felt before. For the first time since he'd become a man, he felt determined to have a child of his own. Jack laughed and whispered to the beautiful baby, "I believe I have just fallen in love." He lifted the child close to his lips and kissed the top of her head.

Doc Hays walked into the room and smiled big. "You are holding one of God's miracles. Every time I deliver a child, I am amazed. The pain is almost unbearable for the mother, screams and tears a plenty, but once that little one slips out into my hands, the pain is gone, and all the little woman wants to know is if her child has all its fingers and toes."

A log crashed down onto the fireplace floor breaking the sweet mood between Doc Hays and Jack. "As I sat out here, I thanked God for making me a man." He smiled and held the baby up for the doctor to give her an examination.

The little one clenched her fist and cried like a mad kitten. "She doesn't like this stethoscope. I should have warmed it before touching her chest with it." After the doctor checked her tiny body from one end to the other, he found that she was perfect, which Jack already knew. The doctor put a clean nappy on the baby's bottom and passed her back to Jack's big warm arms.

"I'll make another sugar tit while you make a bed so she can be close to her mother. That little lady cannot get out of bed for two weeks. Some women are up and around in a week, but you'll have to watch her. She is going to bleed, and it will make her weak and lightheaded. Do you have anything that can be used as a bedpan?"

"Do you think we can get some woman or girl to come here and help me care for her? Some things are very personal, and she is not going to want me to help her."

"Let me think on it. You'll have to pay for the woman."

"I can pay," Jack replied.

Chapter 3

While the mother slept, Jack cleaned out a dresser drawer and padded it with an old quilt to make it comfortable. He set up two of the kitchen chairs and laid the drawer across the top. Jack was proud of himself, and the doctor thought it was just perfect.

"Now, this little gal won't have to get up to care for her baby," he said as the little mother stirred. "She's waking up. I had hoped she would sleep longer because her body will still be hurting. I will leave laudanum for her to take for pain. One teaspoon only once a day and not anymore. She will be nursing in a day or two. I have some herbs that you can put in hot tea that will help with pain, too. Do you have tea?"

"No, but I'll pick some up from town. I hope you can find a woman to help me."

"I am going to check her over once more before I leave. I'll stop at Sadie Parker's cabin and ask if her daughter can come and lend you a hand. That young'un of hers has been doing chores and nursing since she could walk."

***

From the barn, Jack heard singing coming up the trail. He stood and eased over to the wide door and watched a young, barefoot gal leaping and twisting around as she sang "She'll Be Coming around the Mountain."

As she neared the clearing, she stopped in her tracks and observed the area. "This place is as clean as the churchyard. Where are the chickens and the pigs?"

"Hello, young lady," Jack called to her. "Where in the blazes did you come from, especially this time of the evening? It'll be dark soon."

"Are you Mr. Mills?" The young girl asked, still gazing at her surroundings.

"That's me. Who are you?" Jack couldn't help but notice how dirty and poorly dressed the child was.

"Doc told my ma that you need help, and you're willing to pay. Well, here I am, and my ma shore could use some money."

"So, your mother sent you to work for me, but she will take your wages?"

"I reckon. Ma didn't say I would keep any of it."

"How old are you?" Jack noticed that the child had a lovely face and pretty blonde hair, but, Lord, she was dirty.

"Shoot, I think I'm old enough to care for your woman. Doc said she had a wee one, and I have taken care of newborn babes before. I even helped Ma bring my two brothers into this world."

"Your mother didn't have a doctor help deliver her babies?"

"A strange man?" The girl placed her hands over her mouth. "My ma would never let a stranger peek under her skirt, much less see her naked down there."

"Well, I guess you're old enough." Jack felt his face turn red. "Let me get the milk from the barn, and I'll take you inside to meet the miss. Oh, before we go inside, you need to know that this girl is not my wife. She wandered up to my cabin, and she can't remember anything about herself. Even her name."

"Mercy." The girl looked at Jack in wonder. "So, what are you calling her?"

"Nothing right now. We might have to name the lady when she names her baby." Jack knew he couldn't keep calling the stranger, Lady. Once Jack retrieved the bucket of milk, he motioned for the young girl to follow him inside. He placed the liquid on the counter and peered down at the dirty little girl. "Now, miss, what's your name?"

"Sally," she said, her eyes glancing around at Jack's beautiful things. "Golly, you live in a mansion."

"Listen, Sally, I want you to feel at home here. I need your help with caring for the lady and her baby, but the first thing you have to do is get clean. You must be clean when you handle the baby and when you care for the mother. So, here's a nice cloth, water, and soap. Please wash your face, hands, and the upper part of your arms.

Did you bring over anything to sleep in or change into tomorrow?"

The girl hung her chin down to her chest and shook her head. She looked like she had the desire to crawl in a hole. "I didn't have nothing to bring. This is everything I own. Do you still want me to stay?"

"Mercy, child. I need you. Tomorrow, I have to ride into town to get supplies to care for the mother and child. I will add a few more things to the list. Wash good, and I will take you in to see them. I'll cook some supper while you are attending to their needs."

"I can cook, too, if you ever need me to, "Sally said, appearing pleased that he wasn't going to send her home.

"I believe you and I are going to get along just fine. There will be times that I will be away for a day or two, and you being able to cook will be a great help." He watched Sally wash and dry her face and arms. "Come now, let me show you the most beautiful baby in the world," Jack said as he took her elbow and led her through the curtain into the bedroom.

Lady was awake, patting her baby on the back as she made a soft crying sound. "Miss, I hired this young lady, Sally, to help with the baby and your personal needs. She has had a lot of experience taking care of her mother and her brothers."

"Hello, Sally," said the lady as the young girl hung her head down. She reached out to the girl, pulled her close, and swiped her hair away from her face. "My, what a lovely young child you are. I am so happy to have you help me."

"Thank you, ma'am. I'm awful pleased to be here. What can I do for you now? Do you need to pee or anything? I can hold the bedpan for you."

"Yes, Sally. You can help me with a few things, but first, let's shoo Mr. Jack out of the room." Lady laughed at his expression before he hurried out of the room.

Jack stood on the other side of the curtain and listened to the two strangers get to know each other. Sally seemed to know just what to do to make the lady comfortable and settle the baby into her makeshift bed.

After Jack cooked supper and Sally washed the dishes, he filled a tub with warm water for Sally to have a complete bath. He gave her the top of a pair of long johns for her to wear to bed. After bathing, she washed her personal things and her rag of a dress to dry overnight.

Sally helped the lady change into a clean shift for bed. She pointed at the milk stains on the shift. "Lady, your milk is trying to come down, and in a day or sooner, you may be able to feed the baby."

Jack stepped in the bedroom to say goodnight. "Miss, we need to give you a name. What would you like for me and Sally to call you?"

"Hmm. I got it. We must have faith that I will get my memory back, so how about calling me Faith." She smiled, yawned big, and closed her eyes.

"Faith. I like that. How about you, Mr. Jack?" Sally said.

"Yes, I like it very much," Jack answered. "She's right, you know. We must pray that she will get her memory back so she can return to her family." Jack couldn't take his eyes off the beautiful woman with her massive curls spread over the white pillow. Her face was pale, but she had small rosebud lips that looked so irresistible. With Sally standing next to him, he had to control his emotions and not touch the sleeping woman.

"I will start praying tonight." Sally patted the sleeping baby.

"Why don't you climb into this bed with Faith tonight? It's big enough that she won't even know you're in it. I will sleep in front of the fireplace. If Faith or the baby needs anything, you will hear them."

"Land's sake. I ain't never slept in anything so fine," Sally said. "Let me make a trip to the outhouse and I'll be ready for bed." As Sally started to the door, she turned to Jack. "Now, you don't worry about those two in this room. I'll take good care of them both."

Jack watched the young child rush out of the room. He smiled and had to remember to thank Doc for sending her to him.

Chapter 4

Jack removed all the items he had discovered at the girl's wagon and placed them on the porch. When the girl was better, she could decide what she wanted to keep. He raced back into the house to check on the girls and baby before leaving for town to purchase the needed supplies.

Jack drove into town and gave his list to the clerk in the dry goods store. Gibson was a small town, but Mr. and Mrs. Mason, the store owners, sold an adequate supply of items needed by men, women, and children. He allowed most of his customers to run a tab, which was never paid by many. Mr. Mason was a good Christian man who would help anyone down on their luck.

"Jack, what's this I hear from Doc that you got a gal at your place and her with a baby to boot?" Mrs. Mason came from around the counter and stood close to Jack, her eyebrows drawn together.

"Well, Mrs. Mason, I'm afraid you heard right. But, now I have two gals at my place. Sally, a young hill gal, is staying with me, too. She's a mighty fine nurse."

"Goodness, how can I help? Should I come and get the girl and bring her into town?"

"I would like that, but Doc says she can't be moved for two weeks. Did he tell you that she has lost her memory?"

"No, he didn't mention that." Mrs. Mason shook her head and looked puzzled.

"We're calling her Faith, but that's not her name." Jack was glancing around at the items for women as he talked. "I need your help in selecting a few things for the girl—I mean, Faith—to wear. Some underthings, you know. And a couple of dresses about this tall and this wide. She is not very big—now, I don't think. Do you have a robe she could wear when she gets out of the bed?"

"Let me look back here." Mrs. Mason walked through a curtain to their storeroom.

Jack continued to look around but stopped when he came to the children's things. He saw several plain dresses, shifts, and cotton nightgowns in different colors.

Mrs. Mason returned and held out a dark green robe that looked like something a royal princess might wear. It was green velvet with gold braided trim. "This is all I have, but it is warm and pretty. Any woman would love to have this garment, but it's too expensive for my customers."

"I'll take it and some of these dresses for my little hill girl, Sally Parker," he said. "Do you know Sally?" Surprised, Mrs. Mason said she did.

"Sally has come in for her mother, so I can fit her very well." Mrs. Mason replaced the dresses that Jack had chosen and selected several others in a larger size. She picked personal underthings and four cotton gowns. "Sally will think she has died and gone to heaven when you give her these things. Bless that child. She needs them."

"She's smart and a good worker. Sally pitched in and helped Faith and the baby like she'd been doing it every day. She says she can cook, too. Though she told me that she has to give her mother the money I pay her, so I want to give her some things she needs besides just money."

"You are a good man, Jack. You may never get rid of that little gal." She laughed and wrapped his items. "Do you have everything you need for the baby?" Mrs. Mason glanced over her shoulder at Jack.

"Gosh, I almost forgot about that. I'm sure I need some things. Can you pick out some little clothes, blankets, bottles, nipples, and some oil to go over her belly button? Sally did mention that. Oh, and white muslin cloth to make nappies."

"You sure know about babies. Do you have younger brothers and sisters?"

"Yep, I was the oldest, and sometimes I helped my mother shop," Jack said, grinning.

"What about different size nappy pins?" Mrs. Mason asked as she pulled out a box containing different sizes.

"Whatever you think I need, please give it to me. I have plenty of cash today, so don't worry about cost. Just give me anything we may need for the child or her mother." Mrs. Mason smiled and fulfilled his order with pleasure.

As he headed home, Jack was pleased with his purchases. Most of the items would help make everyday living a lot easier, he thought. When Jack drove into the yard near the front door, he knew something was wrong. Bear didn't come out to greet him. Jack jumped down from the wagon and raced into the cabin. He could hear the two girls talking, and the baby was screaming.

He stood at the closed curtain to the bedroom before he asked, "Can I come in?"

Sally glanced at Faith, and she said, "Yes, sir."

Jack looked at the girls and then down at the screaming baby. "What's wrong?" He scooped up the tiny baby into his arms. "She's wet," he said flatly.

"I'm sorry you had to come home to a screaming baby, but I have been taking care of Faith. She has a fever."

"Fever?" Fear raced through Jack. "Should I go get the doctor?"

Sally pulled him into the kitchen and whispered that her milk was trying to come in, but she had a fever in her breasts. "This is normal. Ma got it every time. I have been putting cold water on her, but we need ice to bring the fever down quicker."

"I have ice in the cellar. Here, take the baby and I will chip a pan full. Will that be enough for now?"

"Yes, praise the Lord. We will put it in some cloth and lay it over her chest." Sally hurried back into the bedroom as Jack scurried down into the cellar.

***

Sally changed the baby into a dry nappy. She held the baby while Faith tried not to cry from the pain. "How will I be able to feed my baby?"

"Now, don't worry. Once the fever is down, you'll be back to your old self. Besides, we have cow's milk, and I can boil some water and make it weak. I'll squeeze some into the babe's mouth. Ma and I have done all kinds of ways to feed babies." Sally cooed and walked the baby back and forth until Jack came back in the kitchen.

He set the pan of ice on the table as she pressed the baby into

24

his arms. Sally hurried into the bedroom, and in a few minutes, he heard Faith sighing with relief. "Now hold this close to yourself while I get a clean towel."

When Sally came back to the kitchen, Jack asked how Faith was going to feed the baby. She told him about squeezing the milk into a cloth and dropping it in the baby's mouth.

"Wait, Mrs. Mason put some baby bottles and nipples in my supplies. I'll bring them in and we can use some of the cow's milk."

Sally nearly leaped for joy. "Thank you, Jesus, for watching over the new babe and us."

Jack entered the house with the much-needed bottles. He stood next to the bed, directly behind Sally, as she changed the cold compress for a fresh one. Sally lowered the melted ice pack, and Jack couldn't help but see Faith's full feverish breasts with two large protruding pink nipples. His body reacted directly below his waistline. Jack was glad that Sally was standing in front of him.

The baby was asleep in the drawer for now. Jack went into the kitchen to prepare the bottles. He boiled them in some hot water and drained them on a clean cloth. Then he heated a small pan of milk to allow it to cool.

After listening to the two girls talking about the pain, Jack remembered he had purchased some tea. He hurried into his bag of supplies, poured a few teaspoons in a pan of water, and brought it to a boil. Jack added some herbs that the doctor had left and allowed them to dissolve in a small china cup.

Once the tea was cool enough to drink, Jack carried it into Faith. "Doc said that this herb tea would give you some relief. Drink it up."

Faith smiled at him, took the cup, and sipped the tea. "This is awful," she said, her face screwing up into a grimace, but she drank all of it.

"The doctor left some stronger medicine but it will make you sleepy. The tea is supposed to help with the pain," Jack said. "Let me know if the pain is too bad, and I will give you a teaspoon of laudanum." Jack left the room and decided to cook something quick and easy for lunch. He didn't want to ask Sally to prepare the meal because she'd had her hands full all morning. Jack fried a few ham steaks and cooked a platter of pancakes. He sliced the ham into small bites and poured a little syrup over the cut-up pancakes.

Faith was trying to sit up against the headboard when she saw the delicious food that Jack carried into the bedroom. "Oh my, you knew I was hungry. Thank you."

"Sally, there's plenty more on the kitchen table. Help yourself, and we'll talk about what you can cook for supper. I usually cook enough food to have leftovers for lunch the next day. It helps keep down the work." Jack smiled.

"Shoot fire, that a right good idea. But at my home, the more I cook, the more my brothers and Pa eat. There's never a bean left in the pot." Sally shook her head and left the room.

"How are you feeling? Do you still have a fever?" Jack nodded toward Faith's chest.

"The ice helped, and I am sure the tea must have, too. I can hardly keep my eyes open, but my stomach is growling like a small bear." She stabbed a piece of ham and put it in her mouth. "So good."

Jack smoothed her quilt and looked over at the baby. "You're going to have to name your little beauty. Like you, we can't keep calling her baby." He grinned and walked out of the room.

"Sally, I have some things in the wagon that I need to bring in, but first I have to put away the wagon and feed the team," Jack said as he placed his plate in the dishpan.

***

Sally finished her lunch and went to check on Faith and the baby. Faith was sound asleep, sitting up against the pillows. Removing the tray, Sally pulled one of the pillows out from under Faith's head and covered her with the top sheet. The baby wiggled around in the drawer. Sally changed her nappy and carried her into the kitchen. With a sprinkle of milk on her arm, she tested its warmth. Just right. She sat down in the rocker and placed the new nipple on the baby's lips. A drop of milk ran across her tongue. Sally pushed the nipple into the baby's mouth, and she began sucking. The child took to the store-bought nipple just like it was her mama's.

When Jack returned, he was surprised to find the baby dry and content with a full stomach. "Sally, my girl, you are a jewel." He glanced into the bedroom and saw Faith sound asleep. He reached down and took the baby to her makeshift bed. "Sally, I have a package for you. Let's call this part of your wages." He passed her the brown wrapped package tied with brown string.

"This is for me?" Puzzled, she pushed the present away from her body. "I'm sorry, Mr. Jack. I can't take gifts for payment. You see, I have to have money to give Ma." She fingered the string on the brown paper. Sally had never had a present before.

"Oh, Sally, I'm sorry. I didn't mean that I wasn't going to pay you wages. It would help if you had these things, and I bought some things for Faith, too. You see, girls' needs are different from men's. Please open the package and see if you can use the things that Mrs. Mason picked out for you."

"Well, I guess I can look," she said, as she pulled hard and broke the string. Unfolding the paper, she sighed, placing her hands on her rosy cheeks. "Oh my."

"I hope the dresses fit. They're plain housedresses and a few personal items girls wear," Jack said, as he placed the coffeepot over a hot burner, giving her privacy to look over the new things.

She grabbed one of the dresses and hurried into the bedroom. In a flash, she twirled back in to the kitchen. "Look, Mr. Jack. A perfect fit."

"Mercy, child. You look nice. I hope you'll wear the clothes."

"Well, I'll wear them while I'm here, but I'll have to leave them when I go home. Ma won't like it that I took clothes from a man."

"You'll have earned the items. Surely, your mother will know the difference." He smiled at her lovely face. "There's an empty drawer in the big chest in the bedroom. You can place your new things in it." Jack rewrapped the paper over the things he had purchased for Faith. "Lay these items on the foot of the bed so Faith can have them when she wakes."

Chapter 5

After spending all morning checking his traps and placing the critters on the back of his mule, he headed home. Jack rode straight to the barn and unloaded his bounty onto the cleaning table. Hurrying, he went to the pump to wash up before entering the house. The delicious aroma of food cooking made his stomach growl. He was surprised that the room was empty, so he stood at the closed curtain to the bedroom and whispered, "Sally, are you there?"

When there wasn't an answer, he peeked between the curtains and discovered the room was empty. He rushed back to the porch and put on his boots. Suddenly, he heard laughter coming from the side of the cabin. Jack leaped off the porch and hurried around the place. Sally was hoeing the summer garden while Faith sat in the rocker holding the baby. Relief flowed over Jack as he watched the two girls laugh at a small rabbit chewing a raw carrot. The little fuzzy brown and white bundle wasn't afraid of Bear or the women.

Sally laid the hoe on the ground and reached for the bunny. He kept on chewing while Sally rubbed his fur.

"Faith, the doctor said you were to stay in bed for two weeks. What are you doing out here not following his orders?" Jack tried not to sound like he was scolding her.

"I could see out the window. The weather looked so nice, and I felt good. I wanted to try and walk to the outhouse, so Sally brought the rocker outside for me to sit. Once I was seated, she began weeding the garden. Hope I haven't upset you, but I am recovering nicely. Really." Faith gave him a sweet smile.

"When you get ready to go inside, I will carry you. You must not overdo it until Doc comes back to see you. Understand?" Jack pointed his finger at her like a father would do while lecturing a child.

"I understand," Faith said as she began to rock again.

"I want to keep this little fellow as a pet if it's all right with you, Mr. Jack."

"Sure, you can keep it but not in the house. I'll make a box for him to sleep in and stay safe at night." Jack looked down at the baby. "She's growing every day."

"Guess I need to give her a name," Faith said, as she leaned back in the rocker. "I have been thinking about it for a while, and I can't seem to come up with something I like enough to tag a child for life."

"Why don't we continue this discussion later over dinner? I need to take care of my furs." Jack glanced at Sally. "What smelled so good when I came in the house?"

"Pork Chops. I discovered some in a barrel down in your cellar. I am baking them real slow with some wild onions, little red potatoes, and a few carrots."

"I can hardly wait." Jack turned and hurried to the barn.

Sally placed the bunny down and picked up the hoe to complete the weeding of the rows. As Faith watched Sally's sweet expression while talking and chopping, a memory flashed in her mind. *She was working in the garden, her red hair was pulled tight in a bun with a straw hat covering the curls that often escaped. A man was standing in front of her. Her pa? He was demanding to know why she was smiling. "Who you looking at, gal, with your wicked smile? You'd better lower those eyes and keep your smiles to yourself. You're out here to work, not to try to get the attention of every man that passes. Stop acting like your Jezebel mother."*

The crying baby snapped Faith back to the present. Sally was standing in front of her with her arms held out wide to take the precious bundle.

"Are you all right, Miss? You seemed to be far away."

"Yes, I guess I was." Faith was stunned by the flashback that came to her. *Was that man her pa? Was she running away from home?*

"Now that I have weeded this long-overdue garden, we should have some fresh vegetables pretty soon. Ain't nothing like fresh green beans and red potatoes cooked together?" Sally commented that they needed to go inside and take a long nap before supper. The baby was wet and would want to be fed soon.

***

Sally prepared Faith a cup of specially brewed tea with herbs and placed more ice packs on her breasts after Faith had stretched out on the bed. She made a bottle of milk for the wee one and changed her nappy, then Sally sat in the rocker and fed the baby. Placing her in the bed, she patted her on the back until she fell asleep.

***

Faith couldn't keep her eyes open. Soon she drifted off.

A few hours later, her milk came in, and the front of her gown was soaking wet. Sally immediately changed her gown and laid a soft cloth under her breasts.

"Let's try to feed this young'un." The baby screamed from being hungry, so Faith placed her finger in the baby's mouth. She sucked hard and calmed down. Immediately Faith tried again to put the foreign object into her little lips. After several attempts and a lot of patience, they got the nipple in her mouth. She smacked as she tasted her mother's milk.

"Oh, my, look! Her instincts told her that she's found her dinner." Both girls laughed as Faith leaned back against the headboard and sighed from relief. "Listen, I can hear her swallowing."

Once Faith removed the nipple from her baby's mouth, she let out a howl. Patting her on the back, she burped and continued smacking for more. Faith switched breasts, and the baby attached her lips to the new nipple.

"Once your breasts are emptied, they'll feel so much better," Sally explained. "I'll have to tie a soft cloth tight around your breasts and place padding on your nipples so you don't leak and soak your clothes."

"Child, you're so smart. I don't know how I would have managed without you."

"Oh, shucks. I've been helping Mama since I was this high," she responded as she held her hand up to her waist.

Jack tapped on the wall of the bedroom. Faith quickly tossed a white clean nappy over her breasts and called for him to come in. "I see you have the babe all settled. You know, I think it's time you name this precious bundle." He took one of the baby's hands in his.

"You're right. I've been thinking about it, but I haven't come up with something that I like. I cherish this sweet baby so much," Faith said.

"What about the name, Cherish? I love it, but you have to like it the most," Sally said, looking down at the covered baby.

"Cherish, I like it! What do you think?" Faith searched Jack's face for an answer.

"Yes, I like it a lot. I read something once that went like . . . something like hope, faith and cherish? I believe it's in the Bible. Not sure, but I know I read it somewhere. Maybe it was hope, faith and love instead of cherish, but I like the name, Cherish. "

"I like the name the more I hear you and Sally say it. So, let me introduce you to Cherish." Everyone smiled and laughed. Cherish pulled her mouth away, so Jack left the room.

***

Jack headed toward the barn, inhaled a deep breath into his lungs, and lifted his face toward the warm sunshine. His thoughts went straight to the beautiful, red-haired woman. Who was this girl? Where did she come from, and who was the couple he had buried? If his cabin was near a big city, he could search out other towns and ask the sheriffs if they knew someone described like Faith. He had no idea if she lived nearby or was passing through to another place. She was beautiful and brave, but how was he going to find out who she was in the hills of Tennessee? One thing he knew—if she continued to live in his cabin, he would need the willpower to keep his hands to himself. He wanted to run his hands through her wild red curls. Jack didn't know what he would do when Sally wasn't here acting like a chaperone and nursemaid to Faith.

Jack skinned the beavers and several small rabbits, then fed the beaver meat to his hogs and dressed the rabbits out for cooking, then carried them to his cold cellar until Sally used them for stew. He stretched out the beavers' fur on the wooden frames to dry before preparing them to sell.

***

After going out the next morning to check his traps, he found his mule grazing, but the traps were empty, so he started home. The clearing in the fields sparkled with flowers beneath the afternoon sun. Jack leaped off his horse and picked an armful of lovely dark purple and yellow wildflowers. This was a perfect gift to take to Faith. She seemed to enjoy the simple things of life and would love these for the breakfast table.

His heart slammed against his ribs as he opened the door and entered the empty front room. Fear and chills raced down his spine. "Faith," he called as he pulled back the dark curtain that led into the bedroom. "Sally?" He turned and hurried back outside. Relief flooded over him as he heard giggles coming from the barn.

Sally was feeding her rabbit a carrot. One of the little piglets had escaped from its pen and was trying to get a bite. He would lift his nose and mouth toward Sally's hand. Faith stood swaying Cherish in her arms, laughing.

"Good morning, ladies," Jack called as he entered the barn. "This little piglet needs to go back into his pen with his mother. If she misses him, she will be a determined mother to get him back where he belongs. The sow will even charge the boards until she has broken them down."

"The little fellow was running around in here when we came inside. I'm glad the sow didn't miss her baby. I'd hate to have to run." Faith laughed as she held Cherish.

"Come to me, little one." Jack took the baby from Faith. "This old barn smells, so let's go for a walk outside. We'll leave these two to play with the bunny." Jack cradled Cherish in his arms and strolled to the corral. The two mules trotted over to the fence to see what Jack carried in his arms. The three horses continued to nibble on hay scattered over the ground. Bear jumped and barked as Jack walked toward the porch.

Faith followed slowly across the yard and joined Jack near the front door. "I love your place here," she commented. "Oh, don't misunderstand me. I know I will leave here soon, but I have thanked God for leading me to this safe haven."

"More than two weeks have come and gone, but you don't have to leave my home. Please know that you can remain here until your memory returns. You can't just head out of here with Cherish with no place to go."

"You're so nice. I'm hoping that my memory will return soon. I've had a flash of something in my past, I think. It came quickly and disappeared just as fast."

"Did the little flash of memory give you any idea where you may have come from?"

"No, it didn't make sense. I'm hoping that it was a sign that I will return to normal soon."

"Talking might scare some of your ghosts from the past to the future," Jack said. "When you're ready to talk, please know that I am here to listen."

Faith walked to the outhouse, and when she returned, she took Cherish from Jack and went into the cabin. Sally came across the yard and said she was going to put lunch on the table.

Watching Faith enter the cabin, Jack realized that he loved Faith. The knowledge was like a kick in the gut. He wanted and desired her, longed to hold her silken body next to his, but it was entirely challenging to love a stranger without a memory. He wouldn't allow her to leave this place anytime soon. Jack had appointed himself her protector. Walking inside the cool house, he crouched down in front of the hearth to light a fire.

No, he couldn't allow his feelings to go any further until Faith knew who she was and where she came from. He leaned his head against the stone wall surrounding the fireplace and shut his eyes. She may have a husband searching for her this very day. "Oh Lord, help me help her."

It seemed like an hour, but it was only a few minutes later that Sally called him to lunch. He stood and gazed at the lovely wildflowers sitting in the middle of the table.

"Oh, Mr. Jack, these flowers are so pretty. We love them," Sally said excitedly.

"Yes, it was nice of you to pick the flowers. They are lovely," Faith repeated Sally's comment.

Chapter 6

Smelling fresh bread, Jack stood in the doorway of his cabin. Sally was removing two loaves of cooked bread while Faith sat at the table kneading dough. "Mercy, this place smells like the gingerbread house in Gibson."

"Gibson? Where is this located?" Faith asked.

"Gibson is the name of our town. We are about four miles from there on foot but six on horseback."

"Why the difference? I mean walking or riding a horse?" Faith wondered.

Jack laughed. "On foot, you can take a short cut through the woods, but on horseback, you must take the trail."

"I love to go into town, but it has been months since I have been. Pa said now that I'm bigger, I don't need to go in town and twist my tail in front of the men. He takes my brothers to do all the toting for him." Sally frowned as her eyes darted between Jack and Faith. "I ain't got a tail big enough to twist anywhere."

"Goodness, Sally, I think he was protecting you from some of the old trappers," Jack said. "They may think you have grown enough to do their bidding. Don't be angry at your pa."

"Oh, Mr. Jack, do you think when Miss Faith gets stronger, you can take us into town? We might be able to sell some of this bread and butter; that is, if you wouldn't mind," Sally asked.

"I don't know. This bread smells too good to let some of the other trappers have it. I might eat it all myself." He took a slice of the bread and lavished it with butter.

"We'll have to roll you to town if you eat all of this bread." Faith laughed. "Tell me about Gibson. What is the town like?" Her eyes danced.

Slicing another piece of bread and adding butter with some blackberry jam, Jack said, "Well, of course, there is a livery, a nice place to stable your horse while in town. The saloon, a busy place, is the only source of entertainment for the men. Mrs. Pickles' seamstress shop makes ladies bonnets and dresses. I have never been inside, but I understand she will alter clothing for men and women. There's a café that serves home-cooked meals, bread, and pies."

"That place sounds wonderful." She grabbed the top of the table as a flash of a white building in her mind appeared, nearly causing her to faint.

"Are you all right? Did you remember something?" Jack quickly kneeled beside her chair and patted her shoulder. "Can you tell us about it?"

"I'm fine now." She straightened and offered a weak smile. "I saw a white building with a cross on the top as you were talking."

"That's good. Maybe it's a church in your town. Once we go to town, you may see other things that will help you remember."

"True," Faith commented and glanced over at Sally. "Maybe there'll be a place where we can sell our fresh bread and pies."

"The dry goods store may want your business. Mrs. Mason sells jams and jelly. Sometimes, before you came, I would give her fresh eggs because my hens lay more than I can ever eat. She would give them to some of the families who needed them."

"Mercy sakes, you are a thoughtful man," Faith said.

"Miss Faith, you remember how to bake pies? It might be a good sign that you are getting your memory back," Sally said.

"I don't know for sure. But I might. Isn't that funny?" She rubbed a hand on her face, smearing dough on her cheek.

"There are several pecan trees scattered about, but I have never bothered with the nuts. My hogs have gotten out of their pens while I was away, and they ate them. I'll show you the trees later."

"Does this Gibson have a schoolhouse and a Sunday meeting place?"

"Gibson has a traveling preacher who comes the first Sunday of every month. He travels from Orchard, Alabama, near the big town of Mobile. Everyone attends who can. The building is used for a schoolhouse, too," Jack commented.

"Sally, did your folks send you to school?" Faith questioned the sweet girl.

"One time, the sheriff came out to our farm and told my pa that I was old enough to attend, and they should send me. My pa asked if this was the law, and he said no, but the new schoolteacher asked him to help reach out to all school-age children.

"I can't make you do anything but it wouldn't hurt children to learn to read and write," the sheriff told my folks, but it didn't do any good. When the boys got older, my parents let them go for a while, but not me," Sally said, as she hung her head down to her chin. "I remember my pa laughing and told him to git off our farm. Well, I never got to go into town to get Ma's supplies because I was just plain ignorant and couldn't read the list."

"Sally, that's not true. You're one of the smartest young girls I have ever met. You know how to deliver babes, cook, and clean better than most girls I know. I can help you read and write."

"You can? But if you can't remember who you are, how can you teach me to make pies, read, and write? This seems strange to me."

"I don't know." Faith looked as confused as Sally.

Jack listened to the girls' exchange of words and was just as confused over Faith's condition as they were. While in town, he would visit the doctor's office with a long list of questions. He needed answers about Faith's health.

After lunch, Sally helped Faith and Cherish prepare for a long nap. Cherish had cried until she gave herself hiccups and wore herself out. This had played on Faith's nerves until she was exhausted.

Jack stood and started to the door but stopped short and turned around. "Sally, I'm going fishing at the creek behind the cabin. I have an extra pole. Would you like to go with me for a little while? Maybe we can catch a mess of fish for supper."

"What about Miss Faith and the baby? You think they will be fine alone in the cabin?"

"We won't be more than a good yell from here. Come on. You need some fun." Jack held the door open for her.

"Oh, I haven't fished in years. My pa would never let me go after I grew big enough to help Mama around the house."

Fifteen minutes later, while sitting on a giant boulder with a nice juicy worm on her hook, Sally caught the first fish. "Here, swing your line over to me and let me take it off the hook. You caught a catfish, and its fins can hurt you."

In less than an hour, the two fishers caught eight large fish. "I'll carry these in the barn and clean them. You go on in and wash up. Maybe the girls will still be asleep, and you can rest awhile. Little girl, you sure know how to fish." Jack laughed as he carried the string of fish into the barn while Sally rushed into the kitchen.

***

As Sally was washing her hands and arms, whimpering came from the bedroom. She rushed in to find Faith attempting to feed the baby.

"Oh, Sally. Cherish won't take my nipple in her mouth. She pushes her legs straight out, and she keeps turning her mouth away. What do you think is wrong?" Faith swiped at the tears flowing down her face.

Sally tasted a drop of milk from Faith's breast and nearly gagged. "Oh, my goodness, your milk is sour."

"What? How could that be?" Faith tried to think of something she may have eaten to cause this problem.

"Not sure, but I know this does happen. I need to go home and get Mama to come and help you. She will bring herbs to make you feel better. I do know that I can feed Cherish with a bottle of milk. After I feed her, we will relieve the milk out of your breasts and then I'll bind you tight. I've seen my mama do this."

"How can I get the milk out of my breast?" Faith asked, suddenly very afraid.

"Let me feed this squalling young'un and I will tell you. I won't hurt you, I promise. Instead of me leaving you, I will go outside and ask Mr. Jack to fetch my mama. He can tell her your problem and she'll come."

After the baby was fed, dried, and placed in bed, Sally heated a tub of warm water for Faith to sit in while she heated two more water buckets. She built a fire in the fireplace and locked the front door. With the room toasty, she helped Faith into the tub of water. After the buckets of water was very warm, she poured the water over Faith's breasts. Milk began to flow down the front of her body. "Oh, that feels so good," Faith murmured.

Sounds of Jack's wagon driving into the front yard with her mama caught Sally's attention. "Here comes more water." She poured half a bucket more over Faith's breasts. "My mama has come. Use this towel to cover yourself."

Jack tapped on the door and called Sally. "Your mama is here. I will go back to the barn. Call me if I can help." He helped Mrs. Parker onto the porch.

Sally quickly opened the door and rushed into her ma's sweet arms.

"My goodness, child. Look at you in all your new finery." She held Sally away from her and took in the floral housedress and the pretty ribbon in her daughter's hair.

"Oh, Mama, these things are just part of my wages. I have money for you to take home, but my missus needs help. Her milk is sour, but I am draining it out of her poor body like I seen you do for Mrs. Craft last year."

Mrs. Parker walked around Sally and looked down at Faith, who sat in a tub of milky white water. "Howdy, child. You can call me Sadie. I'm going to help you dry up your milk with some herbs that you'll drink in hot tea. Sally will keep a binder tight around your chest for a few days, maybe a week. My herbs will heal you on the inside."

"Oh, thank you so much for coming. Sally is a wonderful nurse. I don't know what I would have done without her."

Sadie stared at her daughter and reached out to touch Sally's pretty golden curls. "What a lovely young girl you've become since leaving home in the last three weeks." She hurried and grabbed the herbs from her tote bag. Sally gave her a small bowl so she could mash the herbs into small pieces.

While Sadie was preparing the herb tea, Sally helped Faith out of the tub and led her into the bedroom. Sally helped dry Faith's body and dress in clean underthings and a soft housedress. Before Faith was completely dressed, Sally took a long strip of white cloth and tied it around her chest and pinned it as tight as possible. "This will be uncomfortable at first, but your body will get used to having it on. Once your milk dries up, you will feel like your old self again." Sally spoke just like a midwife.

Mrs. Parker packed her tote bag and said goodbye to her daughter. "Wait, Mama. Mr. Jack is going to let me ride home with you so I can see Pa and the boys. Miss Faith, do you mind if I ride along with Mama?"

"No, I feel so much better. I will rest while the baby sleeps the afternoon away." Faith picked up a box that she had placed in the corner of the room. She packed two loaves of fresh bread, several rounds of fresh butter, and three jars of jam. Then she poured a quarter of a jar full of sugar and packed all the items into the box. "Mrs. Parker, please take these items home. Sally and I can bake more bread in the morning."

"Mercy, I sure hate to take this, but I know the boys will enjoy it."

***

Jack opened the door and entered the cabin. He listened to Mrs. Parker and Sally exchange comments about her new clothes.

"I don't know, child," Mrs. Parker said. "Your pa ain't gonna like seeing you dressed in that fine cloth. You still got your old dress?"

Yes, ma'am. I'll hurry and change into it. Do you mind waiting a minute, Mr. Jack?"

Taking the box off the table, he headed to the barn. "No, I will go and hitch up the mules to my bigger wagon."

Chapter 7

Faith stood at the bedroom window and viewed the nice day. Sally was humming as she kneaded dough for fresh bread while she was watching Cherish play with her toes in her bed, which was placed between two kitchen chairs. Jack was working in the barn. This was a wonderful place, and she hoped her past, family and home, were as nice.

***

Later the sheets were flapping in the wind, and pants and shirts were dancing on the clotheslines. Jack walked from the barn and noticed the tubs were turned upside down, telling him that the washing was all done, and Faith must be inside helping Sally with the cooking. He patted Bear on the head, and both went into the cabin. Life was good, thought Jack.

***

After several weeks had passed, Faith opened her eyes at the first ray of sunlight. She held her head while words circulated through her mind that she had heard over and over from someone, probably her pa. The words had made her a prisoner. *She couldn't lift her eyes at any boy or man. Faith reviewed some of the phrases repeated to her. She lay frozen as nasty words were describing her actions because she smiled at one of her brothers.* Oh my, I have brothers, she thought. A wooden floorboard crept, and her nightmare of memories disappeared.

Sally was standing over the bed with Cherish in her arms. Faith smiled at Sally's face. What a lovely young lady she was becoming. Since coming to Jack's cabin, she had washed and bathed each day. Her hair was beautiful, and her tiny figure looked so cute dressed in her new housedresses. She was going to be a beauty when she matured.

"Do you want to relieve yourself before giving the wee one her breakfast?" Sally asked as she changed the babe's nappy. She tossed the wet cloth into a pot of soapy water.

"No, I'm fine. Let me get comfortable on the pillows, and you can give Cherish to me with her bottle."

As Faith fed Cherish, memories flooded back into her mind. A woman was crying. She couldn't make out her face, but she knew it must be her small, fragile mother. *"You'd best teach your gal some manners. She uses her slutty ways to attract men passing in front of the house, just like you did. Everybody knew what kind of wench you were when I was held at gunpoint and made to marry the sorriest trollop in town."*

"Mr. Millstone, please turn me loose. You're hurting me."

"You'd better hear me good, woman. I don't want to have to take a strap to you or our gal, but I will if I see a man hanging around."

Cherish's cry snapped Faith back to the present. She had spit out her bottle. Picking up the baby to burp her, Faith's first thought was, who was Mr. Millstone? Was that what her mother called her husband? Was her last name Millstone? All of these thoughts flooded through Faith's mind.

***

"Good morning, Faith. How's my precious doll this morning?" Jack asked as he entered the bedroom. "How are you feeling?"

"Starved, but I need to get dressed before coming to the table."

"Today is a pretty sunny day with a cool breeze. I have a little business in town and a long list of supplies to buy. I was wondering if you, Sally, and the baby would like to go with me. I can take care of business, and you and Sally can do a little shopping and have my list of supplies filled. If the little princess is good, maybe we can have a bite of lunch at the café. What do you say? You wanna go?"

"Oh my. I think this would be a great treat for Sally. And me. I can't remember anything about my home. Maybe something in town might help me, as you said before."

"Get dressed, eat breakfast, and pack the baby's things. I believe the milk will be fine if you fill several bottles for her," Jack said, with much authority.

Peering at herself in the glass on the wall, she was presently surprised to find the black circles and pale complexion had disappeared. Sally and Jack had taken excellent care of her. She started to smile at her reflection, but she slapped her hand up to cover her mouth, remembering that she wasn't allowed to smile. All those bad memories flooded her mind. She glanced over her shoulder, and there was no one in the room but her. Shaking her head, she peered back into the looking glass. Faith felt joy for the first time in her heart. There was no sin in smiling. She wasn't harming anyone like the dark creature in her memory kept shouting. Jack had told her that one day she would be happy. *Today is the day. I am delighted that I'm going to town, and I will smile*!

The hustle and bustle of several wagons passed Jack's wagon in town. Faith and Sally were giddy with excitement. Jack nodded at the drivers and pulled the mules to a stop in front of the livery. "Settle down, girls. I'll come around and help you to the ground."

Faith and Sally were both jumping with excitement. Faith couldn't remember ever seeing this great number of people on horseback and in wagons and strolling on the boardwalk. Sally was pointing at the different signs and all the children playing in the middle of the road. It had been a long time since the young girl had enjoyed the privilege of going to town.

Jack took Sally down from the high seat, and Faith passed down Cherish, whom Jack placed in Sally's arms. Faith's body slid down the front of his tall, hard body. Her hair smelled of rosewater, and her body felt so good close to his. She struggled to stand on her two feet. Jack wondered how long he'd be able to control himself from kissing her senseless.

***

"Look," Sally said to Faith. "There's the big dry goods store. Let's go there and get a sarsaparilla. I haven't had one since I was knee high."

"What is sarsaparilla?" Faith asked, enjoying the excitement on Sally's face.

"A nice, cold bottle drink. You'll love it, so let's hurry." Faith and Sally waved at Jack, then went into the store and ordered a drink.

Faith took a long swallow of the cool glass. "Wonderful."

Mrs. Mason came from the back of the store and declared," My goodness, what do we have here? Well, Lordy me. Look at you, little Sally. Ain't you the prettiest thing?"

"Aw, thank you, Mrs. Mason. That's mighty nice of you to say."

"Who do you have with you? And look at this beautiful babe with curly red hair to boot."

"This here is Faith and her baby girl, Cherish. She's staying out at Mr. Jack's cabin until her memory returns."

"Oh, yes, Jack told me about you, Miss. He came in a few weeks ago and bought clothes and baby items. But, land's sake, I thought you were gone by now." Mrs. Mason reached to take the baby in her arms.

A few chatting ladies came strolling through the door. They stopped and stared at Faith, Sally, and Mrs. Mason. "Well, my goodness, Mildred, who are these young women?"

"Mrs. Godwin, Mrs. Ledbetter, and Mrs. Smith, let me introduce you to Sally Parker, Faith and her baby, Cherish. You all remember little Sally Parker, who lives a few miles from here with her folks? She's practically grown now."

"You didn't tell us Faith's last name? Is she from somewhere near here in Tennessee?" Mrs. Ledbetter asked.

"Faith was in an accident, and because of it, she lost her memory. She's staying at Jack Mills' cabin until she gets well," Mrs. Mason spoke in a quiet voice.

Faith excused herself after giving Mrs. Mason the list of needed supplies and headed to the back of the store where the baby items were displayed.

***

The three ladies huddled together and spoke under their breath. "We can't allow this to continue. A young, pretty gal living with a single man in our community," one of the ladies whispered. "Mr. Mills needs a wife, and that young woman is lovely," Mrs. Ledbetter commented. "We need to get together with Mildred after the girls leave and make plans. I will have to speak with my husband since he's the mayor, and Reverend Peterson, too. They won't approve of them living in sin right under our noses."

"In sin?" Mrs. Godwin spoke louder than she intended.

"What else would you call it, Sister Smith?"

"Yes, we'll have to take a trip out to Jack Mills' place and see what's going on." Mrs. Ledbetter and her two friends stood in the corner and watched Faith's every move.

***

"You know, Mr. Jack. Those ladies in the dry goods store were sure nosy. They kept asking Mrs. Mason questions and whispering about us, mostly about Miss Faith. I think they're up to no good." Sally sat between Jack and Faith on the bumpy ride back to the cabin.

"Don't worry about those old hens. They don't have anyone else to talk about, so Faith, being a stranger, gives them food for gossip." Jack peered down at Sally and smiled.

"I loved the town," Faith said. "The lunch was grand, especially the pecan pie. I'm going to make us one as soon as I can crack the pecans I have at the cabin."

Later, when Faith woke from a long nap, it was getting dark. She bolted up as if an alarm had sounded, but none had. The memory of her day in town washed over her. She enjoyed all the finery in the small stores. So many people were milling around, chatting together, and shopping. Faith needed to check on Cherish and start supper. Jack would be hungry by now. Sally was sleeping with Cherish in the middle of the bed. Mercy, thought Faith. She'd been in such a deep sleep, she hadn't even known that her baby had been lying between her and Sally.

The evening still lay ahead of her. Faith glanced in the looking glass and straightened her hair, then smoothed down her wrinkled dress. She crept out as quietly as she could and ran straight into Jack as he carried an armful of logs to the fireplace.

"Oh, my. Did I hurt you?" Jack shifted the logs in his arms.

"No, I wasn't expecting to find anyone in the kitchen. Here, let me take a few smaller logs off the top of your load." Faith removed three and placed them on the floor.

"Thanks. You're sure I didn't scratch you with one of these bigger logs?"

"I'm sure." She gave him a sweet smile, then hurried around the other side of the table. "Sorry about supper. Sally and I were worn out after our trip into town. I just lay down for a few minutes, but I must have fallen asleep. Dinner will be on the table in a few minutes. Will a good hot breakfast be all right with you tonight?"

"Sounds wonderful. I spent the afternoon working on my bear rug. I would like for you to see it tomorrow."

"Oh, I would love to see it. Is it large enough to cover this floor?"

"Only in front of the fireplace, but it will be nice and snug. Your feet will be good and warm if you stand on it."

Early the next morning, Faith stood on the porch in the warm sunshine as she washed a full tub of clothes. Two buckets of water simmered on the stove to rinse the items. She eyed the vegetable garden, then whirled around like she'd seen Sally do a hundred times and went into the cabin to prepare pies.

Jack entered the kitchen and grinned. White flour covered both the girls' faces, and they were giggling. He had never seen two girls get along like these two. His three sisters had argued and fussed all the time. Mama would say they were like she-cats who couldn't stand the sight of each other. "What's so funny this morning?" Jack asked the silly girls.

"We'll never tell," Sally said with a chuckle.

How Jack loved the expression on Faith's face. He straddled a kitchen chair as he fought the urge to reveal his feelings. He was struck with the unbelievable fact that he loved this flour-faced girl more than life. Jack wanted to reach out and tell her how much he cared for her, but he thought better of it. She must belong to another. It was like a stab in his heart whenever that thought flashed through his mind. Somehow, he had to find out more information about who she was and where she came from.

Chapter Eight

The sound of thunder brought Jack to the barn door. He stood staring at the black clouds rolling in from the west. It wouldn't be long before Thanksgiving would arrive. This year was undoubtedly going to be different. They would cook a big dinner with the girls here, and he wouldn't have to go to the church and eat with strangers, which he hated, but his friends in town insisted that he come.

But this year would be different. Of course, Sally might want to go home and spend time with her family, which would be fine, but he would miss her sunny disposition. As he turned to get back to work cleaning his fur hides, the pounding of a horse's hooves came near the barn door.

Jack went to the barn door and welcomed Gibson's minister, Reverend Peterson. "My goodness, Reverend, what brings you out here in the bad weather that's coming?" Jack asked.

"I believe I just beat the rain." The minister said as he climbed down off his bay horse.

"Give him to me, and I'll put him in a stall and give him a treat while you visit." Jack took the reins, led the horse into a clean stall, and pitched him a pitchfork or two of dry hay to eat. It was quiet in the barn, with the sweet smell of hay surrounding the two men.

"Thanks, Jack. I know he'll appreciate some good hay. I heard you were in town yesterday with two pretty ladies and a babe. Are they still here with you?"

"Yes, they are in the house preparing lunch and making loaves of fresh bread."

"Jack," the minister took a deep breath and said that he had something important to discuss. Jack rolled over a barrel for him to sit on and took one for himself. "Out with it, man," Jack said, laughing. And then the reverend began to talk. Jack felt the blood drain out of his face. He stormed across the barn floor and turned to stare at the man who sat holding his black hat in his hands.

"What are you saying?" Jack whispered. He could hardly swallow while waiting for the minister to explain the words he had just dropped on Jack's head.

***

The minister took a deep breath. "Now, Jack, the mayor's wife and the other ladies of Gibson, well, a few of them anyway, are upset that you and the girl are living out here together with only a child for a chaperone. They feel that you two should marry and marry very soon. Since this is your home, you can't just up and leave, and from what you said about Miss Faith, she has no place to go. Therefore, they feel that the only right conclusion is that you should marry. We have a nice community, and the women intend to keep it that way. When those ladies gets a bee in their bonnets, nothing can stop them. The mayor slammed out of the room and left me to deal with the women." He peered at Jack, who was as pale as the porcelain teapot back home on his kitchen table.

"What are your thoughts on this matter? The ladies will make all the plans and put together a big spread of food for your wedding reception. They were already making plans for your young lady's wedding dress."

***

Jack sat still for several long minutes. He had to make this man understand how it was with Faith. "Reverend Peterson, I moved out here deep into these woods because I wanted to be left alone. But, when Faith arrived here with only the clothes on her back, with no memory and with child, I couldn't run her off. You and the ladies must understand that Faith has no place to go. But that doesn't mean she must have a husband. For goodness sake, she doesn't even know if she has a husband already. We chose the name *Faith* for her because she doesn't remember who she is. We couldn't keep calling her *lady*. She doesn't know where she came from or why she was

47

even traveling. The worst thing was she didn't even know she was going to have a child. The doctor had to tell her, hours before she had her baby girl."

"I understand all of this, but the ladies don't seem to care. They feel that you must marry or part ways, as of today. I have talked to them until I am blue in the face. You don't have a choice if you want to keep that girl in your cabin."

He stood. "Guess we need to go inside and let you explain to Faith what the women of Gibson are demanding that we do." He stopped and turned to the man. "She must agree to marry me. I will not force her."

After Faith and Sally greeted Reverend Peterson, Sally took the baby into the bedroom to change her nappy and put her down for a nap. Faith offered coffee to the reverend, but he refused.

Jack explained to Faith that the reverend had some important news that he needed to explain to her. "He has already spoken with me, but I wanted him to tell you himself what's going on with the ladies in town." Jack longed to take Faith in his arms, but he folded his arms across his chest instead. He looked into Faith's eyes, large eyes filled with emotion, mostly fear. How he wanted to give her an affirmation of his love, but he couldn't bring himself to declare his feelings in front of the minister.

***

Jack's adam's apple move like he might have something lodged in his throat. One glance at Jack told her he was as embarrassed as she because he was red above his collar. Faith wished she could run and hide from this stranger's presence.

"Miss, I'm sorry to have to deliver this news, but I had no choice. I didn't want the mayor's wife and her cronies—excuse me, I mean her friends—coming out here to accuse both of you of living together in sin. As I explained to Jack, they are distraught that you, being a single woman with only a child as a chaperone, are living with a man. They want you to move on or marry Jack."

"I feel exhausted. May I go and check on the baby?"

"Sally is with Cherish. We need to give Reverend Peterson an answer. These women feel that they have to protect your reputation as if they've known you since childhood, even though we know they haven't," Jack said, making a choking noise in his throat.

"What do you want me to say? Yes, I will marry you?" Pressing her hands against her stomach, she searched Jack's face, hoping he would verbalize what he wanted her to say.

Finally, he stood as straight as he could. "It seems that we don't have much choice. I can't send you away. Mrs. Mason is the only person I know in Gibson who might take you in, but she doesn't have room for two more people. Sally's family has no room, and besides, you don't want to move to their poor farm. This place is the only safe home that you have. Besides, I don't want you to take Cherish and move away until your memory is back and I can take you home to your family."

***

His body stirred as he watched her sit at the kitchen table. He would love to pull her into his arms and press a scorching kiss on her rosy lips. Weeks ago, he couldn't wait until she was well enough to move into town—anywhere but here. Now, he couldn't bear the thought of her being out of his sight. And that beautiful baby. He loved that little one.

One evening he remembered listening to Faith talking low to Sally about leaving and standing on her own two feet. She had no idea where or what she would do to take care of herself and Cherish. His mind clashed at a vision of Faith dressed in a low-cut dress serving whiskey to the old men and trappers who visited the only saloon in the town. His stomach tightened with the dilemma of trying to talk some sense into her. Jack wanted to shake her and say, "You don't have a choice." He stood as still as a stone statue and waited for her to reason out what she was thinking.

"I don't want to discuss our relationship in front of this man, a stranger."

Jack moved closer to her shoulder and whispered, "We don't have time to discuss this privately. The minister knows all about us, and he is waiting for an answer, now."

***

Brushing past her protector and soon-to-be husband, she rounded the table and wrapped a fresh loaf of bread in a white cloth and gave it to the minister. "If Jack agrees to marry me, I will be proud to marry him, but can't we have another day to talk about this situation through?" Faith asked.

"Faith, I have tried to tell the minister you may be married already."

Lifting her chin in an attempt to look confident, she replied, "If I am already married, we will have to face that when my husband finds me," Faith said, feeling physically ill.

The pastor headed to the door. "Well, Mr. Mills, I have delivered the message to you and the young lady. I will tell the ladies that you need a day or two to make this important decision. Don't be surprised if the womenfolk visit you tomorrow. Hopefully, this will give you time to make plans of your own." He tightened his hands and then loosened them. "May I pray with you before I depart back to town?"

After Reverend Peterson finished and amen were said all around, Jack opened the door for the minister and walked him to the barn to retrieve his horse. "Thanks for coming out and warning us," Jack said as the old man climbed on his horse.

***

"Faith, you need to eat and sleep. How will it look if you face those women all tired and starving? They will be sure you need a good man to care for you." He lifted a morsel to his lips and motioned for her to do the same. "Eat," he said grinning.

She didn't speak but nibbled some of the food Sally had prepared. Footsteps made Jack turn toward Sally standing in the doorway of the bedroom.

"I guess after you marry, I'll go home." Sally hung her head and wiped tears from her eyes. "I'm sorry, but I couldn't help but overhear the old man."

"No. I want you to stay. Please, Jack, tell her she doesn't have to leave here." Faith's hands rubbed at her temple.

"Faith is right. We'll still need a chaperone because we will be marrying in name only. Do you know what that means?" Jack looked into Sally's face, but when she didn't respond, he continued. "We have to allow Faith's memory to return before we can move toward the future and live as man and wife."

***

Faith let out a deep breath. She wasn't sure that Jack felt the same way she did, but it was a burden off her shoulders. It would kill her if she found out that she was married, and she had betrayed her husband by living as a wife to another man. Faith rose to her feet.

"Where are you going?" Jack asked.

"Privy." She blushed bright red.

"I have a few things to attend to in the barn. We'll talk later." Jack slipped on his boots and hat and left the kitchen.

When Faith returned to the cabin, she sat next to Sally, drinking a cup of milk. "Sally, I know you're young, but what do you think about me marrying Jack? He wants to save my reputation."

"He's a kind man, and you'll never have to fear him, like so many other men. If you don't want to mate with him, I'm sure he won't leap on you while you're asleep."

"Gracious, child. How in the world do you know so much about men and women?" Faith was stunned to hear such words come from this precious child.

"Shoot fire, Miss Faith. My ma has taken care of neighbors and some of the gals that work in town. They talk around me like I'm grown. I probably know more than I should, being so young, but it has opened my eyes to men who come around our place. When a strange man comes to the house, Mama hides me in the bedroom. When I was real young, I didn't understand, but now that I am older, I do."

"You think I will be doing the right thing by marrying Jack?" Faith stared down the floor. "I'm scared because I don't know who I am or who Cherish's father is."

Sally poured milk into the potato soup she'd made earlier and gave it a good stir. Cherish was moving around in her bed and started whimpering. "You sit here and gather your thoughts together. Mr. Jack will be back in for supper soon and afterward, he'll want to talk."

Faith watched Sally prepare a bottle of milk for the baby and go into the bedroom to care for her. Her thoughts went to the stranger whom she was living with. He said they should marry. Jack was handsome. There was no doubt about that, but that wasn't what made her heart beat faster when he was near. His hands were gentle when he touched her and his large, tall body didn't have an ounce of fat. His shoulders were broad and his buffalo vest made him appear as wide as the door.

There was more to Jack than just his appearance, though. He had been so kind to her and she witnessed how gentle he could be when he bathed Cherish the day she was born. He had been generous to Sally, realizing that the child needed so many personal things, and he readily bought them. He purchased clothes, personal items for her, and many things the baby needed. Jack truly cared, and that was the one quality that made her feel that he would continue to treat her like a lady.

She was ordinary, nothing special, but this kind man was willing to help her in every way. God had led her to Jack's cabin, the safe haven she'd prayed for. Jack deserved a good woman. Faith would try not to do anything that would make her presence in his home shame him.

Chapter 9

Orchard, Alabama
Twenty miles north of Mobile

A tall, skinny man with a long nose and a sharp chin stood in his three-room shack in a long, black coat holding a worn Bible. He pointed his knotted finger at his poor wife, who was so thin that her dress hung off her shoulders, displacing her ragged shift. Slamming his hand down on the face of the Bible, he yelled, "You'd best put a sock in that trap of yours and stop mentioning that brazen whore. She's dead to us, and you'd better tell the boys not to talk about their sister to nobody. I'll beat them to an inch of their lives if I learn they're even breathing her name." The older man was always fantasizing about Satan encouraging others to do wrong.

"Just like you walloped Precious? You nearly killed her, you old fool. She didn't deserve the beating you gave her, and I ain't forgetting it, either. I miss my firstborn, and soon she'll have her child—one I won't ever get to hold." Tears flowed down her haggard face.

"She deserved everything that I did to her and more." When he'd completed his vengeance on his daughter, her body was in pitiful shape for days. Bruised from head to toe, with swollen, blackened eyes, every bruised hip and muscle ached throughout her young body. He locked her in the cellar for several weeks, only allowing her mother to feed her. The only things the girl had were candles, a blanket, and the Bible until she looked decent again.

"People who lie with dogs ain't no better, and she did worse than that. Her man didn't want her after they wallowed around in the hay. Later after he discovered she was with child, he didn't want the babe either."

"You know better, old man. When Precious started showing, his mother loaded him up, and they left for Texas. She told everyone that her boy had a job offer in his uncle's bank. Precious never even told Ned that she was with child." Mrs. Millstone stared at her husband with hatred in her eyes. Like a lunatic, his actions caused Precious and her brothers to despise and fear him more than ever.

"You and I know that was just an excuse to get her lily-white handed, sniffle-nosed son out of Orchard, away from our whore who was ready to trap him into marriage." He stormed out the front door and let it slam. His anger still unspent, he kicked the boys' hound dog and watched as it ran off howling.

Mrs. Millstone sat down at the kitchen table and wept. Her child was a good girl. She wanted more than anything to know where that old couple had taken Precious. It seemed like yesterday that she heard her man pleading with the Amish couple to take her daughter with them on their way to Kansas. Mrs. Millstone listened to her husband as he offered the couple money.

"You take my gal with you to Kansas and teach her your Christian ways. Lord knows I have tried to make her walk the path of righteousness, but I couldn't even beat it in her. You don't have to spare the rod if need be."

"My woman and I will pass her off as our granddaughter. Everyone knows that our daughter had a baby years ago. My people don't ask questions. They will welcome her just like they will us." The old Amish gentleman placed his black hat over his shoulder-length gray hair.

"I don't care. Just go and don't bring her back." Mr. Millstone counted out forty dollars to the old man.

"Great Christian people you chose to take our daughter. They claimed to be God's children but the will hid the truth about our daughter. You'll let everyone in town think that our gal ran away, and you searched for days and couldn't find her. You need to go live with an Amish clan." Mrs. Millstone dragged herself back into their shack.

After a couple of weeks, the townspeople stopped asking about the whereabouts of Precious and believed the story that Mr. Millstone had spread throughout the town that she had run off. One day he came home and demanded that his wife stop her grieving and get back to living.

"People are talking about you. You ain't nothing but a bag of bones and you look like a hundred-year-old woman. I'm sick of it, too. I've a good mind to go and find myself another woman."

Mrs. Millstone refused to look up from the counter where she stood peeling potatoes. "Please do. Get yourself two women. You'll need two to take care of you and your horny, soppy ways."

He slapped her across the face, knocking her down on the floor, then stood over her frail body and screamed, "Woman of Satan, you'll go straight to Hell one day soon." Murmuring to himself, he hurried out of the house.

Chapter 10

Gibson, Tenn.

Jack took a long cool drink of water and said to Faith, "Well, it's after lunch and the ladies of Gibson haven't shown themselves. Maybe the preacher was wrong, and they won't come out here making demands on us."

"We're the talk of that lovely town. Of course, I wish the people had nice things to say about us, especially me." Faith raised downhearted eyes toward Jack.

Sally came from the bedroom. "I hear horses out front."

"I guess I spoke too soon. Let me go and greet our guests." Jack straightened his shirt and vest and ran his hand through his hair. "Do I look presentable?" he said to the girls with a grin.

"Invite them in, and Sally and I will serve some pecan pie and coffee. Maybe after they've eaten, they won't care how you look." Faith tried to smile back at him.

Sally rushed over to the stove and put on a fresh pot of coffee. She reached under the counter and pulled out three plates and two others that didn't match. Faith laid out forks and spoons on the table with white and blue porcelain cups. She was glad that she had found the dishes while cleaning the kitchen.

***

"Will you be quiet, Henrietta? I'll be asking the questions," Virginia Ledbetter, the mayor's wife said. "We want to make a good impression on Mr. Mills and *his woman.*"

Bear was barking and jumping up on the wagon. He growled and bared his teeth at Mrs. Ledbetter.

"For goodness sakes, Virginia, they should be making a good impression on us. They're the ones living out here in sin," Henrietta Smith commented while adjusting the tall yellow feather that had fallen sideways on her hat. "You drove this carriage like we were in a race."

"Oh hush up, Henrietta, and watch out for that big dog. He looks ferocious," Mrs. Ledbetter said. "I wanted to get out here as soon as possible."

"Why didn't we leave right after breakfast as I wanted to? No, we had to wait until Lois could fix your hair. You wanted to look like a queen while Henrietta and I looked like your serving maids," Mary Jane Godwin spoke for the first time after arriving.

"How dare you talk to me like that—" Suddenly Mrs. Ledbetter noticed Jack standing beside the carriage. Blushing bright red, she knew that this nice man had overheard their argument. "Oh, Mr. Mills, how good to see you again."

"Yes, it's nice of you ladies to come out for a visit. I know Faith will be happy to see you. May I help you down from the carriage?" he said, holding out his strong hand to lift each one of the ladies to the ground.

**

Faith returned from the pantry with two cans of open peaches and a tray of sugar cookies. "Who are you going to serve cookies and peaches to, Miss Faith? We already have pecan pies on the table."

Faith whipped around and said, "I don't know where my mind is. I'm just nervous." She set the tray in the middle of the table anyway.

Sally rushed to the door and peeked out. She saw a tall woman who looked like a scarecrow. Her shirtwaist was bright yellow, and her full skirt was floral orange with bright yellow flower print. Her hat was too large for her head with a bowl of fruit surrounding the top. Another lady was so fat that Jack had a hard time lifting her out of the carriage. As she bent her head, the large yellow feather waved and hit Bear on the nose. He growled and jumped to grab the long yellow feather. His jaws bit down on the foreign object, then he raced away with the whole bonnet, and in a minute, he'd shaken it to pieces. The dog stood with part of the long yellow feather hanging out of his mouth.

"Bear!" Jack yelled to the animal, "Sit." Bear immediately lay down with the big feathers under his front paws.

The woman gripped onto Jack's shoulders as one of his knees went to the ground, but he kept his balance. She cried out and placed her hands on his shoulders to keep from falling. He stood her on the ground, and she smoothed her long black dress, which had ridden up over her knees.

"Are you hurt?" Before the lady could answer, Jack interjected, "Madam, I'm so sorry about your hat. I'll replace it as soon as I go to the store."

"I'm Mrs. Godwin, and I am perfectly all right." She jerked her head up and attempted to tidy her hair, her eyes never leaving the dog.

The third woman dressed in an elegant hat and dress stared at Jack and demanded, "Don't allow that creature near me." She pulled on her jacket and offered her hand to Jack. The lady's jacket matched her dress which had rows of white ruffles down the front.

Bear stood with anticipation as the long yellow feathers swayed down from the lady's black circular hat. Jack pointed to the ground, demanding that Bear stay still, but when the feathers passed under his nose, he growled.

"Golly, Faith, you should have seen Bear jump up on one of the ladies and eat her hat. I bet she nearly peed on herself." Sally doubled over laughing. "I ain't never seen such fancy dressed women. They're the ladies who were in the dry goods store yesterday, but they're all dressed in their finery today. Jack made Bear lie down." Sally closed the door, walked back to the table, and stood next to Faith. "Don't be afraid of these brazen-faced women. Mama would say they put on their pantaloons just like we do, so don't be afraid of them."

"Oh dear, I'm already afraid, and they haven't entered the room." Faith's bottom lip trembled.

"Come in, Ladies," Jack said as he held the front door open for each woman. "Faith, Sally, we have company. I understand that you met these ladies yesterday while in town." Jack stood back as the three strangers entered his cabin.

"Please, come in and have a seat at the table. It is so nice of you to come and visit with us today. Sally has made some fresh coffee. May I offer you some along with a slice of pecan pie?" Faith held her shaking hands behind her back.

"Mercy, child, we weren't expecting you to be so gracious to us. We have come out to discuss something very personal, but before we do, I would love some coffee and pie. Sit, girls. Let me introduce ourselves. My name is Virginia Ledbetter. My husband is the mayor of Gibson. To my right is Mary Jane Godwin and to my left is Henrietta Smith. My, the pie looks delicious. Did you bake it?"

"Yes, I did bake them, but madam, did the dog harm you?"

"Like I told Mr. Mills, I'm fine. He just scared me and grabbed my hat. I guess he became excited when he saw the fancy feathers, "Mary Jane replied, offering Faith a timid smile.

Jack raised his eyebrows at Faith and watched her slice the pie and place a piece on each plate. "Jack picked up the pecans, and Sally and I shelled them. We baked several pies." Faith was so nervous she felt herself rattling on while Sally poured the coffee and offered milk and sugar to each lady. The women giggled and ate like they were at a party.

The baby cried out, so Sally rushed into the bedroom and changed her wet nappy before bringing her out to show their guests.

"My, what a beautiful baby," Henrietta said, holding out her arms to take the child. Sally reluctantly handed over Cherish. Henrietta lowered her so the other two ladies could see the darling baby girl.

"Give the baby back to the serving girl while we get down to business," Virginia said to Henrietta like a judge in a courtroom.

Faith frowned at the ladies and held her chin high. "Sally, our young friend, is not a serving girl. She's a neighbor who has kindly come over to help me while I am recovering. Please do not speak down to her in my home."

***

Jack didn't know who was more surprised by Faith's comment—the mayor's wife, the other two ladies, or himself. The older woman's mouth stood ajar before she could offer a reply, and he couldn't stop grinning at the situation. He hadn't thought Faith had it in her to take a stand against the discrimination shown to Sally. How wrong he was. He was so proud of her.

"I must apologize, young lady," Mrs. Ledbetter said, "I

misunderstood your position. I am pleased that Mr. Mills has such fine neighbors." She glanced at her two companions and gave them both a smirking grin. "Now, Sally, if you will take the baby to her room, we grown people will get down to the business we came out here to take care of." Mrs. Ledbetter rewarded Faith with a hard glare. Faith smiled at Sally and asked if she would mind sitting with Cherish. Sally complied without comment and left the room.

"Mr. Mills, will you please take a seat, so I don't have to crane my neck while speaking?" Jack pulled the rocker next to the table and took a seat.

"It has come to our attention, actually the whole town's attention, that you, Mr. Mills, have this young lady and child living with you without a proper chaperone. She is an unmarried woman with a child, and you are a single man. It's not a proper or a suitable arrangement. The people of Gibson feel that you have two choices. One, the young lady and child move out of your home, or you move. The second choice is for you two to get married. And the sooner the better."

Jack and Faith didn't comment at first. Finally, Jack said, "What if I move to the barn?"

"No, that is not one of the choices. There will be no one here to make sure you sleep in the barn, and besides, winter is coming. That arrangement will never work," Mrs. Ledbetter said with authority.

"Mrs. Ledbetter, do you have any place in mind where Faith and Cherish can live besides here?"

"There is no room at the Inn, if that's what you are referring to, Mr. Mills. We feel that marriage to this lovely, young woman is your best choice. If you decided to marry, we, the ladies of Gibson, are prepared to make all the arrangements, help make your bride-to-be a wedding gown, and hold a reception in your honor at the church."

Faith cleared her throat. "Did the minister tell you ladies that I was in an accident before arriving at Mr. Mills' door, and I lost my memory? I still don't know my name or where I came from or where I was traveling to. I don't know if I'm already married. I was with child when I arrived here, so hopefully, I belong to someone." She watched the expression on the ladies' faces, but they showed no emotion. "If Mr. Mills marries me, it might not be legal. I am praying that someone is searching for me."

"Young lady, we are saddened over your predicament, but for

now, you are living in sin, and we cannot allow such an arrangement. If and when your husband shows up, that will be a case for you and Mr. Mills to handle, not the good people of Gibson." Mrs. Ledbetter and the other ladies stood. "We feel you must have a proper chaperone for the next two days and nights; therefore, Mrs. Godwin will be staying with you. She brought a cot to sleep on so she won't be a burden to you."

Now Faith's mouth hung ajar.

"We will take our leave now. You have two days to make your choice. Young lady, either you move out of this cabin and go somewhere else, or marry Mr. Mills. Those are your choices." She stared at Faith, waiting for a rebuttal. When Jack or Faith did not comment, she said, "Come, Henrietta, we must return to town. Thank you for your gracious hospitality. Good day to you."

Mrs. Ledbetter marched out the door with her eyes on guard for the big dog. Henrietta smiled and nodded at Faith and Sally.

***

Jack stood waiting for them at the carriage and took the two horses and turned them toward the trail. Hands posted on his hips, he watched Mrs. Ledbetter drive the team toward town. He looked to the sky and softly said a prayer, "Help me, Lord. Two ladies, but now three, in my small cabin. Give me patience." Jack carried Mrs. Godwin's carpet bag and cot into the front room of the cabin. "I'll place your bag in the bedroom, and you can set your cot up in the kitchen. There isn't much room."

"Oh, anywhere will be fine, Mr. Mills. I'm sorry to be put upon you for the next few days. Mrs. Ledbetter demanded that I stay out here first because I don't have a man to care for and don't have any children at home. I will try to stay out of your way."

***

"We want you to feel welcome while you are staying with us," Faith said. "I am going to prepare supper. Sally put a deer roast in the oven early this morning, so I'll go cut some of the meat and place it in with some vegetables for deer stew." Faith walked into the pantry and brought out a bag of potatoes, several large carrots, and a bunch of fresh pulled onions.

"Once the vegetables are ready to mix with the meat, would you like for me to make a skillet of soda biscuits?" Mrs. Godwin asked.

"You can make biscuits?" Sally asked.

"Please call me Mary Jane, and yes, I love biscuits with stew or soups." She giggled as she gestured to her size. "As you can see, I love to eat."

"I would like to learn how to make biscuits. What ingredients do you need to make them?" Faith asked as she peeled the potatoes.

"Here, give me a knife, and I will scrape the carrots and clean the onions," said Mary Jane, as she reached for an apron and tried to tie it around her middle. Faith placed her knife down and took two large diaper pins and pinned the apron on each side of Mary Jane's dress. "There, now you won't spoil your pretty dress."

"Thanks. To make my biscuits, you need flour, baking powder, butter, and buttermilk. Mary Jane tipped her head to one side and asked, "Do you have buttermilk?"

"No, not until we start churning more butter. We can begin on the butter when Jack brings in the evening milk."

"Well, I can make some golden cornbread to go with the stew." Faith agreed because she or Sally rarely made cornbread.

Later, Jack brought in the milk and Sally sat down to churn. In a few hours, she was ready for the cream and milk to sit and separate. There would be fresh buttermilk in the morning.

After supper, Faith prepared for bed. She fed Cherish her last bottle and changed her into a fresh nightgown and rocked her to sleep.

***

Jack put together Mary Jane's cot and gave her a pillow and a couple of blankets. He dismissed himself and left for the barn while the ladies settled in their beds for the night. When he came back inside, he discovered Sally sleeping on the cot and Mary Jane cuddled in his big bed next to Faith. He lay down on his pallet and listened to the sleeping mumbles of the ladies and all the outside noises.

Bear wasn't too happy because he had to sleep in the kitchen near the fire. "So, you aren't welcome in the bed tonight." The dog whined and placed his big paws over his nose and watched Jack.

Chapter 11

Early the next morning, Jack milked and opened the stalls, allowing the horses and mules into the corral. He watched the younger horses run and kick up their back hooves. The horses were as frisky as the cool air. After feeding the hens, he collected and cleaned five dozen eggs. "Wow, something smells good," Jack said, placing the eggs on the counter near the dry sink.

"Miss Mary Jane cooked biscuits," Sally explained, as she continued to put jams and jelly on the table. "I ain't had a good biscuit since I left home to come here."

"I hope they're as good as your mother's. I don't usually make a big round skittle like this one," Mary Jane said, smiling at Sally.

"I'm going to scramble the eggs now. I think I heard Faith and Cherish moving about in the bedroom."

"Do you put cheese in your eggs?" Mary Jane asked.

"Cheese? Why I ain't ever heard of that, but it sounds good. I like eggs and cheese." Sally glanced at Jack. "What about you, Mr. Jack? Do you want cheese in your eggs this morning?"

"We might have to keep Mrs. Godwin out here with us. She sure has some different ideas about cooking." Jack took his place at the table.

"You take up the biscuits, and I'll scramble the eggs and add the cheese. Be sure to spread butter over the tops of those crusty biscuits."

Faith and Cherish came into the kitchen. "Good morning, everyone," she said.

Jack reached for the baby. "Come to your . . . come to Jack, precious." Taking the baby and noticing Faith's pale face, Jack whispered, "Are you all right?" He had almost made a big blunder by calling himself, *Papa.*

***

Faith turned and hurried back into the bedroom. She pulled the curtains closed and sat down on the big bed. *Precious, Precious,* the name was rolling over and over in her mind. *"Don't hit Precious again. Please don't hurt my Precious."* Someone was pleading with another person not to hit…me? Was my name Precious? Oh my goodness, thought Faith. Another clear flashback of my past. I pray that I will get my full memory back, and all these flashbacks will fit together. My life, if these memories are real, doesn't sound like a happy one, though.

"Faith," Jack called. "Can I come in?"

"Yes, please come in." Faith swiped the tears from her eyes and cheeks.

"Sally is feeding Cherish her morning bottle. Mrs. Godwin has cooked a wonderful breakfast. Are you all right?"

"Jack, I remembered something, I think. Let's eat and I will tell you about it later. I am starved."

***

After breakfast was finished and the dishes were washed and put away, Sally asked Jack and Faith if she could borrow the mules and wagon. "With the money you paid me, I sure would like to take Ma and my brothers to town. My brothers are going to start school and they're in need of clothes. I have enough money to give Ma for flour and sugar." Sally opened her white hanky and counted her wages.

"Of course, you can use the team. I'll hitch the wagon and mules up for you," Jack said.

"I wouldn't ask, but with Mrs. Godwin here to help out, I thought this would be a good time to take the boys and get them fitted for overalls and a new shirt."

Jack watched the happy expression on Sally's face as she spoke about buying her little brothers some new clothes, but one new set of clothing wasn't near enough. "I would appreciate it if you'll give Mrs. Mason a note from me," Jack said.

"I'm happy to do anything for you, Mr. Jack." Sally turned to Faith. "Do you have a list of items you want me to bring back from town?"

"No, I don't think we need anything that can't wait until we make another trip. You should take a couple of dozen eggs and butter to share with your mama."

"She'll really appreciate them, Miss Faith. I'll churn more butter tomorrow, and we'll have more buttermilk for biscuits." Sally glanced at Mary Jane.

"Honey child, we still have buttermilk, at least enough for biscuits tonight."

***

Sally entered her house, carrying the eggs and butter.

"Sally!" Mrs. Parker was thrilled to see her daughter but worried at the same time. "Don't tell me you lost your job."

"No, Ma, I came to take you and the boys to town. Go and comb your hair and put on your best dress. I'll call the boys and get them washed."

Sally carried the eggs and butter over to the counter next to the stove. "Miss Faith sent these things over. She's such a thoughtful lady."

"Sally, I don't have money to buy anything in town. Ain't no sense in me going," Mrs. Parker said.

"I have my wages. I have been tucking some of it back so I could buy the boys some school clothes. I'll still have enough for supplies that you need," Sally said, too excited to stand still.

After the boys washed their faces and arms, and combed their hair, and Mrs. Parker changed into her only other dress, Sally drove them to the dry goods store, explaining to her brothers that they needed pants and shirts to wear to school.

They both made ugly faces but followed their big sister to the men's clothes.

"Pick out a shirt and a pair of overalls and then you can try them on to make sure they fit." She turned to the proprietor. "Mrs. Mason, I brought my brothers in for some things, and Mr. Jack sent you this note." Sally handed it to her and waited for a response.

***

Mrs. Mason read the note to herself.

"Mrs. Mason, please allow Sally to purchase three pair of pants, three shirts, and several pairs of long johns for her brothers. Make sure she fits them for good boots, too. Tell her she has enough money, but I will pay the difference. Don't tell her that I am helping. Jack Mills.

***

"Do you want me to tell him anything?" Sally asked, watching her mother as she looked at all the pretty things in the store.

Mrs. Mason shook her head and asked, "Now, how can I help you today?"

"My brothers need overalls, a shirt, and some long johns. You know it's getting colder and they'll need them for school. Can they try the things on? I want them to have a little growing room."

After the boys were fitted for clothes, Sally chose each boy a pair of blue overalls and a shirt.

"Now, Sally, you have plenty of money. Get your brothers several pairs of overalls and shirts. They need at least two sets of long johns."

Sally glanced at her money and asked quietly, "Are you sure? I mean, I thought clothes were expensive."

"I'm having a sale today. Now, let's walk back to the boots. They need a good sturdy pair of boots to wear to school. You don't want them to go barefooted in the cold weather."

Sally glanced at her mother's feet, and her heart dropped. She had tied her shoe soles on her feet with some thin leather. "Do you think I have enough to get Ma some new ones, too?"

"Of course, you do. Come, Mrs. Parker. Sally wants you to try on some shoes."

Sally's mama looked dumbfounded. "Me? We came to outfit the boys, not me."

"Ma, you need shoes, and I have the money today. Please pick out a pair and try them for size."

***

Mrs. Mason wrapped Sally's purchases in brown paper and tied it with a sturdy brown cord. The look on Sally's face brought joy to her heart to see this young girl spending her hard-earned wages on her family. Sally's pa worked their dirt farm and scraped enough money together each year to replant his field and keep his livestock fed. There wasn't much money left over for personal things.

Before they left the store, Sally asked for three peppermint sticks of candy. She offered the boys each one and gave her mother the last one. Mrs. Mason reached into the jar and pulled out one more and said to Sally, "This one is yours."

Standing in the doorway of the store, Mrs. Mason watched the

Parker family drive out of town. She hurried back to the counter and wrote the extra charges down by Jack's name. "Now, that's a good man," she said, voicing her opinion to no one but herself.

***

Sally parked the wagon near the front door of the house. She hurried around to help her mother get down when she saw her pa's old friend, Tucker Mudd, walking out of the privy. He was pulling on his overalls and stuffing his large hand down inside them to adjust his body parts. The man had no manners at all, thought Sally.

When he rounded the house, he saw Sally. "Well, look here. Ain't you the little beauty queen all dolled up in your finery and a ribbon tied in those pretty blond curls?" He grinned, revealing his tobacco-stained teeth. "Where you been keeping yourself, sweetheart? Glenn and me been missing you."

"I'm not your sweetheart, and it ain't none of your business where I keep myself." Glancing around him she asked, "Where's my pa?"

"He's in the barn. We been fishing, and he's skinning the big catfish that we caught. He said that you'd cook them for our supper."

"Pa never said any such thing. He knows that I've been staying over at Mr. Mills' cabin." Sally gasped, realizing she'd spilled the beans as to her whereabouts. Clamping her teeth shut to contain herself from saying harsh words to her pa's friend, she whirled around to head to the barn.

The burly man stepped in front of her and jerked her around to face him. "Now, sweetheart, you know that I still have my eye on you for Glenn. He sure could use a wife since he's nearly grown."

"Glenn ain't no man. He's hardly older than me."

"Well, that ain't no never mind. You can come and be my gal until he is older. You'll enjoy sharing my bed."

"Get out of the way before I scream for Pa." Sally twisted and tried to pull away.

"Hey daughter, why do you need to scream for me? What's going on?" Mr. Parker came out of the barn carrying a bucket of fish heads and guts.

"Nothing for you to be bothered about, Jed. I was telling your gal how pretty she is all cleaned up."

"Well, gal, you sure do look nice. Where did you get that new dress?" Jed Parker asked. It had been nearly two weeks since he'd laid eyes on his daughter.

Sally walked toward her father as he set the bucket down. She hugged him tightly. "I bought the dress with some of my wages a while back. But Pa, this here friend of yours is nagging me to come and share his bed until Glenn is old enough to marry me."

Sally watched her pa thrust out his chest, getting close enough to stand toe to toe with his friend. His face turned beet red, and the veins in his neck protruded.

"Get off my farm and never show your face around here again. You are disgusting. No man, especially a friend of mine, will speak to my sweet little girl like that."

Tucker Mudd stood straight and stared at his longtime friend, Jed. "I never spoke those words to Sally. She's lying!"

"One thing I know about my kids is they don't lie. I taught them all to be good, honest children. If Sally said you spoke those words, I believe her. Now, you'd best git away from here and never let our paths cross again." Jed Parker stared his friend down.

As Tucker Mudd passed Sally, he mummied, "You'll be sorry, gal."

Sally and her pa watched the man climb on his mule and ride away from the farm. "I'm sorry, Pa. I know you and Mr. Mudd have been friends for a long time, but he has tried several times to touch me. He was always making Glenn come over and get me to go berry picking with him or anything to get me away from the house. Ma would tell him to go home."

"You should have told me sooner, and I would've put a stop to them pestering you," Pa said.

"Mama hid me in the house whenever he came over because she was afraid you wouldn't believe me," Sally said and hung her head.

"Come on. Let's git inside. I haven't seen the boys today." Mr. Parker placed his arm across Sally's shoulders, and they entered the farmhouse. "You know, gal, I don't even know how many years have passed since you were born. How old are you?"

"I ain't sure. I think Ma might know. She told me the new doctor wrote the date the boys were born in our old Bible. Maybe we should ask her to look at the date Wendell was born and add a couple of years to me. I remember her telling me that she lost two babes in between Wendell and me."

The two boys, Wendell and Bobby, raced to their father. He

stooped down and hugged them tightly in his strong, muscular arms. "You boys been behaving today?"

"Sure, Pa. Sally took us and Ma to town, and we got new overalls and boots for school and Ma got new shoes, too. It was a great day."

"Pa, I got new cowboy boots and a peppermint stick," Bobby said.

"I believe I could have guessed that, son." Pa grinned at the red sticky circle on Bobby's mouth.

"Sally, I sure do thank you for working over at Mr. Mills' cabin. He is paying you a good wage, but I know you have earned it."

"Miss Faith and the baby are so sweet. Mr. Mills is going to have to marry her soon."

"Does that mean you'll be coming home?" Ma asked.

"No, Ma. They want me to stay for a while until Miss Faith's memory returns." Sally looked around the kitchen and saw her mother's Bible sitting on a shelf. "Pa was asking me my age, and I told him maybe you could look in the Good Book and tell me when Wendell was born. Remember the doctor wrote the date of his birth in the Bible. You said he was born several years after I was."

"That is true. You and I can't read, but I bet Wendell can read the date and year." She reached for the Bible and flipped open to the doctor's writing. There were only two entries: Name (son of Jed and Sadie Parker) born, Wendell Robert Parker, December 1, 1856; Name (son of Jed and Sadie Parker) born, Robert Abraham Parker, July 4, 1857.

"Wendell, can you read these dates on this page?" Sadie held the book down on the table in front of her oldest son.

"Hey, I see my name, Wendell, right here. The numbers at the end of this sentence says De...cem...ber 1, 1856." Wendell pointed with his finger at each number, proud of himself that he could read.

"December 1, 1856, is when Wendell was born, so, Sally, we can take away three years. I lost two babes at birth before my boy here came in the world squalling."

"Sally was born in 1853," Pa spoke while counting the numbers backward on his fingers. "This year is 1865. Wendell, count from 1853 to 1865."

They all stood at his shoulder while he pointed at each finger. "Sally is twelve years old. What date and month were you born, big sister?"

"Ma, do you guess you might be able to remember? I never even had a birthday party like some of the other kids in church."

"Now, Pa, you started all this. Maybe you can help me remember what month. It was freezing cold, and it was after Christmas." Mama sat down at the table next to Wendell.

"That's right. I believe it was the first of the year because some of the men were celebrating the New Year when I stopped in town to get some flour and sugar. After I arrived home, you were ready to have the baby. I delivered you, Sally, right there in that front room." He walked over to his wife and squeezed her shoulders. Sadie touched his right hand, patting it as a show of affection.

Sally squealed. "I was born on January 1, 1853, and I'm twelve years old. How wonderful to learn something so special about oneself." Everyone smiled as Wendell printed Sally's name in the Bible, just like the doctor had done.

"I guess I'd better get on back to help Miss Faith and Mr. Jack. Boys, y'all take care of them boots so they'll look good for school. I'll bring the mule back for you to ride. Mr. Jenkins, the livery owner, said that you could leave him in his corral while you're in school, and he will feed him some water and hay for a dollar a month."

"That's sure nice of him," Pa said. "I don't like you walking that trail alone to come see us. I get worried about you."

"Mr. Mills will loan me one of his mules or a horse, or he may even bring me. He won't like for me to have to walk either, so don't fret over me," Sally said. "I'd better go now so I can get supper ready."

Chapter 12

Sally could hardly contain her excitement as she drove Jack's wagon and mule to the barn. As she debarked from the wagon, she noticed two strange horses tied to the corral fence. Who in the blue blazes is here?

As she climbed down, Jack rushed out of the house to assist her. "Were you able to outfit your brothers for school?" Jack asked, watching Bear jumped up and down around Sally. She leaned over and rubbed the dog's fuzzy head and grinned at Jack.

"Oh, yes, Mr. Jack. I had enough money to get mama a new pair of sturdy shoes, too. She'd been tying the bottom of her shoe soles onto her feet with leather ties. I wanted to cry when I saw her feet. She didn't want me to spend my money on her, but I could afford to get them because you and the good Lord blessed me with this good job."

"We are the ones blessed to have you here with us," Jack said, taking her elbow. "We'll most likely have company for supper. Reverend Peterson and the traveling minister, Reverend Samuel Wright stopped by to see if we have made a decision about marrying." He sighed and kicked the dirt with his boot. "Faith and I haven't had a chance to talk with the preacher because the baby has been so fretful."

"The women said you had two days to make up your minds. I know that Faith will do what's right. She's worried about her memory. Not being able to remember her past has to be scary," Sally said as she looked toward the cabin.

"Go on inside while I put up the team and wagon. Faith will be happy to see you. Cherish has cried ever since you drove away early this morning. Mary Jane has tried to help, but she fought her, wanting only her mother. Faith has rocked her for hours. She's worried about you, too, traveling all alone. I told her that you know everyone, and no one would try to harm you."

Mary Jane rushed over to greet Sally and helped to remove her coat. "Welcome home," she proclaimed, as if Sally had been gone for weeks. "Cherish missed you. She's cried since breakfast. I did fix lunch, and I have started a roast in the oven."

"Where's Faith?" Sally questioned as she noticed the men standing at the table with Faith nowhere in sight. Before Mary Jane answered her, the baby cried out.

Sally rushed past Mary Jane into the bedroom where she found Faith sitting on the side of the bed swaying Cherish in her arms.

Faith's eyes brightened when she saw her. "Oh, Sally, I don't know what is wrong with her. Cherish started crying after you left, and she hasn't stopped. She won't take a bottle, and she hasn't messed her diaper either."

"I bet she has the colic," she felt Cherish's stomach and it was hard. The baby pulled her legs up to her stomach and hiccupped. She put her fists in her mouth.

"My poor baby," Sally said, kissing her on the cheeks. "My ma has a remedy for colic. She doctored Mrs. Gatewood's baby while I was still at home. Mama put crushed catnip herb in warm tea and gave the baby some gripe water. It has several things mixed in it that Ma never told me about, but I will ride over on a mule and get the medicine. Should be gone less than thirty minutes." She flew past Mary Jane and the two ministers and raced to the barn.

"Mr. Jack," Sally called, "help me on the back of one of the mules. I need to ride home and get medicine for the baby." Sally waited for Jack to lift her on the back of the animal.

"Be careful and hurry back," Jack said. He turned to the cabin only to see the two ministers coming toward the barn. "Mr. Mills, I'm sorry that I didn't get to speak with you and the missus. Reverend Peterson said that the young lady couldn't remember anything about her past. I was wondering if she may have come from down south, near Mobile, Alabama."

"She says she can't remember her name, where she's from, or why she was traveling with the couple who died in the accident," Jack said. "We are worried about whether she's married."

"Yes, I can understand your concern. I thought she might be a couple's daughter that went missing from near Mobile, Alabama.

Her father says that his girl ran away. The mother's expression tells me that something else might have happened to her," the traveling minister said with a flat-toned voice.

"Does Faith look like the young lady you're speaking about?" Jack's spirits lifted.

"I'm sorry. I never saw the girl. One woman suggested a man was involved in her disappearance, and a few of the townspeople are worried that something bad happened to the girl."

"We've got to get back to town," Reverend Peterson spoke.

"You both are welcome to stay for supper. Mary Jane and Sally are both good cooks." Jack smiled at the men, but they still refused.

***

Riding as fast as the mule could carry her on the way back to Jack's, Sally suddenly pulled on the reins of the mule.

Glenn Mudd jumped into Sally's path. He threw up his arms and yelled, "whoa!"

Sally pulled tightly on the mule's reins and moved to the side of the trail. "What are you doing, you crazy fool?" Sally yelled at the boy who lay in the bushes on the side of the road. "I nearly run you down." Sally rode closer to the young boy.

Glenn stood and brushed his overalls clean of dirt. "Where are you headed in such a hurry? I wanted to stop you and just talk. I didn't want you to get hurt."

"I've got to get back to Mr. Mills' cabin. Faith's baby is very sick, and Ma gave me medicine to help her. Now move, please, so I can continue to the cabin."

"All right, I'll get out of you way, but I do want to talk to you. I'm sorry that Pa upset you a few days ago."

"I'm sorry, too. I don't have time to talk today. Maybe later, another time." Sally kicked the mule in the side and rode off, leaving Glenn staring after her.

Sally entered the cabin with the medicine for the baby. The two men had left and she knew that Faith was relieved. She washed her hands and took the jar of herbs out of a cloth bag, then sprinkled a few herbs in the baby bottle, carried the bottle of warm tea into the bedroom, and took Cherish out of Faith's arms. Shaking the bottle with one hand and holding the babe with the other, she motioned for Faith to lie down on the bed. "You rest while I give her this medicine. She will go to sleep soon."

"What are you going to give her?" Faith asked with expectant eyes.

"My ma says its catnip tea. It will give her tummy some relief and help her sleep. I have some gripe water to give her if she isn't better when she wakes."

Faith smiled at Sally and relaxed on the bed while adjusting a whimpering baby in her arms. Sally sat in a straight chair and hummed a sweet song to Cherish as the baby sucked the tea and tried to touch Sally's face.

Mary Jane came into the room and covered Faith with a quilt. "I've heard of catnip tea. I might take some myself," Mary Jane said, laughing. "Cherish's crying has put all of our nerves on edge."

Sally continued with her humming as Faith drifted off to sleep. The baby cried when she was placed on her shoulder to burp. The bottle finished, the baby's eyelids became heavy, and she closed them.

Jack sat at the kitchen table and sighed. Peace in the cabin sounded so good, he thought. Mary Jane came out of the bedroom and sat down next to Jack. "You know, Mary Jane, I don't know how Faith and I could manage without Sally. She is the smartest young girl I have ever known, and I have three sisters older than her at home."

"Country folks teach their children young to do household chores and work on their farms. City kids miss out on a lot of common-sense living. I had a little of both, being raised on a big plantation. Mama made my sisters and I do chores even though we had plenty of household help. I learned to do needlework, cook, and work in the kitchen garden. Mama said every young lady needed to know how to take care of a home." She lifted her head and looked toward the front windows.

"It sounds like you have a very wise mother."

"Mr. Mills, I hear someone outside." Mary Jane stood. Jack was already pushing back his chair. Bear was barking and growling. Jack stepped off the porch. A carriage with a young boy driving a two-horse team pulled up. Henrietta Smith sat on the back seat.

"Welcome, Mrs. Smith. Here, let me help you down."

"Wait, Henrietta. Don't get out of the carriage." Mary Jane hurried past Jack as fast as she could to speak to her friend. "Have you come out here to spend the night?"

"You know I have. Our commander said it was time for me to chaperone Mr. Mills and his lady friend. She said that she would come tomorrow since they have to make a decision about getting married. My man and kids are so upset with me because I had to do my duty," Henriette sniffed.

"I hurried out here to tell you that I will stay another night with Mr. Mills and Faith. I am enjoying myself, so I'll take your turn. Go on home now and don't worry about Virginia. I have everything in hand out here."

"If you're sure. I know my family will be glad I've come home. Thanks, Mary Jane. Let's go, boy, before she changes her mind."

After Mary Jane waved bye to her friend, she came back inside the cabin. Jack stood at the window watching her.

"Mr. Mills, you do remember that you and Faith have to come to a decision tomorrow? Virginia will probably be pounding on your door early in the morning. She knows that you will agree to marry, and she's like a runaway horse heading back toward the barn. That woman is ready for the sewing circle to start making Faith's wedding dress and gather all the others to instruct them on what dishes to prepare for the reception. She wants this to be a big event for the whole town," Mary Jane explained.

"Why does she want to make a big to-do out of our marriage? The townspeople hardly know me, and only a couple of people have met Faith. She's asking a lot out of the ladies to spend their time and precious money on perfect strangers."

"When that woman gets a hornet in her bonnet, there's no stopping her. The town has so little entertainment except for the Fourth of July picnic, and the town's mayor election is coming up soon. It's a good time for her to campaign for her husband—as if someone else wants to run against old Harvey, who has been the mayor for years.

***

Faith had gotten up to use the chamber pot when she overheard Jack and Mary Jane speaking about their wedding plans. She leaned her head up against the wall and sighed. The mayor's wife wanted to put Jack and her on display in the center of the church, it seemed. After completing her personal needs, Faith slipped on her shawl and entered the kitchen.

"We thought you were asleep. Are you all right, dear?" Mary

Jane asked.

"Yes, I'm fine. Sally is lying on the bed resting and Cherish is finally asleep." Faith said, looking at Jack. "May we go outside for a breath of fresh air?" Faith smiled.

"Certainly, let me get my boots on, and we can go and look at the new piglets. Mary Jane, will you listen out for the baby and Sally? We won't be long," Jack said as he held the door open for Faith.

Chapter 13

"I love this small farm and all the animals. The goats and piglets are so cute. How many did the mama sow have this time?" Faith was speaking fast because she was so angry.

"She had nine, but she rolled over one and smothered it. Poor little thing. I try to be on hand when she's giving birth, but I was a little late this time." He watched the piglets crawl around the sow's big belly, looking for a free teat. Jack stooped down on one knee and rearranged a few of the tiny babies. "What's on your mind that you felt we needed privacy?" He dusted off his hands with his red hanky.

"I couldn't help but overhear May Jane discussing the wedding plans that the ladies have organized. I'm sorry, but I'm not going to have any of it. I know the mayor's wife will be disappointed, but we're being forced into this wedding, and I'm not going to stand in church and act like we're head over heels in love. If I agree to marry up with you, we aren't going to be this year's entertainment for the townspeople." She sighed and wiped away a tear that had formed. "I don't need a fancy wedding dress or a church full of strangers watching."

Faith walked over and petted a new baby goat that Jack had bought from a trapper last week. With her voice breaking, she spoke softly to Jack, "I'm not sure who I am, my age, where I come from, where I was going, or if I have a husband who might be searching high and low for me. If and when he finds me, it will be easier to explain that we were forced into a simple, quiet ceremony to satisfy the town's leaders. Do you understand what I'm saying?"

When he didn't answer right away, she was disappointed. She wanted to ask if he had ever felt love for her, and the romance that she craved from him, but she couldn't bring herself to do that.

Jack could feel Faith's embarrassment as she spoke of their

pending marriage. "I agree with you. We can go into town, meet with Reverend Peterson, and get married. All we need is Sally and the baby. Afterward, he can tell Mrs. Ledbetter that we're married and to leave us alone." He grinned at her and loosened the goat's rope and placed him in the new pen inside the barn. "It seems that you have agreed to marry me, but I think you have something else on your mind." Jack leaned against his worktable, crossing his arms and ankles.

Rubbing her hands, she smiled. "Yes, you're right. I have decided to marry you. Thank you so much for understanding. I feel that I've been forced upon you."

"I don't feel that way at all. I hate that the people in Gibson can't mind their own business, but we can't control their actions," he responded with light sarcasm. "When your memory returns, and if you discover that you have a husband, I will personally take you and Cherish to him. I'll do whatever you want me to do."

"One more thing, if you don't mind—" she snuck a glance at Jack. "I would like to discuss our living arrangement."

Jack stiffened and waited for her to continue.

With misty green eyes, she looked at the barn floor. "I would like for Sally to continue to live with us until I know about my past. I'd like to keep our sleeping arrangement as it is for now." She dared a glance at her soon-to-be husband.

"Of course," he said, shifted his attention to the new baby goat. But she noticed a sad, wistful look in his eyes.

***

Later that afternoon, Sally went to the chicken yard to gather eggs and feed her pet chickens. She had been at Jack's cabin long enough to name many of the hens. As she told the girls good night, she closed the chicken yard gate and was immediately grabbed from behind. Turning around, she recognized her attacker, who told her to keep quiet or he would knock her out. Being too afraid to listen to the man, she screamed for Jack. The big man slapped her across the face, keeping his promise to knock her out cold. Falling to her knees, the man began dragging her to his mule.

***

Jack tossed his shovel to the ground when he heard Sally scream and rushed out of the barn into the sunshine. A big man was dragging Sally who was struggling and screaming, "No, I ain't going with you!" She refused to stand which made it harder for her attacker to force her on his horse.

She kicked her attacker with such viciousness and hit him in the groin, her target. He released her and fell forward just as Jack reached him. Jack jerked the man up on his feet and smacked his fist in the middle of his ugly face, spewing blood from his nose. The man fell forward with bloody cheeks, lips, and chin.

Sally jumped up off the ground and asked, "Is he dead?"

"I don't believe so, but he is going to wish he was after spending time in jail. Sheriff Matt doesn't care for men mistreating our womenfolk," Jack said between breaths. "Do you know this man?" Jack turned to Sally as he rolled the big ugly man over on his back.

"Yep, I do. He came around to fish or drink a jug with Pa. He has a shack not too far from our place. Last week, while I was at home, he made some nasty remarks to me, and Pa told him to leave and never come back. His name is Tucker Mudd."

"Don't believe I have ever seen him around town before. I know that I've never run into him out on the trail trapping." Jack spun around, when he heard a grunt behind him. The attacker had raised on all fours and bent forward roaring like a wild bull. Lowering his head, he charged and was hell-bent on hitting Jack in the belly.

The collision sent Jack sprawling backward, but the man's target was off-center. He hit Jack in the side making him stumble back to the hard-packed earth. Jack rolled over and kicked the big man in the stomach with both feet. The man cursed but continued to grab at Jack's ankles. All of a sudden, Jack heard a solid thump and watched his opponent crash forward. Faith stood looking down at the man she'd just hit over the head with a heavy board.

"Oh my, I killed him," she said and covered her mouth with her hand.

"He's not dead, but he's gonna have one bad headache." Jack stood and shook his head, attempting to get his head on straight. He lifted Faith and carried her over to the porch and lowered her against the wall. There wasn't a cry of a bird or a hoot of an owl. The whole area was scared to make any noise.

"Are you hurt anywhere?" Jack asked. He ran his hand over her arms.

Faith pulled her body into a ball. "I'm fine, but you need to check on Sally."

Jack dragged the unconscious man onto his flatbed wagon and carried him into town. The sheriff listened to Jack's tale about how the man tried to kidnap Sally. Once Jack filed charges against the man, he headed home.

It was dark, rainy, and cold when Jack came inside from the barn. He was hungry, tired, and his right hand hurt like the devil. Jack needed to get warm, but Faith couldn't build a fire worth a darn. Entering the kitchen, he was pleasantly surprised the room was nice and cozy. His fingers jerked the laces on his wet vest while his stomach growled at the smell of the stew. He quickly stripped off his plaid shirt and the top of his union suit, tossing them in the corner. "I should have stayed in town until it stopped raining," he muttered.

Faith stood stiff and looked at Jack's bare torso. She couldn't take her eyes off him.

He noticed her staring at his naked chest. "Do you have a dry towel?"

Shaking herself out of her daze, she handed him a towel and stuttered, "Can I get you a cup of coffee and something to eat?"

Jack groaned. "Yelp, if it's not too much trouble."

"No trouble at all," she said, as she placed the coffeepot over the hot burner on the stove. She reached under the counter and took a fresh loaf of bread and sliced four pieces. Filling a big bowl of rabbit stew, she placed the bowl on the table close to the fire and poured a cup of hot coffee. "I hope this will be fine. Sally made sugar cookies. They're in the jar in the center of the table. Help yourself," Faith said, as she noticed all the dark bruising and cuts on his shoulder. His left eye was almost swollen shut.

"You eat while I get the medicine bag down and doctor your eye and cuts. You left so fast with that man that I didn't notice that you were hurt."

"I do need to soak my hand in some salty water. My fist hurts from hitting that crazy man," Jack said as he attempted to flex his hand open and close.

After Jack ate his full, Faith dressed the cut on his shoulder and made a warm poultice to go on his eye as he sat with his right hand in a bowl of hot water.

"Sheriff McDonald said he would hold Sally's attacker in jail until the circuit judge comes to town and holds a trial. You and I will have to go into town and tell our story about what he was trying to do to Sally." Taking a deep breath, Jack lifted his hand and dried it with the towel. "The warm salty water does wonders for soreness. Thanks."

"Yes, I will be willing to do anything for Sally. I hope we will never have to see that big man again after the trial," Faith said, trying not to cry.

"If the weather permits, let's get up early, go into town, and get the ceremony over with. We can be back home in a few hours. I'm going to make a mighty fine groom with a swollen lip, black eye, and one good hand."

Smiling for the first time all day, Faith said, "Maybe Reverend Peterson's wife will think that I had to use force to get you to marry me." Jack reached for Faith's hand as they laughed together.

Chapter 14

Standing at the altar in the Gibson's white chapel, Faith wore a new white shirtwaist and long green shirt that she made from the dress that she'd worn when she arrived.

Jack stood beside Faith in his best shirt, covered with a leather vest, a string tie, and a pair of new stiff denim pants. The minister wasn't long-winded by any means, but the words were just as binding.

***

Cherish struggled in Sally's arms, whimpering for her bottle. Sally had never witnessed a wedding before, and she wasn't going to miss a thing, so she ignored the baby's uncomfortable position.

"You may kiss your bride," Reverend Peterson spoke loud and clear. Jack glanced down at Faith as she lifted her face up to Jack's.

"Congratulations, my pet," Jack said as he placed a sweet peck on his new wife's rosy lips. Faith and Jack stood frozen in time until a shrill cry came from the front door. The couple parted and watched as Virginia Ledbetter stormed toward the front of the church with Henrietta on her heels.

Faith maneuvered to Sally and took Cherish into her arms. "Please hand me her bottle," she whispered.

Reverend Peterson stepped in front of Jack and held both of his hands in the air. "You're too late for the ceremony, Virginia. The deed is done, and the young couple is eager to reach their home before the storm breaks."

"But . . . but, we had big plans for a splendid wedding. Everyone is planning on coming this Sunday. What will I tell them?" she shrieked.

"Tell them the truth," Jack said.

"Pray tell, what is the truth?" Virginia said between clenched teeth.

"We are a young couple, and we couldn't wait another day to be together. Now, excuse us and have a good day." Jack took Faith's arm as she thanked Mrs. Peterson for being so kind to them.

Henrietta stopped Sally and asked, "Where's Mary Jane? She will be in trouble with Virginia because she didn't come in this morning and tell her about this. Virginia had big plans for a celebration to help get her husband re-elected."

"Mary Jane stayed at the cabin to help with morning chores and start lunch. We appreciate all of her help." Sally shook Henrietta's hand loose from her upper arm and said, "I've got to go. It's going to storm, and we need to hurry. Bye."

A fall storm had begun blowing, and thunder was upsetting the team of horses. Jack fought to keep them from running dangerously fast. By the time he rounded the curb on the trail that carried them home, the lightning hit some of the smaller trees. He said a small prayer of thanks that they had arrived home before the rain fell upon them.

"Well, we're safely home and married, for better or worse," Faith mumbled to Jack. She wanted to cry. A loud crack of thunder made her jump and hold the baby tighter. Jack drove the wagon as close as he could to the front porch and stopped the horses.

"Here, let me help you down before those clouds open up." Faith had made it inside the front door when a solid sheet of rain hit the rooftop. In a few minutes, a heavy rain came pouring down, and she hoped that Jack had made it to the barn. She laid Cherish down in her bed as Sally raced around the cabin closing the windows. Bear followed her every step, playfully jumping after her.

Faith stared down at the baby. This was her wedding day. Maybe even her second wedding day. Regret pinged her heart. Who did she marry first? Was her first husband still alive? Would she be able to be intimate with the man she married today? Would she ever hear the words, "I love you," from his lips? Sighing, she had to stop daydreaming and feeling self-pity. This wonderful man, to whom she had said vows, had given up his life, home, and all his personal belongings to her. She quickly bowed her head and prayed, *Lord, please help me regain my memory.*

The storm brought more thunder and lightning and a chill to the cabin. Luckily, Jack came in, slapping warmth into his arms. "I'll build up the fire. The front room is too cold for the baby," Jack said and tossed more logs in the fireplace.

"My old fat bones were getting cold," laughed Mary Jane. "Mr. Mills, will you drive me back to town tomorrow? I have enjoyed being out here with all of you, but it's time for me to return to my place."

"Of course, I will, but we'll miss your biscuits." Jack grinned.

"Well, I will just have to make a big batch tonight." Mary Jane laughed and reached for her apron. "I have pork chops almost ready to come out of the oven. I need to mash the potatoes, and after the biscuits are ready, we can eat."

***

Amish Community
Lawrence, Kansas

"Sarah, I will be back as soon as I can locate my cousin and his wife. Thee will start in the town of Gibson, Tennessee, where he mailed me his note," Elder Leon Studerman said to his wife. "The Santa Fe will make several stops and I will get off and ask around about Cornelius. I know he was traveling in a covered wagon, but he might have been seen by some of the townspeople."

"Be careful. Maybe by the time you arrive home, Thy cousin and his wife might be here waiting on thee."

"Let's pray that will be the case. I hope they will be here soon. I can't keep asking Mr. Johnson to hold the land and house that Cornelius asked me to find for him. Mr. Johnson has another buyer, but I have pleaded with him to wait another week. I don't want an English family moving into our community." Elder Studerman placed his black circle hat on his head and climbed into the carriage. "I'll leave the rig at Mr. Black's livery while I'm gone."

Each time the train stopped to take on water and allow passengers some privacy, Elder Studerman asked strangers if they had seen a man dressed like himself. He received the same answer each time which was disappointing. After two days of travel, he arrived near Gibson, Tennessee. The elder had to rent a horse to ride the thirty miles to the town where his cousin may have camped and written him a note, letting him know that he should arrive in Lawrence, Kansas, in several weeks if the weather remained good.

Tired and hungry, Elder Studerman noticed the dry goods store. He entered the busy store and waited until the clerk behind the counter finished with her customer.

**

"Hello," Mrs. Mason greeted the stranger dressed like an Amish man or Amish standing in the corner of her store.

"Madam." Elder Studerman removed his black hat and rubbed his hand down his long, black beard. "I am Mr. Studerman and am looking for a place to eat, but first I have a few questions, if thee have the time to speak with me."

"There's a small café down the street. Food is good and not too expensive. I do have a few minutes, so how can I help you?" Mrs. Mason eyed the man while evaluating his manner and appearance. Sometimes he spoke with *thee* and *thy* and then in other sentences he said, *you* and *your*.

"I'm from Lawrence, Kansas, and I am searching for my cousin and his wife. He wrote me a note and said that he was camping near this town and was resting his mules and gathering more supplies. He would have dressed similar to me."

"I'm sorry, but I don't recall waiting on a man dressed like you. About how long ago did you receive a letter from him?"

"Oh, I would say about seven or eight weeks. He should have left here and been on the trail closer to Kansas by now."

Mrs. Mason's first thought went to Faith, Jack's new wife. She had arrived about that time with another older couple who had been murdered. Neither she nor her husband had sold them any supplies. She needed to speak with Jack about the couple he buried. "How long are you going to be in Gibson, Mr. Studerman?"

He cocked an eyebrow at Mrs. Mason. "Do thee know something you aren't telling me, Madam?" he questioned her like she was hiding something for him.

"No, I was just thinking back to the time you said the couple was here. Sorry, I don't know anything about your cousin." Mrs. Mason walked behind the counter and placed several cans of tobacco on the shelf. There was something that she didn't like about the man, so she ended their conversation.

***

Elder Studerman circled the room and walked out of the store, heading down the boardwalk to the café. He glanced at the few people who were walking in and out of the other stores. Seeing the boardinghouse sign, he thought he would eat and rent a room for the night.

***

Mrs. Mason listened for her nephew as he came from the back of the store. "Jody, I need for you to take a note to Jack Mills for me. I will write it out, and I need for you to hurry out to his cabin."

***

Jack had packed his mules and prepared to check his traps. "I will be gone for two days. Bear will remain here and guard the house. He'll let you know if there is any danger. Do you think you can use the shotgun I left over the fireplace?"

"Yes, you showed me how to use it, but I'm sure we will be fine while you're gone." Faith tried to use humor to lighten the moment. She was going to miss him. They had been only married one day, but their marriage was in name only. Maybe in time, when her memory returned, they could resolve their feelings. If only her memory would return.

"Sally is here, and that man who tried to kidnap her is still in jail. If she needs to go home, you and Cherish ride along with her. Promise me that you'll stay together."

Bouncing lightly on her toes, she agreed. Jack grinned at her and went back into the barn to gather his horse and pack mules. He hoped the traps were full since he hadn't checked them in several days.

***

Faith and Sally stood on the porch and watched as Jack rode away from the barn. They went back into the warm room and decided that they would churn butter and make a few apple and pecan pies to take into town the next morning.

As Sally settled at the churn, a horse rode up into the front yard. Loud boots were stomping on the porch, then a pounding sounded at the door. Faith flew to the window and looked out at the young man. "I have never seen him before. Sally, come and look."

"Oh, that's Mrs. Mason's nephew. I'll let him in." Sally hurried over to the door before he woke up the baby.

"Sorry, to bother you. I have a note for Mr. Mills from my aunt Mildred. She said I was to give it to him and no one else."

"Well, you are about two hours too late. Mr. Mills has gone to check his traps. Give me the note, and I will give it to him when he returns," Sally said.

With a reluctant smile, he nodded and gave her the piece of folded paper. Jumping off the porch, he leaped back on his horse and rode toward town.

Sally gave Faith the folded paper and went back to her churning. Faith looked down at the paper and wondered if she should read the message. It wasn't sealed, only folded. Jack might think she read it anyway. "Maybe I should read this note." Faith fanned the paper as she spoke to Sally.

"I would if I could read," Sally said, "besides, it must be important for Mrs. Mason to send her nephew way out here with it. She may need Jack."

"You're right." Faith unfolded the paper and read the note.

Jack, an Amish man is asking about the couple you buried. Maybe he might know something about Faith. He is from Lawrence, Kansas. You should come to town and speak with this stranger.

Mildred Mason

"Miss Faith, are you all right? You're as white as a sheet. What's the note say?" She leaned closer to Faith's hands.

"There's a man in town who is asking about the couple that I was traveling with, I think." Faith strolled over to a kitchen chair and sat down, still holding the note. *What should I do?* Faith glanced at Sally. "Maybe I should go to town and talk with the man. I might remember him."

"You should wait until Mr. Jack comes home." She bit down on her bottom lip. "Mr. Jack will know what to do even if you do remember this man." Sally hurried over to the bedroom door and looked in at Cherish who was still sleeping.

"No, Sally. I can't wait for Jack to return. He said he would be gone for a couple of days. Let's prepare to go into town now. I'll pack a couple of bottles for Cherish and some nappies. Can you hitch the mule up to the carriage?"

"Sure, I can, but we should wait. I don't like the idea of talking with a strange man about your past."

"I won't speak with this man alone. Mrs. Mason will be with us, and you and the baby, of course. I'll be safe enough."

"I ain't worried about him harming you, but he might want you to go away with him. You're Mr. Jack's woman now." Sally's hands fidgeted.

"Get going and hitch the mule. We'll go into the store, speak with this man, and be home before dark." Faith placed her hand on Sally's shoulder and pushed her toward the door. "Let's hurry."

Chapter 15

Faith held the baby in her arms while Sally drove the small carriage toward town. She was having a hard time breathing, like something was squeezing her chest. The baby was sleeping, which gave Faith time to think and try to remember the couple that she discovered lying on the ground when she'd awakened from the accident.

Why had Jack chosen to go and check his traps today? Why had this stranger shown up when she was alone? Fear and anxiety flowed throughout her body. If only Jack was here with her, she wouldn't have this empty feeling. *Funny, I should be overjoyed that someone might know who I am and where I'm from.*

After entering the town, Sally drove the carriage to the front of the dry goods store and jumped down. She tied the reins to the hitching post and offered her hands to Faith to take the sleeping baby. Faith sat frozen in the seat, afraid of the unknown.

***

Mrs. Mason rushed to the boardwalk and looked into Faith's ashen face. She glanced around the carriage and asked, "Where's Jack? How come he is not with you?"

Sally answered for Faith. "Mr. Jack left early this morning to go check his traps. He will be gone for a couple of days." Sally stood on her tiptoes and looked over Mrs. Mason's shoulder. "Where's the stranger?"

"He is having a late lunch at the café. He will be here soon. Come on in and lay Cherish down on a pallet in the storeroom. You can sit on that barrel and watch her," Mrs. Mason said as she led the way.

Faith strolled over to the counter and looked down at the items placed in the glass case, not seeing anything. She was so nervous that she thought she might lose her lunch. The doorbell over the door jangled and Faith looked up to see a tall, bearded man dressed in a long black coat and stovepipe hat. He glanced at her and continued to look around.

Mrs. Mason and Sally walked from the storeroom chatting about the baby. Sally hopped on the barrel and fixed the curtain so she could view the baby's every move.

Mrs. Mason spotted the stranger who had asked questions about his cousin and wife. "Mr. Studerman, the man who may have information about your relative is out of town, but this is Faith. She was traveling with the couple about that time. Faith is willing to speak to you, but you must know that this young lady has lost her memory." She smiled at Faith. "Her real name is not Faith."

"Miss, I appreciate thee speaking with me. My cousin and his wife were traveling from the south. They were going to purchase a home and land in Lawrence, Kansas. He mailed a letter from this town informing me that he should be arriving in a few weeks or a month. Can you tell me anything about them?"

Faith bit down on her bottom lip and finally raised her eyes to peer at the stranger. "Sir, I woke up from the accident that must have taken place, and I couldn't remember my name or anything about myself. The couple, a man and a woman, dressed like you are now, were lying dead near the front of the wagon. Both of them had been shot. I have no idea why I was spared. Mr. Mills said their wagon had been emptied except for a few women clothes and baby items, like nappies and several gowns."

"Whose baby, and where is the child?" Elder Studerman asked.

"I got up off the ground, unhitched the two mules, and made my way to Mr. Mills' log cabin. Later that very night, I had a baby girl. She is sleeping in the storeroom now."

"Where's the baby's father?" The tall man stretched his neck around.

"I don't know," Faith answered honestly but blushed a bright red.

"You don't know, or you don't remember?"

"I don't remember; therefore, I don't know who or where he is."

"I see." He studied Faith. "You know my cousin's daughter had bright red hair just like yours. Do you think you might be my cousin's granddaughter?"

Faith jerked her head toward Mrs. Mason. "I have no idea. I came into town today, in hopes of meeting you, that I might remember something."

"Have I helped you to remember anything?"

"No. I don't remember anything. I can't tell you anything about the couple I was traveling with either. Jack, my husband, buried the couple. He may remember something that will help you decide if they are your kinfolk."

"Your husband?" The man was baffled.

"Yes, the townspeople forced Jack and me into marriage because I was living in his cabin. Sally was living with us, but because she is a child, they didn't give us a lot of choices."

"What about when you regain your memory and discover you may be married to an Amish man?" Elder Studerman stood taller and straighter than he had before. He scowled at Faith as if she was a piece of low life. "Would you be willing to go before the elders and ask for forgiveness for your sin in taking another husband?"

"Jack and I discussed problems that we would have to face if and when that happened. For now, we are not living in sin, as you so disrespectfully inferred, as husband and wife. We do have Sally living with us as our chaperone."

"This still may not be acceptable with our order. We have very stringent rules to live by."

Mrs. Mason stepped in between Faith and the tall man. "Well, if your Amish people won't accept Faith, then that's just fine with us, and I'm sure Jack will be very pleased."

"You're not sure if this young girl even has a husband. She may have committed sin by lying with a man before marriage. She doesn't remember."

"I think you'd better get out of my store before I call my husband. He'll toss your religious backside into the street. Our Faith is a decent girl, and I will not have you speaking about her like that. Out!" Mrs. Mason jabbed her finger toward the front door.

"I need to speak with the man who buried my cousin," he pleaded as he headed toward the door.

"When he returns to town, I'll send him your way. Don't come back in my store unless I send for you." Mrs. Mason and Faith stood in the doorway and watched the old Amish man make his way back up the boardwalk to the boardinghouse.

"That is one nasty man," mumbled Mrs. Mason. "I should never have sent Jack that note, then you wouldn't have had to confront him."

"It's all right," Faith replied as Cherish cried out. Sally rushed into the storage room and came out with the fretful baby on her shoulder.

"I'm sure she's ready for a bottle. Let me get it out of my bag, and I'll feed her," Faith said. She turned to Sally. "Why don't you stroll around the store and pick out another dress for yourself. Maybe we will go to church this Sunday. Jack should be home by then."

"I have plenty of things to wear. I don't need to spend money on myself when I know my folks could use some things."

"Please, pick out a new dress, and we will purchase supplies to take to your mother. We can drop them off on the way back to the cabin." Faith headed to the barrel and sat on it. Sally flipped through the dresses her size.

Everyone laughed at Cherish, smacking her lips over the nipple on the bottle.

"That one's a greedy little thing, isn't she?" Mrs. Mason commented as she set bags of flour, sugar, and salt on the counter. She reached into the jars at the end of the counter and counted out ten peppermint sticks, then set them aside for Sally's family.

"Mrs. Mason, will you please cut me six yards of that yellow gingham material? My ma has wanted curtains for our front windows for a long time. Put in yellow thread and some small nails to help hang them when she gets them finished." Sally fingered the material. "I can't wait to see the smile on Ma's face when I give it to her this afternoon."

***

After Mrs. Mason had tied up their parcels, they began their trip back to the cabin.

"Faith," Sally asked while keeping her eyes on the road ahead, "what if that old man can prove you're his kin? Do you think he can make you go with him to Kansas?"

"I don't know. It's possible that the older couple I was traveling with were my grandparents and I could be the man's niece. I have been wondering where the old couple's daughter—possibly my mother—might be."

"Well, if she was old enough to have a daughter your age, she must be married. Maybe, just maybe, when you were with child, she sent you away with her parents who were planning to move to Kansas. That could be the reason you were traveling with them."

"So, you think that maybe I was never married? I could have done something sinful with a boy and got in the family way?" Faith glanced at Sally.

"Look, I ain't accusing you of doing the nasty. Girls can get sweet-talked off their feet by a horny boy. They'll tell a girl anything to get her to lay with him."

"Where did you learn such things about boys and girls? You're only a child yourself." Faith couldn't believe the words that came out of Sally's mouth.

"My ma told me a lot of things about life. Good and bad. She didn't want me to grow up ignorant like she did. Before she was fourteen years old, she was hitched up with Pa because her papa discovered them in the hayloft."

Faith didn't know how to respond to this worldly child, so she just let her continue. "Ma said I was a pretty little thing, and boys would be trying to get me 'alone' with them. When I got a little older, Mama made me go into the bedroom when Papa had menfolk drop by for a cup of coffee. I would peek at them from the door, but I never met any of Papa's friends."

"We will wait until Jack returns and talks with this stranger. The couple whom Jack buried might not even be kin to this man." Faith shifted Cherish around in her lap so she could see her face. At two months, the baby was already moving about and liked to sit up with help.

Once home from a nice visit with Sally's folks and young brothers, Faith was exhausted, physically, and mentally. All she wanted to do was give Cherish a warm bath, bottle, and rock her asleep. She was thankful for the early supper that Sally's mother had prepared for them.

***

Sally rushed to the barn to take care of feeding all the animals.

93

Her chickens pranced and clucked when she talked to them and spread chicken feed over the ground. She laughed at the big mama sow, who rushed to the front of the pen as she poured milk into her trough while the piglets tried to catch a teat hanging down. The goat moved into his cage when fresh hay was placed inside.

Sally moved to the corral and opened the gate to lead the mules and two horses into their barn stalls. She pitched heaping piles of hay in front of each animal and placed buckets of water in their stalls. Afterwards, she ran outside and closed the big shutters on the open windows to help keep the animals comfortable from the cool night air.

The room was dark when she entered the cabin. Faith was sitting in the rocker with a sleeping baby wrapped in her arms. She eased over to the kitchen table and lit the lantern.

***

Faith stirred and glanced at Sally. Smiling, she stood and carried Cherish into the bedroom and placed her in the drawer. "Are you hungry, sweet girl?" Faith asked Sally. "I should have helped you with the evening chores. I don't know what Jack and I would do without you."

"No, I'm still full from supper. You and Cherish were tired, and the animals seem to accept me and allow me to lead them around. The mules can be stubborn, but they aren't hard to control when they see me with food." Sally walked over to the fireplace and placed several large logs and a few smaller ones on the hot coals.

Chapter 16

Orchard, Alabama

Mrs. Millstone sat on the back row of the Orchard Methodist church. She had ironed her only good dress, pressed her ribbons on her bonnet, and twisted her long gray-brown hair into a tight bun. She wanted to look nice if she got a chance to speak with the traveling minister, Rev. Samuel Wright. The sermon was long, but Mrs. Millstone couldn't have repeated any of it, if her life depended on it. All she could think about was questioning him about his journey up north.

After the congregation said a prayer, everyone filed out the front door, shaking the pastor's hand and inviting him to come and visit. He smiled and assured each family member that he would see them sometime soon.

Mrs. Millstone stood on weak legs as she watched him shut the front doors. "Reverend, may I speak to you?"

Whirling around with a surprised expression on his handsome face, he spoke, "I'm sorry, I thought everyone was gone. Of course, you may speak to me. How can I help you?"

"I don't know if you remember, but my daughter has been missing from our home for months now. My husband said that she ran away, but I know that's not true. I was hoping you might have discovered a young girl, maybe a runaway, while you visited small towns on your trip up north?"

"Mrs. Millstone, I traveled on horseback to many small towns, and then I took a train to Gibson, Tennessee, and visited that town for several days. Tell me what your daughter looks like, her age, and any outstanding features that might help me to remember if I saw someone like her."

"Pretty little thing about this high," she held her hand so high. "Lovely bright red hair, lots of natural curls. She has green eyes and a pale complexion."

***

Reverend Wright knew that he had met this lovely young girl at Mr. Mills' cabin. But before he gave this pity-poor mother any hope that he knew where her daughter was, he wanted to speak with Reverend Coatsworth.

"Mrs. Millstone, let me think about what you have told me, and I will pray about it. I promise to get back with you tomorrow."

"You think you may have found my daughter?" Tears came into her eyes. "Please tell me she alive. Please, is she safe?"

"Now, Madam, I didn't say I found your daughter. Please give me time to think about the people I met on my trip." He ushered her to the front door. "I will only speak with you about this, and you must keep our conversation between us."

"Yes, yes, I won't say anything to nobody. I promise."

***

Mrs. Millstone rushed down the steps. Her heart was pounding as she said a silent prayer to God. Just maybe this man had found her daughter. "Please heavenly Father, please let this be true."

***

Reverend Wright leaned against the church's double doors and closed his eyes, seeing Mrs. Mills standing in the kitchen holding her beautiful baby girl. She'd rushed into the bedroom when the baby fussed, but not before he caught a good look at her. Mrs. Millstone had described her daughter's appearance well. It was certainly Mrs. Mills. There couldn't be another girl that fit that description. He pushed himself away from the doors and knew he had to go and talk about this young lady with Reverend Coatsworth who knew about Mrs. Millstone's daughter disappearing.

Reverend Wright pulled out his pocket watch and realized that the reverend and wife would be having dinner at one of the constituents' houses. In the meantime, he would go and have lunch at Mrs. Whitehouse's boardinghouse.

As he removed his black robe, he placed the Bible that had been a gift from his folks when he completed seminary on the table beside his bed. The young maid had been in his room because his bed was made up and his dirty clothes were placed in the laundry basket. Fresh water and clean towels sat on his dresser. He enjoyed his stay at this boardinghouse because he never had to worry that his things would be stolen or misplaced, and the food was delicious.

The other boarders circled around the table waiting for him to sit and bless the food. After amen was repeated by all, the food passed from one hand to another. It seemed like all the men were starving by the amount of food piled on their plates and how fast the big bowls emptied. The serving girl was quick to refill each one. Mrs. Whitehouse bragged that no man would ever leave her table hungry.

The men's conversation took on an interesting topic. One man spoke about an Amish man asking questions at the water depot near Gibson, Tennessee. "I told him I had not seen another person dressed like him while I was in town."

Reverend Wright peered over his fork as he prepared to place it in his mouth. "Did he say why he was looking for this couple or where they were going?"

"No, he didn't say, and I didn't ask. Men dressed in black remind me of undertakers and I'm not ready to be around them yet. So, I jumped back on the train and took my seat," the livery owner said, giving his shoulders a shake. Several boarders laughed at his reaction.

Reverend Wright's thoughts flashed back to the Amish or Quaker couple who had been shot and robbed. Miraculous, the girl had been left untouched. She had recovered enough to find her way to Mr. Mills' cabin where he had taken care of her.

"One more question about your conversation with this Amish man. Did he happened to mention a young girl traveling with this couple?"

"As I said, I didn't spend any time yacking with the man. He gave me the creeps, and I got away as fast as I could. He only asked about a couple."

"Reverend, why are you so interested in the conversation between Slim and this stranger?" Mr. Singleton, the assistant banker asked. He spooned another big helping of mashed potatoes while looking at the preacher.

"Just curious, I guess. I haven't seen too many Amish or Quaker families down here in the Mobile area. Most of them live in Ohio,

Kansas, and the Pennsylvania Dutch country," he replied while holding his coffee cup up to the young server.

Several hours later, Reverend Wright knocked on Reverend Coatsworth's door. He was greeted warmly by Mrs. Coatsworth and told to wait in the parlor. She would get her husband and bring in some fresh coffee.

Once the men were settled alone in the winged-back chairs in front of the fireplace, Reverend Coatsworth asked how he could help the young minister.

"Sir, I don't need any help, but I wanted to pick your memory. While I was in Gibson, Tennessee, for several weeks, I met a young couple. They were living together, not married, and I rode out with Reverend Peterson to tell the couple that the townspeople were going to demand that they marry. The town's ladies said they were living in sin." He took a deep breath and leaned forward in his chair. "What I want to talk about is Mrs. Millstone's missing daughter. The woman came to me today and asked if I might have seen her daughter while traveling from town to town. She described her daughter to me. Have you ever met her daughter, Precious? I believe I heard her name before I left town."

"Yes, I have met the young girl many times. She attended service with her mother and brothers. Her father attended too, but he's a mean, loud-mouth, Bible-toting man who scares the devil out of most sinners. People will cross the road to keep from confronting him on the boardwalk. He beats his wife and children, but no one can keep him from displaying his anger."

"Can you describe what the young lady looks like?" Wright sat back in his chair and tried to control his emotions. He was sure that this girl named Precious was the girl called Faith.

"You are right in calling her a young lady. She was always a sweet-looking child, but she is a beautiful, red-haired lady now. Well, she was the last time I saw her. Her hair is curly, and it was hard to hide it under a scarf, which her father made her wear to hide the devil's handiwork, as he said to me one Sunday. She had the most beautiful, soft complexion, even though she worked outside in their gardens and attended to the animals."

"Do you know why she is missing? Her father said that she ran away with some boy, but I saw another story in her mother's eyes. I don't believe she just ran away with some man without telling her mother," Reverend Wright commented.

"I never believed that story either, and there are many others who don't believe it. I do think that maybe the girl got in trouble with a boy because his family left suddenly. The boy's mother told everyone that her brother had a job for her son in his bank in Texas. The boy didn't look like a young man who could work in a bank, but it wasn't for me to question."

Reverend Coatsworth stood and used a pocketknife to empty the old tobacco out of his pipe and then retook his chair. "Now tell me about this person you think might be the Millstone's girl."

"Well, I only saw her for a few minutes. Her baby was sick and crying, so this girl called Faith carried her baby to the cabin's bedroom. But, she was a lovely girl with bright red, curly hair. I was told that the girl had been in an accident with an older couple, and she had hit her head and lost all of her memory. Reverend Peterson said that she didn't even know she was with child until it was time for her to deliver. Mr. Mills thought she was just a heavy girl."

"Goodness, that must have been a surprise to everyone involved," the old minister chuckled.

"The doctor told Mr. Mills the girl couldn't be moved for a few weeks. He asked one of the neighbors to come and stay with Mr. Mills and the girl to help her and the baby. The neighbor is only a young child but is very efficient. She cooks and cleans. While I was there, the girl rode home to get the medicine from her mother to help with the baby's stomach."

"What a blessing that young girl must be to the couple." Reverend Coatsworth placed fresh tobacco in his pipe, took a small piece of wood from the fireplace, and lit it.

"I believe this young woman is the daughter of Mrs. Millstone. She was traveling with a couple who were dressed in clothes like the Amish or Quakers wear."

"Really? I remembered months ago, an older couple came to town to buy supplies. I spoke to the man. He said that he and his wife were traveling to Kansas to be with their religious order. The man had land and a house waiting for them." The minister stood and walked around the room. "I asked the man why he wasn't traveling by rail, and he said because they were carrying all their personal household belongings. He never mentioned anyone else traveling with him and his wife."

"Do you think old man Millstone might have paid that couple to take his daughter away from Orchard with them?"

"Well, it was a few weeks or maybe a month since anyone had seen Precious after rumors spread that she may be with child. People were speculating that her father might have killed her."

"Did you believe that story?" Reverend Wright stood up from his chair and glanced out the window.

"Come and sit back down. Of course, I didn't believe that, but I drove out to Millstone's place. Mrs. Millstone said that her husband had tried to beat the child out of her daughter. He locked her in the cellar for a while, but he finally let her out. Mrs. Millstone cried, but she had a lot of anger in her voice. I feared for her husband. When I asked if I could see the girl, she quickly said no."

"Have you seen the girl lately?" Rev. Wright quizzed.

"No, and no one else has either. The girl's disappeared, but when Mr. Millstone was asked, he said she ran away with a boy, but he wouldn't say with whom. I don't believe she left with a boy, but I do believe that she left the area."

"Reverend Coatsworth, I believe the young lady in Gibson, Tennessee, is Mrs. Millstone's daughter, Precious. By now, I am sure the girl is married to Jack Mills. The town's ladies were in an uproar about this couple living in sin, even though they had a young girl acting as a chaperone. I will write to Reverend Peterson and tell him what I feel about the young lady, named Faith. Of course, I'm not a hundred percent sure this is the same young girl, but I feel it in my bones. I'm going to leave in a few days by horseback and stop at a few of my villages but will catch the train near Greenville and arrive about thirty miles from Gibson, Tennessee. It will take me a few weeks, but I must go and see if I can help Mrs. Millstone find her daughter."

"If you need anything, please let me know. I don't think you need to tell Mrs. Millstone anything about the girl. I would hate for her to get her hopes up and then be disappointed."

You're right. My lips are sealed, for now."

Chapter 17

From the front of the boardinghouse, Mr. Studerman stood looking down the street of the small town. He couldn't wait until Jack Mills arrived back home. He needed to talk with the man about the two bodies he had buried. All he knew about his cousin and wife was that they had stopped near Gibson and camped. Maybe this Jack could give him a description of the couple. The girl could have been traveling with his cousin, but he had not mentioned her in his letter. The one time he had seen his niece, Cornelius's daughter, she was very pretty and had red, curly hair, just like the girl he had seen in the dry goods store. She could be Cornelius' granddaughter. If she turned out to be his niece, he would demand that she and her child go to Kansas with him. He would be responsible for her now, even if she had married an Englishman.

***

Jack entered the butcher's shop next door to the dry goods store. He had a big haul of fresh, cleaned critters to sell.

"Morning, Jack," Mr. Jones saluted him. "Looks like you brought in a good catch today, and I need fresh meat." He flipped through the stack of cleaned animals. "You shore do clean your catch well, and I appreciate it. Saves me a lot of time."

"I try to skin the animals so I can take the hides home and get them ready to sell." He smiled as he helped Mr. Jones count his critters.

"Uh, Jack, a man is looking for you." He stopped counting and peered at Jack's face. "He's at the boardinghouse because Mrs.

Mason won't let him hang around her store. He made her mad." Mr. Jones laughed as he placed a few pieces into his deep sink. He poured a bucket of hot water over the bloody meat.

"What man? Who is he?" Jack questioned his friend.

"I ain't sure but he dresses differently. He wears a long black coat, pants, hat, and speaks using words like *thee* and *thy*." Mr. Jones shook his head and laughed. "Boy, I don't know what he said about your pretty wife, but Mrs. Mason screamed at him, and he practically ran to the boardinghouse. I was standing on the boardwalk when he came out of her store. She looked like an old mother hen with her feathers ruffled."

"I'd better go next door and speak with her. I need to know about this man before I meet him." Jack entered Mrs. Mason's store and looked all around. He could hear people speaking in the storeroom, so he stood at the counter and waited. In a minute, Mrs. Mason came out of the backroom carrying an armful of material.

Surprised to see Jack, she quickly put her load down on the front counter. "Goodness, Jack. I'm sure glad you're back from your trapping adventure. A stranger came into town asking questions about the couple that you buried. He seems to think that they were his kin and Faith may be his niece."

"Where is this man now? I need to speak with him before I head home."

"He's at the boardinghouse. The man is Amish and thinks he's better than the rest of us. Well, he didn't say that, but I got the feeling he thinks he knows what's best for all of us."

"I will go now, then I'll stop back by and tell you how our conversation went." Jack turned and stepped off the boardwalk and crossed the street to the boardinghouse. He asked the clerk which room the Amish man was staying in.

"Room six, Jack, but listen." The clerk leaned across the counter and whispered that Jack needed to walk softly around the man. "He's scary."

Jack grinned and thanked the older man for his advice. "I'll be careful." He knocked on the door and was greeted by a tall, thin man with long gray hair and a beard. His long-sleeved shirt was wrinkled, and he stood barefoot.

"Please come in. I wasn't expecting company. Please give me a minute." He slipped his boots on over his bare feet, put on his grave black coat, and gave Jack a smile that didn't reach his eyes.

"I understood that you were waiting for me to return to town. My name is Jack Mills, and I am the man that buried the couple whom you think may be your kinfolks."

"Yes, I came to Gibson looking for my cousin and his wife. He was heading to Lawrence, Kansas, but he stopped here and wrote a letter to me. Said he was on his way and should arrive in a couple of months, depending on the weather."

"I did bury a couple who were shot and robbed. A young girl was traveling with them, and she had made her way to my cabin. She told me about the couple, and the next day I buried them, but I couldn't put their names on the cross because Faith, the young lady, didn't remember who they were. She didn't remember anything, and as of today, her memory has not returned."

"Would you describe what you remember about the man and woman? I know they were traveling in a covered wagon with all their household goods."

"The best I can remember is the man was dress like you are now. He wasn't a big man but he had a long black beard and I noticed that he had a scar down the side of his face. The woman was dressed in a long black dress with a white apron and her hair was in a tight bun. She looked younger than the man, but they had been lying out in the open for a day or two. Their bodies weren't a pleasant sight to look upon. I wrapped them in a blanket and buried them on the trail near the accident."

What did you do with their household items, wagon, and mules?"

"The wagon had been emptied except for a box of baby items and a dress or two. The mules are in my corral, and the wagon is parked behind my barn." He studied the man's face as he spoke about the mules and wagon.

"Did you search the wagon? What I mean is, my cousin would have hidden his money in the bottom of the wagon." The older man searched Jack's reaction when he spoke of a hidden space in the wagon.

"The wagon was turned over on its side when I arrived. Faith had released the mules and let them roam freely, but they stayed close to the campsite. I hitched them back to the wagon and brought them to my place. You are more than welcome to come to my place and look it over."

"That's mighty kind of you. I want to speak to the young girl again. I understand that she was forced to marry you, and you aren't the father of her child." He stammered as he made this statement.

"Although the ladies in this town suggested that we marry because we were living together, that doesn't mean that our marriage is not legal. We aren't living as man and woman because Faith still doesn't remember anything of her past."

"Mr. Mills, when I feel that Faith is my niece, I will be taking her and her child with me home. She will be become Amish and live in our community. Your wedding will not be deemed a true marriage by our Order."

"Faith will never go anywhere with you—now or even after she regains her memory. She's my wife, and you'll be very sorry if you try to take her by force."

"When can I come out to your cabin and speak with the girl?" His eyes narrowed into evil slits.

"You can follow me home now, if you like. The sooner we get this settled and you have gone on your way, the better for all of us." Jack flicked a hand in front of his nose as if he smelled something bad.

"My horse is at the livery. I will meet you in front of the dry goods store. That busybody who owes the place will want to know where we are going."

"Mrs. Mason is one of the most respected ladies in this territory. I would be careful how you speak about her." Jack spun around and strode toward the store. He would discuss his conversation with the old Amish man with Mrs. Mason.

***

Jack and Elder Studerman rode in silence as they traveled the wooden trail to his cabin. The birds twittered, and a small doe stood on the path. It quickly darted out of sight in the bushes. When the clearing came into view, Bear barked and leaped off the front porch. He raced to the edge of the front yard, growling and baring his big white fangs.

"Bear, settle down. It's all right." Jack stepped down off his horse and patted his chest. Bear placed his front paws on Jack's chest and gave his neck a sloppy lick. Then he confronted the stranger dressed in black with a growl.

"Go and lie down. Be a good boy," Jack commanded to his pet and guard dog.

"Get down, Mr. Studerman, and I will tie your horse over by the water trough. The girls know that I have arrived home." Jack waited for the older man to climb off his horse and watched him as he straightened his hat and pressed his hands down his coat.

When they reached the porch, Jack called to Faith. She immediately opened the door and stepped back to allow him and the old man to enter. "Faith, I believe you have met this man, Mr. Studerman, earlier this morning."

"Yes, please come in. May Sally fix you a cup of coffee or another refreshment?" Faith asked. Jack noticed her tightened jawline.

"Water would be nice." Sally poured a glass of water and placed it in the old man's hand. She hurried into the bedroom to sit with Cherish.

"Miss," the old man spoke. "I am sure the couple that you were traveling with was my cousin, Cornelius Jansen and his wife. You are their granddaughter, so therefore, you are my niece. Cornelius's mother and my father were brother and sister."

"But, you don't have any proof that I am their granddaughter."

"You are too young to be their daughter. I have met her several times, and she was beautiful with red curly hair, just like yours." He gave Faith a hard stare, his eyes landing on the ring that she was wearing around her neck. "May I see that ring you have around your neck?" He pointed at the gold chain that Faith wore all the time.

Faith looked at Jack and slowly removed the chain from her neck and handed it to the old man. He picked up the piece of jewelry and smiled as if he had just won a big prize.

"This is my grandmother's wedding ring. Cornelius gave it to his wife when they married." He turned to Jack. "Mr. Mills, it appears that there is no doubt that your wife is my niece." Then he turned to face Faith. "Although you may not know who you are, Faith is not your real name. You gave yourself that name. Your last name may be Jansen. Do you remember anything now?"

She continued to look down at her hands and her lower lip trembled. "No, I don't remember anything more today than I did yesterday. I have to say that I don't believe I was raised Amish. If I were, I believe in my heart that I'd know it."

"Whether you believe it or not, you were, and now I want you to pack your personal belongings. I will be here in the morning to pick you up. We will travel by wagon to the train depot thirty miles away, then we will travel to Lawrence, Kansas by train and arrive home in two days' time. My wife will be thrilled to have you and your child. Of course, you will be shunned by our community, but Cherish will be accepted because she is an innocent child."

Faith, Jack, and Sally all sat in total silence as the old man sprouted his instructions as to their travel plans and the action that would be taken with the Amish Order in his community.

Jack stood and faced the man. "Mr. Studerman or Elder Studerman, Faith is not going anywhere with you. She is my legal wife and her child is my daughter. You'd better get on your horse and go back to town, while you are able. I will break your neck if you lay a hand on Faith or Cherish. Now, we are all sorry about the death of your cousin and his wife, but since Faith has lived with Sally and me, she is staying here."

"I will get the sheriff and bring him out here. He will force you to give her to me."

"Faith is a grown woman, and she can make her own decision about where and who she wants to live with—her husband or a total stranger." Jack crossed his arms, mentally ordering himself to calm down.

The old man stood and glanced at Faith and Sally. "I will be in town for a few days, if you change your mind and want to go home with me." He nodded to them and stormed out of the house.

Jack watched the man ride away without a glance backwards. He turned to Faith and pulled her into his arms. "I'm sorry you had to hear from that old man. I don't believe he is your kinfolk."

"Something in my heart says the same. He scares me and I don't believe I want to live like that in his community. Shun means that no one will talk or speak to a person. I'd be an outcast for the rest of my life." Faith looked as if she wanted to cry. "I need to lie down for a while, if you two don't mind?"

"Go ahead, Miss Faith. I'll listen out for Cherish," Sally said.

"I need to go into the barn and clean my traps and get things ready to go out in the morning. The beaver is aplenty and not too far from here. I have a trap set for a wild boar hog. He's killing so many small critters, so I need to check on it tomorrow for sure."

"Before I lie down, can I help you with anything for your trip tomorrow?"

Jack walked over to Faith and touched her shoulder, turning her toward the bedroom. "No, I can manage on my own like I've been doing for several years," he said with a wink and a smile.

Chapter 18

Faith woke up from a long nap and smelled something delicious. She glanced over at the drawer where Cherish slept and saw that it was empty. Stretching and running a hand through her wild curls, she walked into the kitchen. She lifted the lid off the giant pot that was sitting off the fire on the stove. Sally had prepared a beef stew. A cloth covered a pan of golden cornbread. Walking onto the porch, she could hear people talking in the barn.

***

Sally had taken Cherish outside to get a breath of fresh air and went into the barn to visit with Jack while he readied for his trip. Cherish loved watching the goat and the little piglets. She waved her arms and kicked her feet when she got near the small animals.

"Jack, what do you think about that old man who says he is going to take Miss Faith away from here to live somewhere in Kansas?" Sally jiggled Cherish in her arms.

"Don't you worry about Faith and Cherish. That man is not going to touch a hair on their heads. I will do him great harm if he tries." He stopped packing the mule and turned to look at Sally. "You know, when I first discovered that lovely red-headed girl in my kitchen, all I wanted was to hurry and get rid of her. I wanted her gone. I never wanted her in my cabin."

***

Faith froze in her tracks at the front door of the barn. Jack and Sally are talking about me, she thought. Leaning up against the wall she listened to their conversation.

"I never wanted a woman in my cabin, much less a stranger. I tried in every way to get rid of her, but that wasn't to be. I thought she was just a pretty fat gal, but that night she gave birth to Cherish. I begged the doctor to take her away with him, but well, I was stuck with her."

He was stuck with me. He wanted me gone, but he couldn't get rid of me and Cherish. My goodness. I thought that Jack cared for me, but he was only feeling responsible for us. I'm nothing but a burden to him. With tears streaming down her face, she whirled and raced back to the cabin. She hurried into the bedroom and sat down on the bed to think. *I must give this man his freedom. I can't live with him and continue to be a burden.*

***

"Sally, I care for Faith and I love that baby girl likes she is my own. Faith is my wife, and when she gets her memory back, we'll face whatever is in her past. I feel that someone in her life had mistreated her. Every day I pray that something will make her remember who she is. I don't care about anything in her past, but she needs to know for herself."

"I know I will just die if she is forced to leave us. I want her memory to come back to her so she can tell that man she isn't his kin." Sally shifted Cherish as she began to fret. "I'd better take her to the cabin and give her a bottle. Maybe Miss Faith is awake and ready to have dinner. I have it ready when you're finished out here." Sally walked toward the cabin as Bear jumped and leaped beside her. She discovered Faith sitting at the kitchen table with swollen eyes and a red nose. "Oh, my, Miss Faith. What's wrong?"

"Just feeling sorry for myself, I guess. The nap helped me, but I can't help but think about that old man who says that I'm his niece. I don't want to leave here, but I wonder if God has sent this man to take me to his home where I belong."

"But, you don't know that for sure. This is your home now and Mr. Jack is your husband." She rested Cherish in Faith's arms, then placed a bottle on the table and warmed a small amount of milk. After pouring the milk into the bottle, Sally screwed the nipple on it, and took Cherish from Faith. "I will feed her and prepare her for bed while you and Jack eat dinner. I hear him coming from the barn now."

Faith stood and scooped the hearty beef stew into two bowls and poured two fresh cups of coffee. She positioned herself at the table just as Jack entered the room.

"Boy, something smells wonderful, and I'm starved." He sat down and looked into Faith's sad face. "Are you all right?" he asked as he placed a white cloth napkin in his lap.

"Yes. Do you want to bless the food?"

Without answering Faith, he bowed his head and closed his eyes. He reached for her hand and squeezed it. "Lord, thank you for these girls in my life. I don't know what I would do without them. Bless this meal and the hands that prepared it. Amen."

In total silence, the two ate their meal. Faith passed Jack the cornbread without him having to request it.

***

Bear whined from the front porch to come inside. Jack stood and walked to the door and let the dog inside. He took the bowl of scraps and placed it on the floor in front of the sink and sat back down. He cast shy glances at the woman he loved more than life, but she wouldn't look his way. She had something on her mind, but he knew better than to ask at this time. Faith had shut down, and he recognized all the signs.

***

Faith went into the kitchen to get the peach cobbler Sally had prepared for their dessert. "Would you like a dish of cobbler with your coffee?" She asked with a painful, dry throat.

"I'll wait to have some later. The stew and cornbread filled me," he replied, patting his stomach. "Sally is a wonderful cook for her age."

"Her mother has taught her well, but unfortunately, she has never known a young girl's childhood. She has helped with chores since she was old enough, but she never was permitted to go to school. I had wanted to teach her to read and give her some adventure in her life through books, but I haven't had time to do it."

"She's still young, and you have plenty of time to teach her. I will ask Mrs. Mason to order you a list of books for her. I know she will."

"Thank you. That will be a big help," Faith said as she stared down at her empty hands. She felt guilty knowing that she wouldn't be here to teach her little friend to read.

"Faith, do you want to talk about Elder Studerman and his plan to take you with him?" He waited with arms crossed.

Without speaking, she shook her head. Her eyes never looked up at Jack.

"Well, I have more chores to do before we turn in tonight because I will be leaving early in the morning before breakfast. I'll cook myself something later in the day, after I trap a few big beavers and other critters down by the creek bed. Should be gone for two days if the weather holds. Will you be all right while I'm gone?"

"Of course. Sally and Bear will be here with me."

Jack smiled as Bear eased over to him after hearing his name. He patted the dog and said, "Come on, fellow. Let's go to the barn and settle the animals down for the night."

***

Early the next morning, the sun slipped over the barn as the rooster crowed to wake up the other farm animals. Jack squatted in front of the fireplace and placed several logs over the hot coals to ensure the kitchen area was warm before the girls woke up. He picked up his pallet and placed it in the corner where he stored it every morning. Dressing quickly, he slipped on his boots and coat and left the cabin. He fed his horse while he packed his two mules. Afterward, he fed the mules and saddled his horse.

All the while he was preparing to leave on his trip, he felt uneasy about Faith. She was troubled, but she wouldn't talk to him about it. Maybe, she would work out her feelings while he was away. He prayed that the old Amish man would be on his way home today and not come back and nag Faith about leaving with him. He didn't know what he would do without her and the baby in his life.

He was planning a trip to his hometown. His folks would undoubtedly be surprised he was married, but they would love Faith and Cherish. Giving the cabin one last look, he saddled up, took two mules, and headed down the long trail to the creek. Jack hoped he would get a chance to shoot the wild boar that was scaring all the critters in the woods.

***

Allowing the curtain to drop back in place, Faith sighed as she watched Jack and the mules head down the trail. She was going to miss this man with whom she had fallen in love.

As she put small pieces of wood in the stove, Sally walked into the kitchen. Yawning big, she hurried over to the window. "Was that Jack I heard out in the yard?"

"Yes, he just left. He said last night he would eat on the trail today." Faith placed water in the granite coffee pot and put coffee grounds and a cracked egg into it. She reached for a clean bottle and filled it with milk. Jack had milked the cow before he left and drained the cream off the top. He was in a hurry to go on his trip, but he'd thought of the baby before he left.

"Cherish is babbling this morning and playing with her feet. She is growing so much every day," Sally said as she went into the bedroom to care for the little one.

"Sally, come quick. I believe your brothers are riding toward the barn," Faith called to her friend.

With Cherish straddled on her hip, she hurried to the front window. "My goodness, it's both of them." She passed Cherish to Faith, opened the door, and headed outside behind Bear who was barking and growling.

"Quiet, Bear. Down, boy." Sally ordered the dog. He immediately stopped still but soon wagged his large tail as he watched Sally hugging her brothers. "What in the world brought you two over here so early?"

"Mama is sick and she told us to come and get you. She's been up most all night. Says it's her stomach, but she won't let Pa touch her. Should we go get the doctor?"

"Take me home with you. The three of us can ride your big mule. If I can't help her, you can ride for the doctor."

Faith was standing on the front porch listening to the conversation between Sally and her brothers. "Come in and dress and hurry off with the boys. Cherish and I will be just fine here with Bear."

Faith said a silent prayer for Mrs. Millstone, but this illness offered an opportunity for her to take Cherish and leave. She would hitch the small carriage, drive into town, and return home to Lawrence, Kansas, with Elder Studerman. He said she was his niece, and she was wearing his cousin's mother's wedding ring around her neck. Faith didn't like this man, but she had to give Jack his life back. He didn't love her. She and Cherish had only been a burden. Jack had to pay Sally to come and care for her. Elder Studerman said her marriage to Jack would be annulled, and he could go on with his life.

After feeding Cherish her bottle and dressing her, she walked to the barn and retrieved a small brown trunk. Jack wouldn't mind if she took it. She dragged it across the yard into the house and laid Cherish in the middle of the big bed she had never shared with Jack. Tears streamed down her cheeks as she folded the baby's clothes and nappies in a pile.

She selected two dresses and several pieces of personal underclothes, stockings, and slippers. Packing her hairbrush and other toiletries, she carried all the items to the open trunk. After placing Cherish on a pallet on the floor, Faith took a piece of paper and a pencil from under the kitchen counter. What should she write to Jack and Sally? More tears fell from her eyes. "Lord, forgive me for leaving like this. I feel like a sneak. Please don't let Jack hate me. I do love him, but I cannot tell him. Amen."

Dear Jack,

I am so sorry for being a burden to you these past few months. You are a wonderful man and I will never be able to thank you for all you have done for me and Cherish. I have gone to be with my family in Lawrence, Kansas. You will be free to live your life now that we are gone.

Give my love to Sally. I love her like a little sister. Please watch after her and her sweet family.

Your wagon and team are at the livery. I will write to let you know we arrived safely.

Regards, Faith

Faith folded the paper, placed it in the middle of the kitchen table, and finished packing. She hitched the mule to the small carriage and drove it over to the porch. Taking the large clothes basket, she placed Cherish in it and put it on the front seat. Dragging the trunk into the yard, she picked it up and placed it in the back seat. She bent down and hugged Bear. "You cannot go with me." She looped a long rope over his neck and tied it to the porch rail. He jumped and tugged on the rope, not happy at all to remain alone.

Faith glanced over her shoulder one last time at the cabin in the dell. How she loved this little home where she had lost her heart. She smiled at Bear as he jumped and pulled on the rope that held him captured. "Bless your heart, Bear, be good." A lump grew in her throat as she tapped the mule's back.

Chapter 19

Faith drove to town and stopped her rig in front of the livery. Mr. Jenkins came to the front double doors, wiping his hands with a brown rag. "Morning, Mrs. Mills. You're out mighty early. What can I do for you?"

"I want to leave Jack's carriage and mule until he comes for them. He will be away for two days. Will you do that for me, and he will pay you when he comes?"

"Shore, no problem. I'll take good care of them. Do you want me to deliver your trunk somewhere?" Curious eyes peered over spectacles at her.

"I don't think that will be necessary, but thank you. I will come for it in a little while." Mr. Jenkins lifted the clothes basket out and placed it in Faith's arms. "This little tyke has fallen asleep."

"Good morning, sir." Faith said softy to the day clerk at the boardinghouse. "Is Mr. Studerman still here?" She had never been inside this place before. The reception area was very homey.

"Yes, but he is in the dining room having breakfast. Come, I will take you to him." Faith followed the short, bald man.

A chain of keys around his waist jingled as he walked. "Excuse me, Mr. Studerman, but this young lady wishes to speak with you."

Elder Studerman jumped up from the table, nearly spilling his cup of coffee. "Morning," he said to Faith. "This is a pleasant surprise. Please give me the baby, and I'll place her on the floor between us. She sure is a beautiful child."

"Thank you." Faith glanced around the room. Several people she had seen before were staring at her, probably wondering where Jack might be. She took her seat beside the tall stranger who claimed to be her uncle. "Elder Studerman, I have decided to go with you, if you still wish me to. Are you leaving for the train today?"

"Yes, I'm packed and ready to leave this town. I placed a cross on thy grandparents' grave. We will travel by wagon to the train depot, which is about thirty miles away. The train will depart at three. We can arrive in time to catch the northern train, if we travel quickly. I have rented four horses to pull my wagon."

"My memory has still not returned, and I am not sure we are kin. If and when my memory returns, and I am not the granddaughter of your cousin, will you help me to return to my home?"

"Of course, my dear. I give thee my word. If thy memory returns and thou know for sure that thou aren't from Lawrence, I will see that thou return home. It is still puzzling to me how thou came to be traveling with Cornelius and Mary if thou aren't their grandchild."

"Right now, only God knows that answer. I have to trust Him that I am doing the right thing by leaving Gibson with you."

"Thou are a child of God, and that is enough proof for me to know that my cousin raised thee." He stood and laid a quarter on the table. "Let's go retrieve my wagon and be on our way. Do thou need to do anything before we start?"

"One thing. I need to say goodbye to Mrs. Mason at the dry goods store." Faith lifted Cherish out of the basket and placed her head on her shoulder while she slept.

"That old woman may try to talk you out of going away with me. Maybe you should just skip telling her where you're going."

"Please, I must speak to her. I won't be but a minute, and I've made my mind up. I'm leaving with you, no matter what she has to say." Faith hurried up the boardwalk and entered the store. The bell jingled over the door, and Mrs. Mason came from the storeroom.

"Goodness, child. What are you doing in town so early?" Mrs. Mason peered at the baby and reached out and patted her back.

"Mrs. Mason, I am leaving town. I am going to Lawrence, Kansas, with Elder Studerman. I have to go, even though Jack is my husband." Tears flowed from her eyes before she could control them. "I have only been a burden to him, so I must go. Elder Studerman said that the ring I am wearing around my neck belonged to his cousin's wife. She must have been my grandmother."

"I don't believe it. You can't go. Jack loves you and the baby. Sally will just die. I don't want you to leave. Please don't go. Where is Jack?" She looked around and went to the door to see if he was outside on the road.

"Jack is trapping for a couple of days, and Sally left this morning to help her mother, who's sick. Maybe you can check on Mrs. Millstone?"

Faith heard the rattling of wheels drive up to the front of the store. "It's time to go. Thank you for being a good friend to me. I will always remember you," she mumbled with a big lump in her throat.

"Oh, child, please don't go. I love you like a daughter, and I will miss you so much. Jack is going to be lost without you." She blinked back tears.

Faith wanted to turn around and give her a tight hug, but she knew she would burst into tears and probably change her mind about leaving. She opened the door and rushed out to the wagon.

Elder Studerman took the baby and helped Faith onto the seat. He passed Cherish to Faith and quickly climbed up on the seat next to the girls.

Faith wiped her face with her hanky and cradled Cherish in her arms. She hummed a sweet tune as they traveled miles out of town. The sun was high and warm, and the sky was covered with lovely white clouds. There was just enough of a cool breeze to make the trip comfortable. After three hours of travel, Elder Studerman drove the wagon off the road to rest the animals. He went to the back of the wagon and retrieved a basket that held a few sandwiches and fruit. A jug of fresh water sat next to the basket.

Faith reached down into her bag and pulled out a bottle of milk for Cherish. The baby smacked her lips and reached for the nipple. Faith placed it to her lips and she sucked greedily. "Slow down, sweet girl," laughed Faith as she placed the baby on her shoulder to burp her. After placing a dry nappy and a clean bib on the child, Faith rocked her until she went to sleep.

Elder Studerman reached and took the sleeping baby and helped Faith down from the wagon. "There's a small stream down that slope. Thou can have a few minutes of privacy and wash. I have buckets in the back, and I'll carry water up to the team."

"How far away are we from the train depot?" Faith asked.

"We will be there in about two hours if the horses continue at the same speed," Elder Studerman responded.

Faith had rolled up her long sleeves and loosened the buttons around her neck. She dropped her hanky into the cold water and wrung it out, then wiped the road grime from her skin. Suddenly, she felt as if someone was watching her. Slowly she turned her head and looked up the sloop. Elder Studerman was standing there, sporting a lustful stare. Once he noticed that Faith had spotted him, he quickly pretended that Cherish needed her.

Faith buttoned the neck of her dress and rolled the sleeves down, then followed up the sloop after him on shaky legs. She would have to be careful around this man who called himself her uncle.

After several hours of travel, they pulled up to the train depot. Elder Studerman jumped down and tied the reins to the hitching rail before strolling inside the sturdy building. Faith wished to get down and use the necessary behind the building, but she stayed where she was until her uncle came back.

"We arrived just in time. The train will be here in about twenty minutes. I've purchased our tickets."

"May I get down and have a few minutes of privacy? I also need to change Cherish and make her comfortable before we board the train."

"Here, I will help thee down. I have to make arrangements to have the wagon and team of horses delivered to Lawrence."

After completing her personal needs and changing Cherish into a fresh nappy, she walked into the depot. She asked if the clerk sold milk and was pleased that he had milk in his kitchen in the back. He gladly filled two bottles of fresh milk for Cherish but would not take any payment.

"Thank you so much," Faith said, then headed to the platform. Holding Cherish up for some fresh air, she was surprised when the baby screamed after hearing the train whistle announcing its arrival.

"Shut that brat up!" Elder Studerman yelled.

Faith immediately cradled the baby to her chest and patted her back. "Who are you calling a brat? If that's the way you're going to speak about my baby, you can cash our tickets back in. I will not tolerate that kind of attitude toward my child."

"Forgive me. I didn't mean to speak ill of the child. The loud whistle just caught me off guard."

Faith needed to get away from Gibson and Jack, so she prepared to board the train. She didn't speak until after they were seated in the passenger car. Fortunately, there were few travelers so she could lay Cherish down on the seat next to her. The window view was nice. She could look at the scenery as they traveled. She didn't remember seeing any of the hillsides, small farms, or animals before she arrived at Jack's cabin.

Cherish was such a good baby. She hardly ever cried or became fussy when moved around. After she took her fresh bottle of milk, she dozed off into a deep sleep after Faith changed her nappy.

"What are thou doing with the child's dirty wet things?" Elder Studerman asked.

"I have them wrapped up and placed in my carpet bag," Faith answered.

"Give them to me and I will toss them in the trash. Thou don't need them. When we get home, thou will have plenty of new ones."

"That is so wasteful. There's nothing wrong with the way I have them stored, and I will wash them once we get settled."

"If they started stinking, I will take them from thee."

"Elder Studerman, I need to ask you a question. Are you always so bossy, or is it just me that you feel you must order around?"

"I am head of thy family, and I'm responsible for everyone's actions. Therefore, thou must follow my orders or else." He gave her a sinister smile.

"I see. Since I will be living with you and your wife, I must obey your orders, whether I like them or not?"

"Now that we have that straight, please do as I ask without any of thy sass."

Early on the third morning, Faith watched the conductor walk toward them, calling out Lawrence. "We will be pulling into the station in five minutes. Gather all your items and prepare to get off if this is your stop." He continued out the door into the next car filled with passengers.

With Cherish wrapped in her arms and her basket dangling from her hand, Faith stepped down onto the station's platform. Looking over her shoulder, she saw Elder Studerman waiting at the door of the stock car. He watched as men retrieved their team and wagon.

All the strange noises from the train and men yelling caused Cherish to start fretting. Faith cooed in her ears that all was well, and mama would take care of her. Her eyes were bright and large. Cherish felt safe in Faith's arms, so she just looked around without crying. Elder Studerman called her name. Faith stood and walked to the steps that took her to the ground and hurried over to the wagon.

"We'll be home in a little while. My farm is about two miles from the center of the community." He reached for Cherish, who began to cry, and offered his hand to Faith. "I will be glad when she gets used to me. I can't stand a crying baby."

"I want to apologize for my baby's actions. Children are like animals. They can sense a good or bad person."

"Are thou suggesting that I am a bad person?" he demanded with narrowed eyes.

"Cherish feels something is wrong whenever you take her in your arms." Faith said with a lifted chin.

After Faith was settled on the seat, he practically tossed Cherish back into her arms. Immediately, the baby settled down and started playing with her toes. Faith kissed the top of her head and smiled down deep.

Chapter 20

Sally slipped off the back of the horse and raced into the house. Her mother was lying in bed covered with a heavy quilt. Ma's hair was soaked and sweat dipped off her forehead. Sally rested her hand on her mother's forehead. She was burning up. When Wendell, her oldest brother, came into the house, she asked about her pa.

"He's lying in the bedroom. Ma was up taking care of him when we rode over to get you," Wendell explained.

Sally rushed into the bedroom and found her father lying covered in the bed. She tried to wake him, but he was cold and stiff. "Oh no, he's dead," thought Sally. "Wendell, please ride into town and get the doctor." She took his face into her hands. "Look at me, brother. Pa is gone."

"No, he's not. He's in bed!" He darted around Sally to go and check on him.

Sally took his arm and pulled him close. He stood tall and straight, staring ahead. "He's gone to be with our heavenly Father." She sniffed her runny nose and tried to stay strong. Their mother needed them now. "Please hurry to town and bring the doctor back. Ma is burning with fever," Sally instructed.

Without a word, her oldest brother raced past Bobby.

Sally held out her arms and hugged her baby brother. "Pa has died, baby. Wendell has gone for the doctor. Now, I must take care of Ma. Why don't you go out and take care of the morning chores? I'll cook some breakfast as soon as I care for her."

Sally hurried over to her mother's bedside, took some cool water, and wiped her face, neck, and arms. A few red spots were festering. Measles, thought Sally. Oh Lord, I don't remember if my brothers had the disease. She'd had a mild case when she was young. Glenn had gotten sick, and his pa brought him to Ma for help. Later, Sally had broken out with a few spots but didn't become as ill as Glenn.

As fast as she could, she took off her mother's dirty dress, shift, and pantaloons. After bathing her mother, she dressed her in clean underpants and a cotton gown. Sally continued with the cool baths until her Ma's fever went down. As Sally was attempting to persuade her mother to drink some water, she opened her eyes.

"My child. Pa and I have measles. Your pa is real sick. Take care of him first. I had measles years ago. I'm surprised I got them again, but I'm not as sick as your pa."

"I have taken care of him, Mama. Now you drink this water. The doctor is on his way. Your fever's down."

Her mother grabbed her hand. "Listen, the boys had a few spots last week, but they're all right. An Indian man came by with a little boy, and he had spots on him. That is where we got measles. The Indian wouldn't let me nurse his boy. Later my boys got sick, but they're okay now. You had this disease when you were small. Do you remember?" She sounded so exhausted to Sally.

"Yes'um. Please close your eyes and sleep. I'm not afraid of catching it, but I will make the boys stay in the barn until you're well. I want to make sure they won't catch measles again. Drink this water. What can I do to make you comfortable?"

"Use some of that baking soda, make a paste out of it, and put it on my spots." Her mother fell into a deep, restful sleep.

"Thank you, God," Sally prayed. As she mixed the baking soda and water into a paste, Doctor Hays opened the door. "Oh, am I glad to see you." Sally rushed to the doctor, wiping her hands on the side of her dress. She looked over his shoulder and said softly. "I'm afraid Pa is dead. When I arrived, he was cold and stiff. He died during the night while the boys thought he was asleep."

"Let me take a look at him," Doc Hays said. In a few minutes he came back to her mother's bedside. "You're right about your pa. He's been gone for hours. I want to check your mother." The doctor took out his stethoscope while Sally pulled down the quilt, then listened to her heart and lungs. He pointed at a festering spot on her neck. "Does she have many red spots on her body?"

"No, sir. I only saw about a half of dozen or so. Ma said she had the measles a long time ago and was surprised that she caught the disease again. Pa had never had it."

"Your mother is going to be all right. A lot of rest and liquids will help her get well soon. She is not to go outside and aggravate those spots. I see you are making a paste. Keep that on the sores until they dry up, and she will be all right. There's no fever, which is great. Give her a cool bath twice a day."

"Thank you so much, Doctor. I will go over and get Mr. Jack to help me and the boys bury Pa. He should be home tomorrow. Will Pa be all right lying in the bedroom until then?"

"Yes, just stay out of the room, and after Jack moves him, open the windows and scrub every inch of the room."

Sally was trying hard to hold back the tears. After the doctor left, Sally cooked breakfast for herself and the boys. Bobby had done all the chores which made Wendell happy. She told the boys that she was going to go over and tell Faith that she had to stay home for a few days. "Wendell, watch over Ma, and Bobby, stay out of the house while I'm away. I know you are going to miss school, but it is more important that we take care of Ma."

Both of the boys bobbed their heads. Wendell rushed to the corral and brought out the big mule for Sally to ride over to the Mills' cabin.

"Be careful, and don't worry about Ma. I will take good care of her and Bobby." Wendell thrust out his chest like a gentleman.

***

Sally rode up to Jack's cabin and tied the reins to the hitching rail at the corral. Bear was barking and jumping up and down, tied to the porch rail. She walked around him and opened the kitchen door. The room was dark, except for the sunlight coming in through the windows. There wasn't a fire in the fireplace and the stove looked cold. Hurrying past the curtain into the bedroom, she found the room neat, but the drawers stood open and empty. The only things in the dresser were her clothes. She saw a note on the kitchen table. Though she couldn't read most of the words, she did recognize her name.

Oh my goodness. Faith has left, thought Sally. She wrote a note to Jack and me. I need to find him . . . now. Sally rushed out the door and untied Bear. Bending down in front of the dog, she said. "Bear, go find Jack!"

Hurrying to the mule, she led him over to the fence where she could leap on his back. She yelled to the dog. "Go, Bear, and take me to Jack."

Bear ran down a trail for a few miles, then rushed though some bushes and down into a creek bed. He barked as she yelled Jack's name. Up a hill and down the sloop by a wide creek, Bear stopped. He jumped and barked. Sally leaped off her mule and yelled, "Jack, oh Jack. Where is he, Bear?"

Bear pawed at the ground and growled. He snarled and showed all his teeth. Sally whirled around to see what Bear was so viciously preparing to attack. Standing about thirty feet from her was a black hairless-faced, wild boar. He had long ears, small eyes, and a blunt snout—the most fierce-looking animal that she had ever seen. He was snorting and digging his short paws into the ground, preparing to charge.

"Run, Bear, run," she screamed as she ran down the slope and climbed a tree that was in her path.

***

A duck squawked at his companion and then dove beneath the water. Jack loved this forest and enjoyed the peace of his surroundings. He bent to wash his hands in the cold water when he heard a blood-curdling scream. He stood and listened. Did he hear the word, 'bear'? Was someone calling his dog, Bear, or was it a real black bear?

Jack grabbed his rifle and raced up the hillside toward the sounds of a growling animal. Coming into a clearing, he spotted the wild boar that he had wanted to kill. The boar was getting very close to Bear, his dog. He eased forward as close as he could, hoping not to alert Bear's attention. Raising his rifle, he bent down on his knee and aimed.

Unfortunately, Bear had spotted him and raced toward him. Before Jack could fire, Bear leaped into Jack's arms, knocking him over. His gun exploded and the wild boar ran off into the deep forest. With the wind knocked out of him, he heard someone screaming for help. "Jack, help me!" The voice was familiar. Jack jerked his head toward the tree where Bear had run and stood barking. A leg dangled from a tree limb.

"Sally, is that you?" Jack leaped up and hurried over to the tree, but before he reached it, he stepped in a deep, grass-covered hole. His foot and part of his left leg went down into the narrow pit. Pain shot up to his hip. All he could do was lay face down in the tall, dirty grass.

***

Sally peered through the leaves and branches. Tears coursed unchecked down her cheeks. "Mr. Jack, I'm coming down. Move, Bear. I'm going to scoot down." In just a minute, Sally swung to a lower tree limb and dropped to the ground. She brushed at her bottom and hurried to where Jack lay.

"Oh, Mr. Jack, are you hurt bad? Let's get your leg out of that deep hole. Do you think you broke it?" Sally got behind Jack, placed her hands under his armpits, and pulled while he pushed. His left leg broke free of the hole.

"I feel like I'm going to pass out."

"Oh, Mr. Jack, should I remove your boot or just leave it on? I'll need to go to your cabin and get the flatbed wagon to carry you into town."

"No, just get my horse. He's tied down the slope. Be careful and go get the doctor. He will drive the mule and a wagon out here." He flinched when he touched his leg. "You can't lift me by yourself."

Sally rushed down the hill and came back up, pulling on the horse's reins. She quickly removed the bedroll and spread the blanket under Jack's back and made a pillow out of another one. She laid his rifle beside him for protection. "Are you comfortable now?"

Jack winced and nodded. Sally rode a bit in front of him before she stopped. "No, Bear, you stay with Mr. Jack. Go lie down beside him." Bear immediately lumbered to Jack and rested his head on his paws.

Jack was glad that Sally insisted that Bear stay with him. He prayed that Sally could find the doctor and that the wild boar would not return. Bear would put up a good fight, but the wild boar would win the match. His mules brayed close to the creek. That was the last sound he heard until the doctor woke him up.

***

A few hours later, Sally stood over Jack's bed in the doctor's office. He was awake but medicated enough to keep down the pain.

"Sally, come closer." Jack tried to raise his head to speak. "Why were you looking for me?"

"I wanted to tell Miss Faith that I needed to stay with Ma for a few days, with Pa dead and her sick. Ma got sick with the measles, but bless Mrs. Mason's heart, she came out to our cabin with some medicine to check on the boys. Glenn went into town, and when he heard about Pa, he knew I would need help with the burial. He already had the measles when he was younger."

"I am so sorry about your father. Of course, you can spend time with your family." Jack squinted his eyes at her, and she quickly assured him that she had already had the disease and they were keeping the boys out in the barn.

"I went to your cabin to tell Miss Faith that I was going to be helping Ma, but she was gone." She wiped at her teary eyes. "Miss Faith left this note." She reached in her dirty apron and pulled out the folded paper. "I can't read, but I knew it was important. Please read it. She wrote my name in it."

Jack took the note and read it. He couldn't believe that she had left with that old Amish man to go to Lawrence, Kansas. How could she leave? She was his wife and he was sure she loved him, like he did her.

"What does she say?" Sally demanded.

Adrenaline rushed through his tired, broken body. He was suffocating from the news. Jack wanted to run all the way to town and save his wife from going away with that strange man. Sally's worried face stared down at him. She had just told him that her pa had died, but thank goodness, Glenn had helped with the burial. Her brothers were too young to take on that big responsible. He couldn't just take off and leave Sally, her mother, and little brothers unattended before he went after his wife.

Jack looked toward the ground and repeated what was said as a question. "She left with that old Amish man." He dropped the note beside his leg. "The con artist convinced her that he's her family. She wants you to know that she loves you very much, like a little sister."

"Oh, toad frogs. How could she believe that old man? She ain't no kin of his, I just know it. He must have forced her to go with him." Tears streamed down Sally's dirty face.

A slight tick jumped in Jack's cheek while his throat was closing. He was reining in unkind words that he wanted to say about the old man, but he didn't want Sally to know how upset he was with his wife. Jack loved Faith and the baby. He was the first to hold Cherish in his hands, and he felt that she belonged to him, not to that stranger.

Quaking shoulders told him that Sally was silently crying. This child had just lost her father, and now two more people she loved were gone. He had to take care of this child and her family. Jack rested his head down on the pillow and watched Sally slowly leave his bedside. Then he closed his eyes and let the medication do its work.

"Listen, Doc. I've got to get out of here. I have to travel to Kansas and find my wife." Rubbing his hand over his whiskered face, Jack attempted to sit up.

"Jack, for goodness' sake. Lie still before you do more damage to that leg." Doctor Hayes was losing all his patience. "I'm trying to get the swelling down so I can put a cast on that leg. You cracked your bone, and it needs to mend, or you're going to be a young cripple."

"Will I be able to walk with the cast on?"

"Heck no! You'll have to stay off this leg for a couple of weeks."

"That's impossible. I have to travel by train to Lawrence, Kansas. Do you have a pair of crutches that I can use? I'm sure I can hop on my good leg and keep off the broken one."

"I don't have any crutches, but I will check around town to see if anyone has a pair. Oh, Mr. Albert might be able to build you something. He can build almost anything." He rocked on his heels and studied Jack's leg. "Jack, listen to me. Even if you can hop to Kansas, you'll need someone to travel with you to help with your luggage and going up and down stairs. You're not in any shape to go after your lovely wife and child. Have you thought this through? Maybe you can hire someone to help find Faith and bring her home."

"It's more complicated than just that. I have to find Faith and convince her to come back here. She felt she had to leave. I'm the only one who can fix things between us."

"I see. It surprises me. I thought you were the perfect couple." He placed his bowler on his head. "Now you listen, and you listen well. Try to rest, and tomorrow I'll put the cast on your leg. If you want to travel to Kansas, I can't stop you, but please don't travel alone." He patted Jack's shoulder. "I've got other patients to visit, so I'll be gone for a few hours."

Chapter 21

It was late in the afternoon when the train arrived in Lawrence, Kansas. Faith glanced out the window and saw many small houses spaced apart. In the back there were fences that seemed to connect to each other with livestock in all of them. Off to one side was a garden that seemed to go on and on with many women and children working in it. As the train pulled into the depot, she could see many businesses.

"Get your things together and that baby. We'll be getting off in a few minutes," Elder Studerman demanded in a harsh tone. He pushed himself past other passengers to the door without offering to help with her carpet bags or her child.

"Madam, may I give you some assistance?" A young train conductor asked.

"Oh, that would be nice. If you would place my bags on the platform that would be a great help." Faith smiled sweetly at the young man.

Before the man could pick up Faith's bag, Elder Studerman stepped in front of him. "She doesn't need your help. Now, hurry along and help some elderly woman."

The young man looked surprised. "Sorry, sir, I didn't realize this lady had her father traveling with her." He bobbed his hat and rushed down the aisle to help another family.

"You don't need to flash a smile at everything that wears long pants. Keep your eyes down, or you'll be sorry."

Faith's body stiffened as she closed her eyes. She'd heard those same words before, but who said them? Her father? She suddenly felt lightheaded.

"Stop daydreaming, gal. Get that young'un and follow me." Elder Studerman marched to the door, stepped down on the platform, and walked toward an old black covered buggy with a small porthole window on each side. An elderly woman dressed in a long black dress with a black bonnet tied under her chin waved at him.

"Move over, Sarah. I brought Cornelius's granddaughter home, and she has a child. Try not to spoil the baby, and remember she is not your responsibility," he said.

"A baby? Oh my. It's been so long since we had a child in the house." Sarah scooted over on the front seat but craned her neck to see her new niece and her child.

Elder Studerman placed Faith's carpet bag in the back, and for the first time on the trip offered her his hand to assist her into the backseat of his buggy. "Sarah, this is Faith, but that's not her real name. She's had a memory loss and doesn't remember anything about her past—so she says."

Sarah peered at her, and her eyes lit up. "Gracious, child, you have beautiful red hair. And look at your baby girl. Her hair is just like yours." Sarah smiled so sweetly that Faith's heart felt better. "Thank you, ma'am. Her name is Cherish, and she is almost three months old."

"Turn around and look ahead. There's plenty of time for you to get to know each other." He snapped the reins at the horses.

***

Sarah's heart was racing. There was going to be a baby under their roof again, one that she could hold and love. Cornelius's granddaughter seemed very young and would probably be glad to have help with the care of the infant, and she was just the one to do it. Oh, to just hold that beautiful baby in her arms, Sarah thought, as she turned her head to sneak another glance at the girl in the rear seat.

***

Arriving at the whitewashed boarded house with a small picket fence in front was a surprise. Faith thought that this man would own a farm away from town. She was pleased to see that other people lived near them.

Sarah quickly jumped down from her seat and reached to take Cherish out of Faith's arms.

"Thank you," Faith mumbled as she climbed down and circled the buggy to retrieve her carpet bag.

"Follow me while Mr. Studerman puts away the horses and the buggy," Sarah said.

"You call your husband Mr. and not Leon?" Faith was surprised to hear Elder Studerman's wife call him by his surname.

"Oh, yes. It's a sign of respect. All the wives call their husbands by their last name. You must show respect to him by calling him Elder Studerman. Now don't forget because he will get angry if you don't."

"Mrs. Studerman, may I call you Sarah or Aunt Sarah? Your husband told me that your sister was my grandmother. Is that correct?"

"That's right. My sister and her husband were coming to settle here near us. I didn't know that you were traveling with them."

"Do you know why my mama wasn't traveling with them, and when was the last time you heard from her?"

Hurrying to the window, Sarah peeked through the curtains. "Good, he's out in the barn. I don't have any idea, deary, and I can't remember seeing my niece since she was very young. My sister never even wrote about her." She picked up Faith's carpet bag. "Follow me. I will show you your room. We can freshen it up tomorrow. I would have had it all ready for you if I had known you were coming."

Faith walked into the small bedroom and sat down on the bed. "Oh, this feels so good. Do you think Cherish and I could lie down for a short nap? I sat up on the train for nearly two days, and I'm exhausted."

"'I'll tell Mr. Studerman that you are ill and need to rest. I'll wake you when I have the evening meal on the table." She walked over to a chest at the foot of the bed and pulled out a lovely quilt. She laid it across the bed and left the room.

Faith opened the carpet bag and retrieved a fresh nappy for the baby. After changing her into a clean gown, she rocked her until Cherish fell into a deep slumber. Faith walked to the window and placed her forehead on the windowpane. She glanced at her surroundings and wished she'd been able to see more of the countryside. Looking down at her lovely baby, she laid her on the bed up against the wall, then stretched out beside her and fell into a deep sleep.

***

A couple hours later, Elder Studerman strode into the house while his wife was putting dinner on the table. "Where's the girl?" the old man growled as he removed his large black hat. He lowered his suspenders and rubbed his shoulders.

"The two lay down for a nap right after we arrived home. They both were exhausted from the long train trip. I told her I'd wake her to eat supper." Sarah moved toward the bedroom door.

"I'll wake her. This will be her last nap during the day. I didn't bring her here for you to have to wait on her hand and foot. She's going to help you do everything, or I will make her regret coming here."

"Why will I regret coming here, Elder Studerman?" Faith stood in the doorway holding Cherish in her arms.

Elder Studerman stormed across the kitchen and towered over Faith. "Don't you get sassy with me, girl. You'll be sorry if you use your smart English mouth while speaking to me." He whipped around and strode back to the table. "After supper I will give you a list of things you are to do here and things you cannot do outside this house. I spent the last two hours speaking with our bishop about your predicament."

***

Faith stepped across the room, took a deep breath, and straightened her spine. She jerked the chair away from the table and sat down, adjusting Cherish in her arms so she could feed her a mouth or two of soft food. Anger flowed through her body. She had made a big mistake coming to Lawrence with Elder Studerman. Now, she had no choice but to survive living with this couple.

After a lengthy blessing, Sarah passed the bowls of food to her husband first who helped himself to a portion enough for two men. Sarah moved the bowls in front of Faith and smiled. She took a large tablespoon of mashed potatoes and a few soft green beans. Cherish smacked the metal spoon and jumped up and down in Faith's lap for more. Sarah smiled as Faith adjusted the baby in her lap and wiped her messy mouth.

After a few more slices of buttered cornbread, Elder Studerman drank a full glass of buttermilk, gave a loud burp, and stood. "You wash the dishes while my wife rests." Tossing his napkin down in the middle of his plate, he stalked upstairs.

Faith watched the tall, angry man climb the staircase. She glanced at Sarah and whispered, "Has he retired for the night? I thought he wanted to discuss my chores and what the bishop said about me being here."

"I think he forgot that he was going to talk to you, but he's gone to bed. We'll be able to hear him in a little while. He snores loud enough to be heard by our neighbors." She covered her laughter.

Faith walked into her bedroom and took the quilt from the bed. She returned and made a pallet on the floor and laid Cherish on her back. The baby cooed and grabbed her toes and tried to rock back and forth.

Quickly grabbing an apron from a nook on the wall, she cleaned the table and stacked the dishes. Sarah sat on the floor beside the baby and took a foot and kissed it. Faith smiled as she filled the dishpan with the dishes and raked the leftovers into a pail sitting on the end of the counter. She rinsed the dishes and took the teapot filled with water and poured it over the plates and bowls. After she wiped the table and swept the floor, she took a dishcloth and dried all the dishes. After placing the plates, bowls, and cups on a shelf over the sink, she folded the drying rag on a hook.

Faith smiled down at Sarah as she continued playing with Cherish. She asked if she needed to fill the wood box and bring in fresh water for in the morning.

"Mr. Studerman will pull up fresh water from the well." Sarah looked around the kitchen. "You did a good job cleaning this room. Thank you."

"For some reason, I remember how to cook and clean. I have a few flashes of memory but not enough to tell me where I came from and who I am. God will help me when He's ready for me to know."

"It pleases me that you have faith. Isn't that funny? You have faith and your name is Faith?" Sarah stood and picked up Cherish from the pallet.

"Jack, Sally, and I chose my new name. I said that I needed to place my faith in God, and we all laughed and decided that Faith was a good name for me. I do wish I knew who I was and where I came from. I can't help but wonder if I was married, and what he must think about me being gone." Sarah sat quietly and took Faith's hand. "I also wonder about my folks and if I have brothers and sisters. There is so much I feel like I am missing out on in life."

"Child, you are here now with your new family. My sister was your grandmother, and she was a sweet woman. I am sorry that you don't remember her." Sarah stood and said that morning came early so they'd best go to bed. "Please get up early and put the coffee on for Mr. Studerman. He's an early riser and very demanding."

"Yes, I will try to be up before he is. What does he eat for breakfast?" Faith picked up Cherish and wiped the drool off her mouth and chin.

"He eats whatever I cook as long as there's plenty of it." Laughing softly, she passed by the stairs, entered another room, and closed the door.

Chapter 22

Faith had hardly slept at all during the night. She was afraid of oversleeping and not being up before Elder Studerman rose. The coffee was ready, and a pan of biscuits was golden brown in the oven when she heard the man stomping down the stairs. He was an ill-mannered man who cared about no one but himself.

He pulled up his suspenders and flopped down at the kitchen table. Faith rushed over and poured him a cup of coffee. She set the pot on the stove, opened the oven door, and retrieved the biscuits. "Do you want your eggs fried or scrambled?"

"Four fried eggs, well done. Butter me several of those biscuits," he growled.

After the eggs were placed in front of him, she set several more buttered biscuits and the strawberry jam in front of him. She stood in front of the stove and poured herself a fresh cup of coffee.

"Sit down, girl. I want to tell you what I expect of you. Here's a list. Do all of these things every day. Sarah will watch over your brat." He picked up another biscuit, spread butter on the hot bread, and poked the whole thing in his mouth. He wiped his mouth with his sleeve and looked at her. "The bishop said that our community will shun you." He scowled at Faith as she stared back at him. "That means that you cannot leave this house except to do your chores outside. You will attend church each Sunday, but you will sit on the bench behind the other ladies. You will not speak to anyone. Shunned means you are treated like an outcast."

"Why?" Faith asks.

"Why what? Why are you to be shunned?" But before Faith could ask again, he continued. "You have no idea who you are and how you became with child. You could be a loose woman, and we can't have you around our women and children."

"Why did you bring me with you to this community? You knew I had lost my memory and that I was married to Jack Mills. You knew I had a child and didn't know the man with whom I had this child—my husband?"

"You are my niece. I have a responsibility to take care of you. Besides, you have a baby that Sarah has always desired. She can love and care for the child."

"Yes, Sarah can love her niece," Faith slowly responded, "but she is my child. I will take care of her. Do I make myself clear? Cherish is my baby."

Sarah stood in the doorway of her bedroom. "Faith, dear, of course, Cherish is your baby. I only want to help you with her."

Elder Studerman glared at his wife, slipped on his boots, and stormed out the door. He grabbed his hat off the hook on the porch and strode toward town.

Faith stood at the window, watching the man walked down the trail. "Sarah, did he bring me here to take my baby away from me?" She waited for the woman to answer, but no sound came from her. "Please know that I will never give my baby to you or anyone. She is part of me, and I would die before I was forced to give her up."

Sarah nodded. "I understand, dear. I will never take your baby away from you."

"Good, I am glad we understand each other. I have baked biscuits and there is plenty of coffee on the stove. I need to go to the barn and complete this list of chores your husband left me. Will you call me when Cherish wakes?" Faith went to the door and smiled at Sarah.

Faith walked out into the morning daylight. It was a beautiful day without a cloud in the sky. She entered the barn and smelled the horses, goats, and the cow. The manure was deep in the stalls, and black flies were swarming the piles.

Searching for a wheelbarrow and a shovel, she placed them beside the horses' stalls. She led the two large horses into the corral. Tossing several pitchforks of hay to them, she led the goats outside too. Faith placed two buckets of oats in front of them and dodged one of them as he tried to butt her in the side. The chicken pen looked like it had never been raked, but she had to clean the horses' stalls first and milk the cow.

Faith went into the chicken house and scattered feed around for the sitting hens and two big roosters. She would collect and clean the eggs later.

After two hours of back-breaking work, she was proud that she had cleaned the stalls. Listening to the cow moo and stomp around, she placed a pail of feed in front of her. She finally set a stool beside the hefty animal, took a bucket of water, and washed her teats. After placing a clean pail under the animal, she laid her face against the cow's warm hide.

As she milked the cow, she closed her eyes and could see herself walking around in another barn, humming as she fed a small goat and several piglets. *Where was she?* The thought floated through her mind. She opened her eyes and glanced around the nearly clean barn. Faith completed her milking and pushed the cow into a stall where she gave her a pat on the rump. Several windows had wooden shutters opened from the inside. Quickly she pushed the shutters open and allowed cool, fresh air to flow.

As she headed over to the chicken yard to collect eggs, she could smell honeysuckle. On the far side of the fence, a bush grew over a wire. She walked around to the bush and threaded the long thin stem through the wire so it could grow and bloom.

"Hey, you."

Faith glanced around and looked everywhere.

"Hey, over here." The voice came again. On the side of the barn stood a wiry older woman motioning for Faith to come. Faith stood still and looked at the little shriveled-looking stranger.

"You calling me?" She asked the woman.

"Don't be afraid. I'm your neighbor. My name is Dottie. I know your name."

Faith glanced over her shoulder to make sure no one saw her talking to this stranger. "Do you know that everyone is shunning me?"

"Of course, I know. That's why I am in hiding, trying to be your friend." Dottie spoke like Faith didn't have any sense.

"Why do you want to be my friend, and where do you live?"

"Next door with my daughter and husband. You are going to need a friend, and I want to help you. I'm English, too. I do whatever I want and drive my family crazy because I don't talk and act like they do." She placed her hand over her mouth and laughed.

"Dottie, I've got to get back to work. I have a list of chores to do, and if I don't finish before Elder Studerman comes home, he'll be mad."

"That fool of a man is mad all the time. You watch yourself around him. You're a pretty little thing, and he's claiming you're his kin. I bet you ain't." She leaned up against the barn and said, "I'll go now, but I will see you each morning. Come to me if you need protection."

Faith watched the little woman scoot around the barn out of sight. "Protection?" Faith rolled that word around in her mind. Why would she need protection from Elder Studerman? After a few moments Faith walked into the henhouse and gathered several dozen eggs. She took the basket to the water pump and washed each egg until they were clean. A glance at the list showed that she had done all the chores outside. Hurrying into the house, she needed to put something on to cook for the midday meal.

Cherish was sitting in Sarah's lap eating soft oatmeal. She was dressed, and her lovely red curls had a bow pinned on the side. A cold chill went down Faith's back. "I asked you to call me when she woke up. I like to have a few minutes with her every morning before I prepare her for the day."

A sad expression came across Sarah's face.

"I'm sorry, and I do appreciate you caring for her." Taking a chair at the kitchen table, she sat down in front of her baby. She looked at the pretty bow in her hair and smiled. "This is her first bow. She looks so cute and girly."

"What do you think you're doing?" Elder Studerman yelled. Neither Sarah nor Faith had heard him enter the front door. "You have a list of chores to do. I will not allow a good-for-nothing living under my roof. You'll be sorry if I catch you being lazy again."

"Mr. Studerman, the girl just came in from outside from doing all of the outside chores." Sarah stood and gave the baby to Faith. "She needs coffee and something to eat."

"Don't you dare speak to me in that tone of voice?" He grabbed his wife's arm and shook her hard. "You're my wife and I don't won't to harm you, but I will make you sorry. Do you understand me, woman?"

"Yes, sir," mumbled Sarah as she hung her head.

He pivoted toward the door. "I will be back in two hours for the midday meal. Have it ready." Slamming the door, he left.

"Are you all right, Aunt Sarah? Does he ever go out that door without slamming it?"

"No, I think he wants all the neighbors to know that he's coming their way." Sarah struggled to her feet and looked out the window.

Faith took Sarah's hand. "Sarah, are you well?"

Sarah sat down in the rocker in front of the fireplace. "I have good days and bad ones. My side hurts something fierce, and sometimes the pain is unbearable."

"Did you fall and break a rib or something like that?"

"Not quite like that, but I do think that something is broken."

"Come and sit on my bed. I can bind your ribs tight, and maybe that will help." Faith stopped suddenly. *How did I know about binding?* She felt that she might be getting her memory back.

Once she'd wrapped a binding around Sarah's ribs, she started the midday meal. She insisted that her aunt continue to sit in the rocking chair and rest. Cherish was lying in the laundry basket taking her morning nap.

Faith walked down into the dark cellar, lit a lantern, and found a pork barrel. She dug down into the lard and retrieved six, excellent-sized chops. After preparing the chops, she put them into the stove to cook slowly. She peeled potatoes, cleaned green snap beans, and kneaded the bread, setting several loaves to rise.

Working on the side porch, she prepared the wash water and gathered all the dirty clothes that needed attending. After an hour of washing, rinsing, and hanging the items on the line, she went back inside and continued cooking the potatoes and beans. Faith punched down the bread to let it rise some more.

Cherish was awake and wanting to be picked up. Sarah offered to hold her, but Faith declined. "You don't need to pick up anything heavy for a while. We want to get your side better."

Faith fed and changed her baby. She saw Elder Studerman walking toward the house, so she immediately began mashing the potatoes and buttering a few hot rolls. He stormed into the house and scared Cherish who began to fret and tear up. Hiding her face into Faith's shoulder, she became calm.

"Mr. Studerman, you scared the baby. Do you have to be so loud every time you enter?"

"Shut your trap, woman. I will do as I please in my home." He glared at his wife and snatched a chair out from the table and folded his large frame into it.

"Are you going to pour me some coffee, woman? Get yourself over here and help with the food or take the brat from her."

"My child is not a brat, and she has a name."

With bulging eyes, he grabbed Faith's arm and pulled her close. He jerked her arm up behind her back as high as he could without breaking it.

Faith let out a scream, and he pushed her away. With her eyes closed she clutched her arm against her chest and rubbed it. She rocked on her toes, afraid to move forward. Time held no meaning as she stood looking at her so-called uncle.

"Don't ever speak to me in that voice again, or I will break it next time." His eyes moved up and down Faith's young body.

Faith noticed his reaction but didn't show it because she was too angry. A flush of adrenaline rushed through her body like never before. If he had hurt Cherish during this alteration, she had no idea what she would have done to the man who called himself her uncle.

Sarah screamed and rushed to Faith, taking the babe out of her arms. "Hush, baby child, Aunt Sarah has you now. Don't cry, please," she whispered to Cherish. Faith stretched her left arm and was glad that he had not broken it, but it hurt like the dickens. The table was set for one. She poured her uncle some hot coffee and placed a bowl of steaming mashed potatoes in front of him.

"Who told you to go into my cellar and get this meat?" He banged on the table with his fist.

Faith took a few steps away from the table. "I had to have something to cook for your meal, so I went down into the cellar where most people keep fresh vegetables and meat in barrels."

"Don't go down there again without my permission, understand?"

"How will I find food to cook?"

"Sarah can go down there and get whatever is needed." He glared at his wife and asked why she was all bent over.

"My side is aching today, but Faith wrapped it with a binder. It is better already."

"Don't be coming to me with excuses for not doing your duty," he demanded.

Sarah nodded to him, embarrassed that he would mention what went on in the bedroom. She weighed the danger of disobeying her husband. Even at his age, he was a demanding lover, something he liked to call himself.

***

Faith sat at the table and fed Cherish a spoon filled with mashed potatoes. She smacked as the food spilled from the side of her mouth.

"Don't ever feed that young'un while I am eating. She is making me lose my appetite," Again Elder Studerman pounded his fist on the tabletop, which caused Cherish to jump and cry out.

"Look what you have done." Splaying her hands out wide, Sarah tried to take the baby from Faith.

Faith scrunched up her face and then released her breath. She tried to remain calm as Mr. Studerman stalked from the kitchen. Watching Sarah pace with her baby, she confessed her plan.

"Sarah, I haven't been here a week, but I can tell I have made a big mistake in coming here with your husband, who claims to be my uncle. The man hates my baby and me. I don't know why he kept insisting that I come, but I know the reason I agreed."

"Why, dearie? Why did you come with him?" Sarah rubbed her ribs after she placed the baby in her mother's arms.

Faith began feeding her again. She cooed and reached for the spoon, but Faith dodged her hand and gave her a bite of food.

"Set yourself a plate and eat something." Sarah said as Faith continued to feed the baby. "After our talk you need to go and rest."

"I overheard Jack, my new husband, talking, and now I am beginning to believe I didn't fully understand what he was saying to my young friend and helper. I want to go home and try to work things out with Jack, and just maybe, in a better environment, my memory will return."

"My husband will never let you leave. He is already making plans for your future." Sarah sat at the table in an unnatural stillness.

A bleak mood came over Faith as she watched the older woman staring off into space. "You must tell me what he's planning. He scares me, and I'm afraid for my baby. At first, I thought he wanted to take my baby and give her to you, but now I know you would never do that to me."

Sarah shifted to face Faith. "I can't explain to you what is going through his mind, but walk softly around him."

Helping Sarah into bed, Faith walked into the kitchen and watched her baby as she drifted off to sleep. A tight knot of dread lodged itself in the pit of her stomach. Her nerves were on edge. She circled the pallet and washed the dishes. After she dried them, she placed the china into a handmade cabinet. Standing in the kitchen she felt afraid and alone. Faith conceded to her emotions. She had to make plans to leave—get away from Elder Studerman. He was a bad man who pretended to be a good Amish man. If only his bishop knew the real man that Elder Studerman was in private.

***

His loud measured stride alerted her to his return home. He saw her quickly pick up her baby and rush into her bedroom. While laying Cherish into her bed, he entered her room and he stood so close to her she could smell the file-odor of ale on his breath. He wrapped his arms around her chest and captured her arms from behind.

"You are so beautiful, and I can hardly keep my hands off your lovely, young body." He wanted this girl so much he couldn't control himself whenever she was near. He couldn't tolerate the awful glares she gave him. Soon, he would claim her as his own. He heard Sarah moving around. Tonight might not be the time, but he would soon claim her as his mistress. No one would know with her living under his roof as his niece.

***

Faith was scared out of her wits being held captive by this brute of a man. She had to get free from his tight hold. "Let me go before I scream loud enough for the whole community to hear." She leaned forward and butted him with her backside. "Can't you remember that I'm your niece for one minute? Get out and stay out."

He turned her loose and stood frozen in place. In his drunken state, he shook his head and left the room as quietly as he entered.

Suppressing a groan, she listened as he stomped up the stairs to his bedroom. Rushing to the door, she locked it, and took the straight chair and propped it under the doorknob. If he returned, she would surely hear him, she thought.

Chapter 23

Sunday morning was a perfect fall day. The wind was blowing a cool breeze and the few trees surrounding the town and small farms had turned bright gold and orange. Sarah had come into Faith's room earlier and laid out an outfit for her to wear to church. On the dresser was a new, long white gown with a matching bonnet and tiny crochet socks for Cherish. Faith couldn't remember ever seeing anything prettier for a baby to wear to church.

After the morning chores, she would come in and get herself and Cherish ready for their first Amish church service. She remembered that the community would shun her. But her uncle said that she would still attend. She wondered where she would sit in the church. Sarah had told her earlier that the men and women sat across the room from each other. The younger unmarried girls would sit on the second row behind their mamas. At this church, there would be no music or singing.

After washing up and removing the barn smell from her body, she could hear Sarah moving around in the kitchen, so she hurried with her attire. A long purple skirt with a bib and straps that crisscrossed in the back fit her perfectly. A long-sleeved white blouse covered her upper body. A small white bonnet with long strings to be tied under the chin hid her hair.

Faith walked into the kitchen carrying the bonnet and asked Sarah if she would button her straps in the back and help with the bonnet. After the buttons were fastened, she placed the cap over Faith's thick wild red curls.

"All of your hair must be tucked under the material. No curls can be seen or hang loose." After five minutes, Sarah had done an excellent job and Faith looked just like a beautiful Amish young lady.

"The wagon is out front. Gather your things and get outside." Elder Studerman voice roared from the front door. He turned and went out on the porch. Sarah reached for her shawl and picked up the basket that would be used if Cherish fell asleep. Faith wrapped Cherish in a soft white blanket that matched her new outfit, snuggled her close to her chest, and scooted past her uncle to the wagon. The mules were shifting and flapping their ears at the big horse flies that were swarming around. Sarah managed to get in the wagon and reached down for the baby. Faith climbed in the back and took Cherish from Sarah. After they were seated, Elder Studerman urged the mules forward toward the church.

Elder Studerman stopped the mules beside the church and waited while some other families unloaded their wagons and entered the white building. He watched several more minutes and then shuffled his large frame around and faced Faith. "Listen to my instructions, girl, and obey me." He surveyed Faith's face to make sure she was listening to him. "You are not to raise your eyes to anyone—man or woman. If the bishop speaks to you, keep your eyes lowered to the ground. You will not speak to anyone, and if you are spoken to, keep your eyes downcast and remain quiet. The whole church is shunning you, but some of the members may not know it yet. Do you understand me?"

"Yes, Mr. Studerman, I hear you very well." Faith agreed only to avoid a confrontation in front of the few church members standing at the door.

Elder Studerman jumped down from the wagon and helped the two ladies and baby down. He was acting the perfect gentleman in front of the congregation who stood watching and wondering who the young woman was with him and his wife.

Bishop Merriweather greeted them, then Sarah took Faith's hand and led her to the women's side of the church. She whispered to Faith that she must sit on the back bench with the baby in her basket as long as she was quiet.

All the ladies were twisting around and craning their necks to see Faith. Most of them probably wondered why she was sitting all alone and not being friendly to anyone. The men acted like they had not seen Faith at all. Most likely the men already knew about Faith and her past. Men conducted their business in their own homes and only told their wives what they needed to know. The ladies got their information about the community through gossip whispered in the marketplace held on Saturday morning at the edge of town.

Faith lifted her eyes to glance around the room without being noticed. She could tell that the younger men were watching her every move. Some of them were jabbing each other in the side and smiling as they looked her way.

"Let us pray," a voice boomed from the front of the room. The men and women fell to their knees facing their chair and prayed silently as the bishop's voice droned on and on.

Faith sat as still as night. She wasn't told to do whatever the ladies did in the service and if Mr. Studerman didn't like it, so be it. He should have given her better instructions. Cherish got tired of being in the small space of the basket and fretted. Faith reached down and pulled on her foot which made her laugh. She quickly picked her up out of the confines of the small basket and bounced her on her knees. It seemed that every eye of the congregation was watching her actions.

Another Amish man stood and walked to the front, and the bishop took his seat. The man cleared his throat and read a scripture from his big black Bible. He said with a loud, clear voice, "This is what our God says about fornication; a voluntary sexual act between a man and a woman." The room was so quiet a dog could be heard barking down the street. The man certainly had all the young people's attention. He read Corinthians 5:1.

Faith could hear her own heart beating from the silence in the meeting room.

The man closed his Bible, and the slight noise caused most everyone to jump. "Let me explain the Word of God to the best of my ability. It has been reported that there is sexual immorality among us that is not and will not be tolerated."

The man talked on and on, but Faith blocked his words from her mind. She couldn't believe that Elder Studerman told the bishop and this man that she was an immoral woman because she had a child and couldn't remember anything about the act of conception.

Faith realized that all the women in the congregation knew the man was talking about her. She could see the stiffening of their spines, the occasional glances back at her, and how they held their eyes facing forward from the moment the man took his seat.

Bishop Merriweather announced that Elder Studerman's niece had come to live with them and had a child. "For a period of unknown time, his niece will be shunned by our community. Please follow the rules of our Order and do as you are requested. If you break the silence with this young lady, you will also be shunned. Now, let us pray and go and have a good week."

Faith didn't move a muscle. She held Cherish tight while keeping her eyes downcast. She could see her uncle's boots standing next to her.

"Girl, these people would like to look at your baby. Let the woman hold her." Faith eyed the older man and woman who looked like all the other members of the church. The grandmother-looking woman was wearing all black and the man had a long gray beard.

"Cherish doesn't take to strangers," Faith replied and held her baby tighter.

"Don't make me take her from you. Now give her the baby so we can get on home," he said through clenched teeth.

"That's all right," the older woman said. "I can see she's a beautiful child. Anyone would love to have a baby girl like her." Cherish took that moment to smile and showed her one front tooth that was trying to erupt. "Oh my, she's teething already." The woman was glowing with happiness.

Faith gathered the baby's basket, stepped around the couple, and hurried outside to their wagon. *What is going on here? Does this couple believe that I am going to give up my baby to them?*

Once Elder Studerman led his team away from the church, he snapped at Faith. "How dare you be so ugly to my friends who wanted to look at your baby? You'd better learn how to behave or you are going to be sorry."

"How can you say that to me? You told me I would be sorry if I spoke or even looked at anyone while in the church. You brought over these strangers and acted like it was perfectly all right to visit with them. How did I know that you weren't just testing me?"

***

Elder Studerman was pleased that he had found a home for Faith's brat. The older couple would be staying at the hotel for a few days, waiting for him to bring the baby to them. Faith would have more time to spend with him, and the two thousand dollars would fill his pockets with the money the couple was willing to pay him for the child. Sarah was his only problem, but he was planning on sending her to visit her sister in northern Kansas. He just wouldn't send her money to return home. Problem solved. Child gone, Sarah gone, and Faith all to himself whenever he wanted her in his bed.

***

"I don't won't to visit my sister at this time. My ribs still hurt, and it will be hard on me to travel. I will go later." Sarah smiled at her husband. "I thank you for thinking of me."

"Sarah, you will go. I have already purchased your train ticket, and you'll leave tomorrow morning. Don't sass me, woman, or you may have more than hurt ribs. Do I make myself clear?"

Sarah couldn't believe that her man was sending her away. She had seen the way he watched Faith when he thought no one was watching, and she was sure that he had tried to touch Faith because she was afraid of him. If she had to leave her home, she would make sure Faith and her baby was safe. Dottie would help her with removing Faith from her home. It was too late tonight, but she would tell Faith why she had to leave.

After Elder Studerman had left the house, Sarah gathered the strength to walk outside and looked over the fence at her neighbor's small farm. The Jefferson's were nice people, but they stayed to themselves because of her husband's attitude. They had tried to be good neighbors, but Mr. Studerman had practically told them to stay home.

Dottie Anderson was the mother of Mrs. Jefferson and everyone believed that she was a little crazy, but in all reality, she had everyone fooled. Because she allowed them to believe that she was "off her rocker," she didn't have to obey all those dumb Amish rules. Everyone just overlooked her actions or whenever she spoke about issues in the Order, they didn't pay her any mind.

Sarah walked along the edge of her fence line and watched for any sign of Dottie. Finally, Dottie spotted Sarah holding onto the fence for dear life and rushed out to her.

"What wrong, Sarah? Has that man of yours hurt you again? If he has he will be sorry before today's sun sets." Dottie looked over Sarah's shoulder and around the farm area.

"Not this time, but I do need you to help Faith. My man is sending me away to my sister's tomorrow. You and I can guess why." She hung her head and wiped away a tear. "He wants to be all alone with Faith."

"What does he plan to do about her little girl?" Dottie had watched Elder Studerman slip around and try to peek in Faith's bedroom window. She had watched the old so-called Amish man practically drool at the mouth.

"He is selling the baby to an older couple that came to the prayer meeting Sunday. Their daughter wants a baby so badly, and they are willing to pay him a large amount of money. He wants Faith's attention showered on him and no one else, especially a baby and old woman. Please, Dottie, I need to you watch after Faith. He might have to lock her in the house to keep her from running away. She's already spoken to me about trying to leave."

"I'm sorry to see you leave, but it is best for you now. Your man is crazy about that girl and he could hurt you again. He cracked your ribs, so please don't deny it. You are married to a mean-spirited man, and one day he will be punished." Dottie climbed through the fence railings and placed her arm around Sarah's shoulders. "Come, I will help you back to the house."

Chapter 24

Jack was determined to leave on the next train heading to Kansas. The doctor had discovered a pair of adult-size crutches, and he could move around without putting any weight on his bad leg. He had asked Glenn to travel with him to Lawrence, Kansas, like the doctor had advised.

While the leg was mending enough to get around, he questioned Mrs. Mason over and over about the morning that Faith had come into town and told her that she was leaving with her uncle.

"She was sad, but she kept saying that she had to leave and go and live with her kinfolks," Mrs. Mason repeated their conversation and explained that she had begged Faith not to go away until he returned.

Jack made plans to leave as soon as possible. He arranged that Sally and her two brothers would look after his place and Bear in the afternoon when the boys returned home from school. He stabled his six horses at the livery while he was gone so the boys wouldn't have to be bothered with them. The goats, pigs, and chickens had to be fed every day, and the cow needed to be milked. Mrs. Parker could use the milk and the boys could gather and wash the eggs. Whatever their mother didn't need, they could sell to Mrs. Mason at the dry goods store. As an incentive, they could keep the money. Sally would still have her wages to give to her mother once he returned. Jack instructed Mrs. Mason to put whatever was needed at his place and the Parkers' on his account.

Mrs. Mason saw Jack and Glenn off at the train depot. She waved and wished him good luck finding Faith. Jack wondered why Sally didn't come into town and see him off. He guessed she had a lot to do, and she had promised to keep Bear with her at all times for protection.

***

Glenn shifted and scratched at the new clothes that Jack had purchased for him to travel in. With his hair slicked back and a new hat, he was almost handsome. He had been living all alone since Pa had been placed in jail. Without money he was nearly starved because he couldn't purchase any food. Living off the land was hard for an amateur. His pa had set all the traps, and Glenn had cleaned the furs and cooked their meals.

Once he set about helping the boys bury their pa, Sally had insisted that Glenn sleep in their loft and eat meals with them. He was happy working around their place from sunup to sundown. Mrs. Parker seemed pleased to have him staying with them.

Jack had offered to pay Glenn a fair wage if he would travel with him and help with anything he needed. Glenn was reluctant to leave Mrs. Parker, but Sally insisted that Jack needed his help so he agreed.

Glenn helped Jack up the train's steps and laid his crutches on the empty seat beside him. After making sure his boss was comfortable, he told Jack he would be right back.

***

As the train began to move, Jack was concerned about Glenn because he had not return to the passenger car. As he gave the conductor two tickets, he asked him if he had seen his companion.

"Yes, sir. I believe she's headed this way." The conductor tipped his hat and moved forward taking other passenger's tickets.

"She?" Jack whirled around in the hard seat and saw Sally walking slowly toward him.

"Hi, Mr. Jack." Sally eased down in the seat facing her friend and boss man. She was carrying a picnic basket, which she set on the floor. "I hope you won't be too mad, but Glenn and I swapped places. I need to go with you to find Miss Faith and the baby. I have been nearly crazy with worry about her." Her voice was soft and breathless.

Jack just stared at Sally. He couldn't believe these two young people had pulled this trick on him. "I can't believe you did this." His voice hardened like cold hard steel. "I need Glenn to help me, not a young whippersnapper." He knew that he was using his courtroom voice, snappy and uncaring.

"But Mr. Jack, I can do whatever Glenn could do for you. Besides, Miss Faith may need me to help her and the baby. Please don't be upset with me." The color drained from her face, and Jack was immediately sorry for his thoughtlessness. Sally had been more than a helpmate to Faith and him during the time she had worked for them. She had become family, and he really cared for the child. Jack reached for her hand, and her eyes widened. "I'm sorry, sweet child." His voice broke and he blinked before he said anymore. "I haven't been myself since I learned of Faith's departure with that old man."

***

His soft words were hardly a whisper, but Sally heard and felt his torment. He was a man in pain, emotionally and physically.

"How is your leg feeling? Do you need to place it up beside me?" Sally asked frowning.

"No, it's fine for now. Maybe later." Jack smiled as he adjusted himself to get more comfortable in the train seat.

"Does your mother know that you are traveling with me? A man?"

"Yep, she said for you to tell everyone that I'm your little sister, and no one will think anything bad about us being together. Besides, she thought it was a good idea because Glenn can handle the animals, chop firewood, and help the boys do the chores over at your place. He really surprised me. I thought him to be lazy and shiftless, but he's a good worker. Ma is treating him like family, but he sure can pack away the food." Sally grinned.

"Well, we know his pa was no good, but Glenn had no one else. He had to obey his pa or get a beating."

***

"He won't ever be mistreated at my home. Ma will teach him manners, but she'll never raise her hand to him," Sally said, darting glances at Jack. After traveling several hours, Sally reached down and placed a basket in her lap. "Are you hungry, Mr. Jack? Mama prepared us a nice lunch, and I'm ready to eat something."

"I'm always hungry for something good to eat," he replied and sat a little straighter. "We could eat in the dining car."

"Well, we might have to in the morning. I did bring some money tied in my hanky stuffed down in my deep pocket." Sally patted the side of her new dress.

"You just keep that bounty of yours hidden for now. We might have to use it later." He lifted the napkin covering the food and smelled the fried chicken.

"Well, little sister, did you kill one of your pet chickens for us to eat?" Jack knew how she talked to her chicks as she fed them each day.

"No! This bird is from Ma's chicken yard. The boys always gathered the eggs and fed the chickens at home."

"Oh well, that will make this bird taste so much better." He took a big bite of the chicken as she passed him a large square napkin.

Jack ate several chicken pieces, boiled eggs, and two large slices of fresh bread with cheese. Sally poured him a jar of fresh, cool water that her ma had wrapped in two damp dishtowels. "This water is so good. I'll have to thank your mother when we return home."

Before nightfall, the train stopped at a water depot. Sally helped Jack off the train and watched him hop to the outhouse. After he came out, she went inside for some privacy. Once all their personal needs were taken care of, they climbed on the train and settled down for the night. Sally asked the porter if she could have two pillows. "Certainly, miss, but they'll cost you a nickel a piece to use."

"Mercy." Prices are sky-high away from home, she thought. "I still want two please." When the porter left, she untied her hanky and took out two nickels, then quickly retied it and put it back in her pocket. Sally walked back to Jack. "Let me put this pillow under your leg and lift it onto the seat beside me."

"Where in blue blazes did you find those pillows?" He moved back in his seat and lifted his leg high, so she could position the pillow and make his leg comfortable.

"Oh, I have my ways," she said, smiling. "Does that feel better?"

"Wonderful, thank you."

"Lift your head and I'll place the other pillow behind your neck, so you can press up against the side of the window." He did as she requested but asked where her pillow was. "I don't need one. You just rest and it will help your leg heal."

"So now, you aren't just a nurse; you're a doctor, too." He laughed and settled back against the window and closed his eyes. In just a few minutes, he fell asleep.

Sally gazed at the sunset outside her window. She had never

been away from home, and the passing countryside was beautiful because God had started turning the leaves orange, brown, and yellow. The chug of the engine, the train whistle, and the rattling of the wheels were soon music to her ears. Her eyes grew heavy, so she moved across the aisle from Jack to the empty seats and made herself comfortable. She curled her small frame into a ball and slept.

The next day was the same, except Jack and Sally had breakfast and a light lunch in the dining car. There was a large family, whom they recognized as Amish, who was enjoying a lunch sitting at the table next to them. The children were quiet while their mother fed the youngest child. Sally couldn't keep her eyes off this family. She wondered if the family had been in Lawrence when Faith and her uncle arrived.

"Jack," Sally whispered, "I wonder if that family has seen Faith and Cherish in Lawrence. Why don't you question them?"

"It looks like they are traveling home. Maybe they haven't been in Lawrence for a while, but I will ask." He leaned forward. "Good afternoon, folks," Jack smiled at the man, woman, and children.

The woman cast her eyes downward at her food, but the man responded, "Good afternoon."

"I was wondering if you are traveling to Lawrence, Kansas," Jack asked.

"I don't know if that is any of your business where we are going. Why do you ask?" The man seemed disturbed that an Englishman was even speaking to his family.

"I have an older sister and her baby who were going to Lawrence, and I am worried about her because she hasn't written to our mother. I was hoping that if you live in Lawrence, you may have seen her. I know not many English people are welcome in your community."

"Well, sir, what does this girl look like?" Before Jack could answer the man continued. "I do remember Elder Studerman brought his niece and her child back from Tennessee right before I left to go and retrieve my family. I saw them at our prayer meeting last Sunday. Pretty young girl with a lovely girl child." He wiped his mouth with his napkin and picked up his coffee.

"You've been a big help. I'm sure that's my sister. She wanted to visit with my uncle and aunt for a few weeks." Jack reached for his coffee cup and drank it all, while watching the expression on the man's face.

Sally smiled at Jack and helped herself to a piece of cake. "I believe we have found them."

"Yes, you're correct. Faith is at her uncle's farm. Should be easy to find her." Jack appeared better than he had in days. Just knowing that Faith was in Lawrence was probably a big load off his chest.

Chapter 25

The big black engine pulled up to the station in Clarksville, Kansas. Lawrence was located six miles from this train depot. Sally helped Jack down the train steps, and they waited for their bags to be brought to the train depot. Jack took a seat on a wooden bench while they waited.

"Sally, we're going to have to rent a carriage to use while we're here. Can you go inside and ask the ticket agent if he knows if there is a livery nearby?" After Sally entered the building, the Amish man on the train stopped at the bottom steps of the depot.

"Sir, I heard you asking your sister to go find information about renting a rig. The man who owns the livery is my brother. My buggy and horses are boarded with him, and he will be coming for my family and me in a few minutes. If thee would like, I can ask if he can help thee. Would thee like for me to do that?"

"Yes, I certainly would appreciate your assistance. You're very kind to a stranger." Jack tried to stand without losing his balance on his good leg.

In a flash, a sizeable black buggy drove up to the depot. A tall, young man jumped down and raced over to the Amish man. A person could immediately tell that the two men were kin to each other. The lad wore a blue shirt, dark trousers with black suspenders, and a circled black hat. He was clean-shaven and cast a big smile at his brother's children.

"Thanks for the buggy, Luther. Come, children, climb inside so we can go home." The man helped his wife and children in the buggy and turned to Luther.

"Brother, this man will be visiting Lawrence for a while and is in need of a rig to rent. Do you have one for him to use?" The man leaned over to his brother and whispered, "This man is kin to Elder Studerman."

"I will be happy to help this man with a rig for as long as it is needed. I can use the business." Luther turned to Jack and shook his hand.

"Let me go to my livery and get thee a nice rig with one strong horse. I charge a dollar a day for the rental. Is that all right with thee?"

"You have me over a barrel, young man. The price is high, but you are the only business in town, so yes, I will pay your fee. Do you want payment in advance?

"How long are thee going to be in town?"

"Not sure. I am willing to pay you for three days now, and if I stay longer, I will pay when I bring the rig back to you. Agreed?"

The young man smiled, turned, and trotted down the street to his livery.

***

Jack and Sally drove down the street to the hotel in the center of Lawrence. Sally parked close to the boardwalk, jumped down, and assisted Jack to the ground. She drove the rig to the livery.

Jack hobbled inside the lobby and looked around. A lovely, old Amish lady asked in accented English if she could help him.

"Please, I need two rooms. One for me and one for my sister who has gone to the livery."

"Thee is in luck. I have two nice front-side rooms for fifty cents a day. We have clean sheets, clean towels, and hot water each morning upon thy requests. We have a small dining room that serves breakfast and the evening meal for a small price." She seemed pleased that this Englishman didn't complain about her prices.

Sally came into the lobby carrying their bags. She gave Jack and the older lady a big smile. "This is a nice town. I mean, community. There are so many cottage-like homes, and there seem to be farms located close together further out of town. The livery boy knows our uncle and aunt. He told me where they live. Ain't that great, brother?"

"Oh, who is your kinsfolks here? Are they members of our Amish Order?" the lady queried.

"Elder Studerman is our uncle. My sister came to visit him, but we are worried about her because she hasn't let us know if she made it here."

The older woman frowned. She closed her registration book and began to dust her counter.

"Do you know the Studermans'?" Jack watched her body language.

"All the Amish know each other. We all attend prayer meetings together. I am sorry, but I must return to the dining room."

Jack and Sally watched the lady hurry away. "It seems the lady knows our uncle real well." He picked up the keys to their rooms and slowly hopped up the stairs, taking one step at a time. Awkwardly, he made it to his room, but his injured leg hurt something awful. Jack closed his eyes, breathing deep as he made his way to the bed. Of all time to need to use the water closet down the hall. Jack wished he had thought of this before Sally went to her room.

Jack stood and hopped to the door, taking more deep breaths as he hobbled down the hall. He groped for the door handle and went inside. After he finished, he placed the crutches under his armpits and made it back to his room without falling on his face. *Thank the Lord for small favors.*

After a restless night of sleep, Jack knocked on Sally's room door. She immediately opened the door and was shocked by his appearance.

"Oh, Jack, you look like you've been up all night. Was your leg paining you?"

"Yes, tonight I will take some medicine, but last night I was afraid someone would tell old man Studerman that we're here. We shouldn't have told everyone that we are looking for him. Let's get some breakfast and try to find his farm."

***

Elder Studerman was happy that the train had left precisely on time this morning, carrying his pitiful wife away from Lawrence. Later today, he would deliver the baby to the older couple and collect the fee. With his wife gone and his pockets lined with money, a beautiful red-haired young gal would be in his bed. He felt like the luckiest man alive, at least in this God-forsaken place that his pa had left him.

He still remembered that day, at the age of nine, he was left at his uncle's farm, with no words of explanation. His pa's brother hit him on the top of the head and said, "Stop that blubbering. You are lucky he gave you to me. You'll get three square meals a day and a clean bed to lay your head on every night. That's more than I got out of the deal."

Shaking his head to clear the ugly words and thoughts of his childhood away, he smiled to himself, thinking about Faith waiting patiently at home for his return. She would have a nice hot lunch on the table, more treats later on.

***

Cherish cooed as Faith gathered all their clothes and personal items and placed them on the bed. She had to stop and feed the baby and then hurry down in the cellar and grab her traveling bag. She would leave this house in broad daylight so all the neighbors would hear and see her leaving. Elder Studerman wouldn't dare make a scene in front of the community people.

From the open window, she could hear her uncle coming down the pathway to the front door. Before she could race into the kitchen, he entered, so she stalled at the bedroom doorway. He was looking around the kitchen, sniffing for food, and frowning at the empty table. He glanced over Faith's shoulder and saw all of her things spread out on the bed.

"Well, Faith, I can see you are planning to go away, too. Must you leave me now that my sweet wife has left?"

"You are alone because you sent Sarah away, and we all know it." She stared at him. "I don't know why you felt that she had to go now. She isn't fit to travel with her side hurting her."

"She wanted to go, my dear. I have always wanted to please my sweet wife," he said with an unnatural stillness. With a smile that quickly faded, he reached out to pull Faith into his arms.

She darted away from him and placed Cherish in her basket. "I am leaving today, and you cannot stop me. I must go to the cellar and get my carpet bag." She started to move, but he stood between her and the door. "Please, move out of my way."

He sidestepped and gestured with flourish as she passed him.

She carried Cherish outside with her and set the basket down near the cellar door. Hurrying as fast as she could down the ladder, she found the matches, and lit the lantern that sat in the center of a table. As soon as the room lit up, the cellar down slammed and the lock slid in place. Rushing up the ladder, she banged on the door. From her dark prison, she heard her baby cry out.

"Cherish, Cherish, don't cry. Mama will come and get you in a minute."

"No, my dear. You'll not get out until I return. I will tell your darling baby goodbye for you."

Through the cracks in the door, she watched him pick up Cherish and disappear. She tried to see more of the outside, but she could only see a tiny light peeking through the boards. Wiping away tears with shaky fingers, she took one step at a time lowering herself down the ladder. As she stepped down on the next to last rung, it gave way. She tried to catch her balance but to no avail. Faith held tight to the ladder, but she slipped further down and tumbled to the hard surface, hitting the side of her head. When she tried to sit up, her prison whirled around and around until everything turned total black.

Someone was looking for her. She could feel it as she tried to open her eyes. Faith wanted to go to the voices that swam around in her head. Bright lights, sweet words, and baby cries surrounded her. A familiar voice called her. "Precious, come back." Who was Precious? Suddenly, a huge man slapped someone and began calling out nasty names—slut, whore, Jezebel. *Oh, dear Jesus, help.*

***

Dottie went outside to see why her two dogs were barking. They were running back and forth along the fence line, but she didn't see anything that would make them so upset. Glancing over at Sarah's place, she remembered that she hadn't seen Faith outside doing the morning chores. Looking closely at the back of the house, she saw the basket that Faith used to place the baby down when she needed to. It was positioned at the mouth of the cellar door.

Dottie hurried to the cellar window, stooped down on the ground, and tried to see down into the cellar. A lantern flickered from the middle of a table, but she couldn't see anything at all. A lantern shouldn't be lit in the cellar unless someone was down there. Dottie circled to Faith's bedroom window and peeked inside. On her bed were stacks of clothing. She glanced toward the kitchen, but no one was in the house. Something was very wrong. Sarah had asked her to watch after Faith because she was afraid of what her husband might do to her. Sarah had even said that he planned to sell the baby. "Oh, Jesus, please help me find the girl." Though Dottie wasn't

Amish, perhaps God would hear her prayer.

Dottie shaded her eyes and looked down the path to see if Elder Studerman was around. She hurried around to the back of the house. Using all the strength that her small frame would allow, she lifted the cellar door about a foot wide but dropped it because of its weight. Looking around the area, she saw a wooden crate to prop the door open. After propping the crate under the door, she crawled down into the cellar using the ladder. Once she almost reached the bottom, she felt the broken rung, but she lowered herself to the last step and finally landed on the dirt floor. Hurrying over to the lantern, she could tell it was almost out of fuel. The light from the door helped her to see all around.

Easing around the table, she bumped into something on the floor. "Oh my goodness, child," Dottie said. Faith lay on the floor—dead or unconscious. What had that man done? "Are you all right?" When she received no answer, she lifted Faith's bloody head in her small hands. "Mercy," she said aloud to herself. "I've got to get help."

***

"Here, let me help," Sarah said softly as she stooped down next to Dottie.

Dottie screamed and grabbed her chest. "You nearly scared me out of my drawers." Peering at Sarah from head to toe, she asked, "Where in the dickens did you come from? I thought you left on the train this morning."

"I did, but I got off about a mile down the tracks. The conductor was madder than a hive of disturbed bees when I pulled the emergency cord, but I didn't care. I had to come back here and help this child. Move and let me check her over." Sarah's ribs were hurting so bad she thought she might pass out from the pain. She had walked along the train track all the way home, but she couldn't think about herself now.

"Listen, I hear someone coming," Dottie said. "Leave her and let's hide over there in the dark until we know who it is. If it is your man, I'll hit him over the head with a board."

Chapter 26

Jack and Sally drove to the farmhouse where they were told the Studerman's lived. He reached for his crutches as Sally tied the reins of the horse to a post. After Jack eased down to the ground, they surveyed the area. The place appeared deserted.

Jack knocked on the front door while Sally walked around to the back of the house. He joined her. "Sally, I knocked on the front door but no one is home. Maybe some of the neighbors will know where they are."

***

The two ladies down in the cellar listened to the voices above the ground. "That must be Faith's husband. She said he might come looking for her," Sarah whispered to Dottie. They pushed further back into the darkness and watched a young girl peer down into the darkness.

***

"Jack, come back! Their cellar door is propped open, and there's a lit lantern with a little light," Sally yelled from behind the house. Jack hobbled toward her.

Once he saw the door propped open, he grabbed it, and pulled it wide open. With no thought of his damaged leg, he practically leaped down the ladder. With the afternoon sunlight shining down into the cellar, he peered all around.

A moan came from his left, and he glanced down on the floor. Jack couldn't believe his eyes. There lying in a pile of black material with wild red curls spreading around an angelic face was his long-lost wife.

Jack bent down on his good leg and lifted Faith's head off the floor. She lay so still he prayed she was alive. "Breathe, Faith, breathe." She continued to lay rigid. He prayed. *Please let her survive.*

"Sally," Jack yelled. "Come down here. I need your help."

"Let us help," a female voice came from beside the table in the center of the room.

Jack's heart stopped and he glanced up at two small, frail women who almost looked like twins.

"Who are you?" Jack asked as one of the women approached. "Where did you come from?" They had to be in the cellar already when he came down. "What are you doing down here? What have you done to my wife?"

"Jack?" Sally screamed with joy. "You found our Faith. Thank you, Lord Jesus, thank you," she whispered loud.

Jack was holding Faith's head while Sally scooted around the table and bent down beside her dearest friend. "Her head is bleeding, and she may have some broken bones." Her eyes widened as she glanced up at the two ladies.

Sarah answered first. "I'm Sarah. This is my home and Faith has been living with us. I'm her aunt, I think. This is my neighbor, Dottie, who has been helping me watch over Faith and the baby."

Suddenly, Faith's chest took in a deep breath and she slowly exhaled. "Help me," she whispered. "Hide me. Bad man." Faith reached to touch Jack's face as he ran his hand over her cheek. Blood caked in her hair.

"My name is Precious," Faith whispered, "I don't belong here." Her eyes clouded with tears. "My baby. Bad man took her."

"Where? What do you mean?" Jack clutched Faith tighter.

Sarah bent down and smoothed Faith's hair away from her cheeks. "My husband took her away. He is selling the baby to an older couple who wants to give Cherish to their daughter. He left with her earlier today." Sarah dabbed at errant tears.

"Faith, Precious, we need to get you up and out of this nasty cellar." Jack turned to the ladies. "I need another man to help me carry her up the ladder. With my hurt leg, I'm crippled."

"I'll go get my son-in-law. He will be happy to help." Dottie pushed back a white flappy band on the front of her cap. She didn't wait for Jack to answer but climbed the ladder like a young'un and was back in less than five minutes. "Mister, I have help. He was out in the barn and he heard me calling."

A tall man practically jumped down. "My name is Jerrod. How can I help thee, sir?" The young man looked from Jack to Faith.

"Please carry her up the ladder. I have a rig that can carry her into town to the doctor. Do you know where the doctor is located?"

"I will drive you to him while thee hold her. If thee agrees?"

"That'll be a big help." Jack climbed slowly up the ladder and hopped over to the buggy.

The young man dressed like the other Amish men carried Faith like she was weightless. Jack crawled up to the front seat of the rig and Jerrod placed her in his arms.

"Sally, climb in the back. Do you ladies want to go with us?" Jack looked at their anxious expressions but before they could answer, Jerrod told Dottie to take Sarah home with her and hide her from Mr. Studerman. "I will be back soon with Bishop Merriweather." The ladies nodded and hurried away.

Jerrod drove to the doctor's office, while Jack's eyes darted from side to side of the road, hoping to catch a glimpse of Elder Studerman. Faith moaned several times, and Jack soothed her with sweet words of love.

"How well do thee know Elder Studerman?" Jerrod asked as he slowed the horse down for another buggy that was in front of his.

"I only met the man once when he came to Gibson." Jack said, his tone clipped. "I was off on a trapping trip when he somehow convinced Faith that he was her uncle. I would have never let her leave with him if I had been home." Jack looked ahead and then asked Jerrod, "How well do you know him? Since you're neighbors, you must know him well."

"Well, we're taught not to speak ill about our neighbors, but me thinks the man is not a real Christian. I believe he's evil, but my family just stays away from his farm. Dottie, my mother-in-law, is English so she goes about her own business and watches everyone. She has helped Mrs. Studerman when he becomes so angry that he beats her. Dottie sneaks and gives Mrs. Studerman comfort when the man is away. She has watched Faith and the baby and has spoken to me about how she is afraid for the girl. My mother-in-law says Studerman watches her and has desires that are not normal for an uncle. I have spoken to our bishop, but he says that my mother-in-law must mind her own business. He said for us to stay away too, because thy wife is to be shunned by everyone. I can't control Dottie, but now I'm happy that she has done the right thing."

"Why was Faith being shunned?" Jack knew something of the religion because years ago he helped a Quaker family with the deed to their farmland. Amish, Quakers, and Amish were not very different, it seemed.

"Elder Studerman told the men in the community that Faith had lost her memory, and she most likely had her child out of wedlock. He wasn't sure, but it was best that she be shunned and not be allowed to associate with the women and children of our Order. I was very angry and told the bishop that it was unfair to jump to the conclusion that just because she couldn't remember she was unfit." He drove to the doctor's office and jumped down to take Faith out of Jack's arms. Sally circled to Jack and handed him one of his crutches.

After a thorough examination, the doctor determined that Faith did not have any broken bones, but the gash on the side of her face needed two stitches. He didn't have to give her any medication because she was still unconscious. From time to time, Faith would open her eyes and mumble a few words and then drift away. The doctor told Jack that this was normal since she had taken a hard fall. "She'll come around in good time. Don't rush her." He looked at Jack and said to take her home and allow her to rest.

Jack asked Jerrod if he would carry Faith back to the wagon and he and Sally would take her to the hotel. "I need to put her to bed, but I must find Mr. Studerman before he sells Cherish to the older couple. I have to get the baby back today. Cherish is like my own baby."

"I will help you. First, we'll see the bishop, and he will gather others to help us search for him and this couple. They can't be too far away."

"I need to report this kidnapping to the sheriff," Jack hopped to the rig. Jerrod gave him a hand-up to the seat. Once Jerrod placed Faith back in Jack's arms, Sally took Jack's crutches and climbed into the back.

"The bishop might not want thee to contact the authority yet. Our Order takes care of the problems our people are involved in. If we cannot settle the problem, then we allow the sheriff to be called."

"This old man may want the protection from the sheriff when

we catch up to him. I could strangle him with my bare hands." Jack looked down at his lovely wife, but Jerrod didn't comment.

As the black rig hit every bump in the dirt road, Jack took his time to explore Faith's features at a close range. He surveyed every inch of her beautiful complexion, even with the two stitches on the side of her face. Her delicately shaped face held a dainty nose, and he had never witnessed such long eyelashes. They were a rusty shade, much lighter than her hair. She had generous, rosy, curved lips. Jack drank his fill of her because he doubted it would be anytime soon that he would be holding her this close again—at least until they settled the problems that faced them with gaining her memory back.

***

The sky rumbled and the air smelled of rain. The men didn't appear to notice the ominous clouds. Jerrod took Faith out of Jack's arms and rushed her to the front door of the bishop's home.

Mrs. Merriweather, the bishop's wife, opened the door and her eyes widened. "Mr. Merriweather, you're needed," she called over her shoulder. She motioned for the men to enter and go into the parlor. "How may I care for this young lady?" the bishop's wife asked.

Sally stepped forward. "Do you have a bed where she can rest while the men talk?"

"Yes, Jerrod, follow me and place the young lady on my extra bed."

After Faith was made comfortable, the men went into the parlor to discuss how they were going to find the baby, Mr. Studerman, and the older couple. The bishop was very disturbed by Mr. Studerman's actions.

"Jerrod, ring the church bell and have the men gather in the church. We will organize a search party immediately."

In less than thirty minutes, many of the Amish men had joined the group and were out in the community searching every house and farm. They questioned the stationmaster and the livery owner. No one has seen anything of Mr. Studerman or the older couple.

Several men saddled their horses and rode down the main trail in search of buggies traveling away from Lawrence. Bishop Merriweather asked two men to ride to Clarksville in search of the missing people.

"How could they get away so fast?" Jack asked the bishop.

"I remember the older couple visiting our church this past Sunday. They are from the Clarksville's Amish Order. I never met their daughter, to whom I'm sure Mr. Studerman was intending to sell the child." The bishop walked over to his wife and whispered a few words, then he returned. "Mr. Mills, are thee able to ride the six miles to Clarksville? I want to go there and speak with their bishop. He will help us."

"I can ride, walk, or run six miles to get my baby back." He said, grabbing his hat from the rack on the wall.

"Thy baby?" The bishop raised his eyes in question.

"I was with Faith and the doctor when she brought the baby into this world. I was first to hold her, bathe her, and clean her up. I love her like she's mine."

"Now, I understand," he said as he placed his black hat over his long, gray hair. "My wife and thy sister can care for the young lady while we are gone. Let's go." The bishop led the way outside to a carriage.

***

Faith lay still, alone, and unable to move. The room swayed as if she was on a vessel. Her head hurt and she felt nauseated. Whispered voices surrounded her, but she couldn't make out what they were saying. She peeked from under her eyelids and saw a large wooden cross nailed to the wall before her. Maybe she was in a church, but she smelled something cooking. Faith wanted to get up, but something heavy restrained her.

The voices were closer to her and she peeked again their way. A younger woman was crying, and an older woman hugged her. The older lady seemed to be sincere and touched the younger one with gentle fingers. In her home, she had never been shown affection as a small child or young adult. Oh, how she wanted to get up and hug her baby. Suddenly, her eyes opened wide. "Sally, where's my baby," Faith sat straight up and screamed.

Sally and Mrs. Merriweather jumped apart, and Sally grabbed Faith's shoulders. "Please, Faith, lie back down. It's wonderful that you are awake. We have been so worried about you."

Slowly, Faith let Sally ease her back down on the bed. Faith took Sally's hand and held tight. "Where's my baby? My uncle took her while I was down in the cellar."

"We know that he took her away," Sally said, "but Jack is out searching for her now. Do you remember Jack?" The young girl knelt down next to the bed.

"Oh, yes. I know you, too. My sweet Sally. I know everything." She reached for the young girl and pulled her face closer to hers. "I don't belong here. I'm not kin to these people. My pa paid that couple in Orchard, Alabama, to take me away with them. It is a sad story, but I want to explain it all to Jack first. Do you understand?"

"I hate to be a told-you-so, but I told Jack right away you weren't kin to that man."

Mrs. Merriweather pulled Sally away. "I'm Mrs. Merriweather, the bishop's wife. You need to rest and let the menfolk find your baby."

"Thank you for caring for me," Faith said. "I have caused a lot of trouble by coming here with Mr. Studerman. He was so sure that I was his niece, or so he pretended I was. I hate it that the old couple with whom I traveled from my home to Tennessee were murdered. The old man kept me tied, but his wife was good to me." Faith winced, and her hand went to the side of her forehead. "Sally, I have to close my eyes. My head hurts so badly."

"You rest, Miss Faith. I will be close by while you sleep," Sally said as she brushed hair off Faith's forehead.

"Come, child, let's have some tea," Mrs. Merriweather said. "This child has lived through some bad times, but I know that God was with her."

"Yes, I am sure of that too. I know another thing. Even though she didn't have her memory, she was good to me and Jack. Faith loves her baby more than I could ever say. If she doesn't get her back, I don't believe she will want to go on living."

"Well, we have to be positive. God is in charge, and I believe the men will find the baby," Mrs. Merriweather soothed.

Chapter 27

The old woman slowly closed the door after the bishop and the young man had entered. She'd told them that she and her husband had waited for hours for Elder Studerman to come to their home. But then these two men showed up on horseback and told them the story about how the elder had stolen the baby. Elder Studerman had lied and told her and her husband that the baby's mother wanted to be free from motherhood and wanted someone else to raise her child. They would never give their daughter a stolen baby and have her heart broken again when the story came out about the missing child.

"Don't you worry, mister? If that man shows up here with the baby, we will take the baby and tell him to return tomorrow for payment, but we will notify you immediately. We only want to help return the child to her mother." The older man waved goodbye to Jack and Bishop Merriweather.

***

As the bishop drove away from the home, Jack frowned. "I wonder where Mr. Studerman has gone. He didn't take any supplies from his house for the baby—not a bottle, diaper, or blanket."

"I don't believe Elder Studerman is in his right mind. He has shown a bit of temper to other members of our Order when they disagree with him. I had planned to have a talk with him but he'd already left for Gibson, Tennessee, to search for his cousin."

"I met him in Gibson," Jack said, "and he wasn't a nice man. He wasn't overly concerned about his cousin and wife. They'd been robbed and murdered, and he didn't even want to know who did it or why it happened. I showed him their grave where I buried them together and told him that I would return and place a marker on it. Studerman didn't ask why Faith wasn't murdered, since she was traveling with them. The man didn't seem to care about contacting the sheriff or finding out why his kin was the target of such a bad crime. He only wanted Faith to go back home with him, even though she didn't know him."

"Studerman wasn't home but one day when he came to me and said that the girl was unfit to be around our women and young girls. I asked him why he brought her to our community. He said he had no choice. She was alone, destitute, and needed a home for herself and the baby. Mr. Studerman believed her to be his niece because she had been traveling with his cousin and wife, so she was their granddaughter."

"Of course, you had no way to know any difference, but all were lies. She was married to me, had a home, and Sally to help her with the baby, housework, and cooking. I don't know why she felt she had to leave, but now that her memory has returned, we will have some answers." Jack searched the woods that whizzed by as they drove back to Lawrence.

By the time they reached Lawrence, the sun had vanished, and all the men who had helped with the search had gone home. Most of them told Mrs. Merriweather that they would assemble in the morning to continue the search.

After returning to the bishop's home, Jack and Sally carried Faith back to Elder Studerman's home where Sarah and Dottie had watched and waited patiently for them.

Sarah's eyes brightened. "I was hoping you would come back here and stay with me while hunting for my man and your baby. Did you find the older couple who wanted to buy Cherish?"

"Yes, but he hadn't gone to their home. Nor did he buy a train or stagecoach ticket either. We figure he must be traveling in an Amish rig," Jack said after he laid Faith down on the bed she had been using while living there.

"All of the baby's things are still in Faith's room. I can't imagine what he's doing for nappies and bottles. Cherish is mostly likely screaming her head off." Dottie shook her head and sat down.

"I pray he doesn't hurt the child," Sarah murmured.

Sally came out of the bedroom and asked if she could cook some food. "Jack has to be hungry, even though he would never ask for anything."

"Yes, why don't we cook a big breakfast? I have plenty of bacon, ham, and eggs." Sarah scooted around in the kitchen, pulling out everything.

Dottie touched her friend's arm. "Sarah, you set the table while the girl and I prepare the food. You need to rest if your ribs are ever going to heal."

"All right, and then I will sit beside Faith in case she wakes up. She seems to have regained her memory. Has she told you anything, Mr. Mills?"

"Please call me Jack. Just that her name was Precious, and she wasn't kin to your husband. That's about all for now. I will not be questioning her until she is feeling better. The doctor said her head had to be hurting pretty bad, and rest would help her."

A week passed without any information about Elder Studerman or the child. Every house, barn, cellar, and cave was searched, but nothing turned up in the Lawrence community or the small town of Clarksville. Jack was nearly frantic with worry while Faith was delirious. She was almost out of her mind with concern for her baby.

Jack had sent many telegrams to the authorities in the surrounding towns and faraway cities. Unfortunately, he had not received any response, so he was preparing to go out on his own when he heard a knock on the front door. He opened it to a young man, who stood holding a brown box.

"Mr. Murphy at the train depot said for me to delivery this box to you." He held it out for Jack to take.

"Thank you, young man," Jack said, as he reached down into his trousers' pocket and gave the young man a dime. Peering down at the box, Jack looked for a return address on the front but found nothing. He sat at the table as Faith stood across the room watching the young boy climb on his mule and ride away.

Jack took his pocketknife and cut the rope that held the lid on tight. He looked down into the open box and lifted out a note from Mrs. Mason. There were several other pieces of mail, but he unfolded the note and read it to himself.

Jack,

You will find a telegram from your mother that was sent to Clarksville. The station depot master sent it by horseback to my store. Forgive me for reading it, but Mr. Mason said we had to in

order to know if it was important. I have included your other mail.
Glen says that your place is fine, and Sally's mother and brothers
are fine, too. Mrs. Mason

Jack immediately read the telegram from his mother. Assuming
the worst-case scenario, because his dad had been sick for a while,
he was thrilled to know that his father was still alive. He wiped his
hand across his forehead and took a deep breath.

Faith stooped down beside him. "What's wrong?"

"My father is very ill, and Mother needs me to come home. This
couldn't come at a worst time." Flashes of leaving Lawrence
without Cherish was like a stab in his heart.

"You must go. I will pack your things."

"Faith, I am not going to leave you here. We must go together,
and while we are traveling south to Montgomery, Alabama, we will
keep searching for Studerman."

"What if they find my baby and I am not here? I can't go."

"Yes, you can and you will. Sally will get your things together,
and we'll leave on the first train in the morning."

"Jack, I haven't told you anything about my past. You haven't
pushed me to open up to you, but I feel that I must tell you about
myself. You might not want to introduce me to your mama as your
wife." She covered her face.

"Faith, look at me." He lifted her chin and glanced into her tear-
filled eyes. "I love you, and no matter what you tell me, I will never
turn my back on you. My folks are good people, and they'll accept
you for the lovely person that you are. Now, let's go into Sarah's
room while Sally gathers our things for the trip."

***

"Jack, my pa wasn't a preacher, but he paraded up and down the
streets of Orchard. He waved his black Bible and screamed the Word
of God and the devils to anyone who was within hearing distance.
People would avoid him by crossing the street or turning around on
the boardwalk. He terrorized small children and made babies cry.
The preacher of Community Church tried to talk to him, but he only
scorned him. When Pa drank, he was awful. Sometimes the sheriff
would put him in jail.

"When he came home, he would be in a foul mood. His temper
knew no bounds. He would beat Mama for no reason, and he
threatened me. Pa would slap me around, but he never took the strap

to me like he did Mama. There would be days that he beat her so bad she couldn't get around, and I had to do the cooking, washing, and caring for the animals.

"If any man came around to buy some moonshine, which he made in a shack behind the house, I couldn't look at them. If I was weeding the garden, I couldn't lift my eyes and look in their direction. If I did, he would slap me and call me every kind of whore, Jezebel, or any other nasty word he could think of. Sometimes he would lock me in the cellar for days at a time. Mama would sneak down with food when he was gone to town. One day Mama went into town and told the sheriff to come out to our place. The next day he showed up and asked about me. Pa said I had gone fishing, but mama nodded toward the cellar, and he demanded to look down there. I was near death that time." Faith wiped away a tear. "The sheriff told him that if he heard of me being locked away again, he would put my pa under the jailhouse."

Jack didn't interrupt Faith. He was afraid that she wouldn't continue with her story, but his fists clenched in anger against the man.

"Several times, when Pa was gone, I went into town with Ma. One day I saw this handsome young man in the dry goods store. I had seen him once before, but we didn't make eye contact. This time he said hello and I smiled at him. One night, I heard rocks hitting my bedroom window. I looked down into the yard, and there stood this young man name Ned. I had heard the store owner call him by his name.

"I slipped on my robe and slippers and eased down the back stairs. He took my hand and we raced into the barn. Soon, I was pinned up against a post, and he was kissing me and running his hands over my body. I tried to make him stop, but he wouldn't. He was a stranger to me. A boy that I had only seen twice. In just a few minutes, he forced me down in the hay, covered my mouth, and had his way with me." Faith cried softly as she looked down at the floor. "I told him if he ever touched me again, I would hurt him bad. He only laughed and said that he would be back the next night, but thank goodness, he didn't come." Faith wiped tears and blew her nose. "You do believe me, don't you?"

Jack didn't answer; he waited for her to continue.

"A few months later, I couldn't keep food down and as I was

throwing up my guts, Pa came into the bedroom. He seemed to know that I was with child, something that I didn't know myself. He grabbed me and threw me down on the floor. Standing with his long legs spread apart, he demanded to know the name of the pig I had lain down with."

"I didn't answer him. Mama ran into the bedroom and screamed at him to leave me alone. He called her every filthy name in the world as he stripped his wide leather belt from his pants. He hit me so many times I lost consciousness. I do remember him saying that he would beat the brat out of me. When I woke up, I was down in our dark cellar."

"Mama came down and doctored the bleeding welts on my back, arms, and legs. I could hardly move my body from the makeshift bed in the corner of the damp, dark room. There was a basket containing a few candles and matches by the ladder. She took out bread and jam and a quart jar of fresh water.

"'This is all I could get for you without your pa noticing. If you hear him, hide these things. He said that I could come down here once a day to check on you, but you couldn't have food or water until you told him who was responsible for your condition. Pa said that you had shamed him and you will be sorry.' Mama grabbed me and hugged me tight, causing me to moan from the pain. 'Oh, my baby, I'm sorry.' Turning to hurry out of the cellar, she said she would be back when Pa went into town." Faith covered her face and cried openly. "I'm sorry."

"Sweetheart, how did you come to be with that old couple?" Jack tried to give her time to tell her story her way, but he was anxious to know how she got all the way to Gibson, Tennessee, from Orchard, Alabama.

"After two weeks' time, my scars had healed some, but I was still purple in many places. Pa opened the cellar, pulled me to my feet, and said that he had found me a new home. He wouldn't allow me to live under his roof any longer. No scum of the earth would shame him ever again."

"'Where am I going?' I managed to squeak out.

"'No matter to you. A Christian family, Amish from Kansas, are taking you home with them. They will teach you and your child to be good Christians since I haven't been able to. You will be leaving as soon as you get dressed in the clothes that they have brought you.'

He pitched a few things at my feet and said for me to get dressed.

"'ll be back in a few minutes. Cover those wild red curls with that cap that they have brought you.' He climbed the ladder in three quick steps and slammed the door shut.

"As fast as I could, I put a purple skirt on with a white blouse. The skirt had long straps that buttoned in the front and crisscross in the back. The white cap was small but had two long ties hanging down the front that had to be tied under the chin. The skirt waist didn't touch my body, but the straps held it up, and the blouse stayed tucked in. I had lost so much weight that I could feel my ribs. I slipped on my boots and sat on the bed waiting." Faith looked at Jack. "I'm almost completed with my horrible story."

He smiled and rubbed her back.

"Finally, I met the couple. Cornelius and Mary Jansen. They were an older couple who were traveling to Lawrence, Kansas, to start a new life with the Amish Oder. Their family was helping them buy a farm near them." Faith swallowed hard when she said, "I saw my pa and Mr. Jansen exchange money. Pa remarked to the man that he was to beat me if I didn't behave like a lady." Lowering her face, she said, "My pa paid that couple to take me off his hands."

Jack pulled her over onto his lap. "There's more to your story, isn't it?"

"My poor mama cried and pleaded with Pa not to do it, but he shoved her back into the house. One good thing—the old couple was good to me, except Mr. Jansen kept me my wrist tied so I wouldn't try to escape. I soon learned how I could help Mrs. Jansen around the campfire at night, and that pleased Mr. Jansen. We got alone real well."

"We traveled for weeks. Once Mr. Jansen had to trade his horses for a good pair of mules. Mostly the weather was good, and traveling was easy. We camped out every night, and I slept under the wagon while the couple bedded down inside. As we traveled, I had to confess to the Jansen's that I was with child. I had gained so much weight that when I walked, I wobbled. The couple was upset at first but then accepted the fact. Mr. Jansen's said he would tell everyone that I was their granddaughter and my husband died on the trip. So much for good Christians. My pa was a liar and he gave me to two more liars."

"I guess they thought they were protecting you." Jack said softly.

Faith only looked at her husband but made no comment.

"One night, as we were preparing our evening meal, three men rode up into the middle of our camp. Before Mr. Jansen could retrieve his rifle, one man shot him and Mrs. Jansen. The men search their wagon. Look under the boards on the wagon floor, while I introduce myself to this lovely young lady, one of the men yelled. I had stood frozen while the men rode around me with their horses stomping on everything in sight. A young man crawled into the back of the wagon, while another searched Mr. Jansen's coat pockets. The bigger man grabbed me and ripped off my white cap. Look here, fellows, he yelled. A spit-fire redhead. Just my type!"

Sighing, Faith took a deep breath. "He pulled me close, and I screamed and placed my hands over my belly. Please, I begged, don't hurt me or my child. Please, I will do whatever, but don't hurt my baby." Faith wiped her eyes and continued.

"The big guy laughed like he enjoyed what was to come and pushed me down on the ground. My head hit a rock, and I felt as if I was going to pass out. Suddenly a young boy grabbed the big man and told him to leave me alone. 'She's going to have a baby, you fool. Leave her be or I'll shoot you.' Laughter was all around me, and then I heard horses stomping the ground near my body. I tried to sit up but I lost all consciousness."

"After you woke up, you made your way to my cabin, but you couldn't remember anything—right?"

"Right. I guess the young boy took pity on me and made the men leave me alone," Faith said, as she snuggled in Jack's arms.

"Now, we'll feel better knowing how you came to lose your memory. So your name is Precious Millstone, and you are from Orchard, Alabama." Jack wiped tears off Faith's cheeks and said playfully, "Nice to meet you, young lady."

"I think I would like to remain as Faith, if you don't mind?" Faith smiled at Jack. "How much of my story do you need to tell your folks? I don't want them to know how I conceived Cherish."

"Ever since I was a small boy, I never kept secrets from my parents. If I was straying off in the wrong direction with my plans, my father always questioned me about my decision. He offered his opinion and asked me to think over my problem in great detail. You see, Faith, he let me be my own man. I don't like hiding important things from either of my parents. Secrets have a way of coming out, and sometimes they can do more damage than the truth. Later, when we need to, we'll tell them together that Cherish is not my baby. Soon, I hope to be able to consider us a real family. I feel like Cherish is mine already. They don't have to know the details, just enough to know that our baby has been abducted by a crazy old man who is trying to sell her."

Jack took Faith's hands and hugged her tight. "Now, you help Sally pack our belongings, and I will go purchase our train tickets. We'll travel to Gibson and check on our home and Sally's folks. We will leave her with her mother."

"I hope she will understand why we are leaving her behind," Faith wistfully commented.

***

Standing in the bedroom doorway, Sally overheard Faith's comment about leaving her behind in Gibson. She loved this couple and wanted to be with them all the time. However, her mama needed her, so she would stay home and not make a fuss about it. If that man came through Gibson, she would recognize him and alert the sheriff.

After Jack left the house, Faith came into the bedroom with Sally.

"Miss Faith, I overheard Mr. Jack say that I would stay home with Mama and the boys. I understand." Sally tried to smile, but a tear slipped out of one of her eyes.

"Oh dear, I don't know what I'm going to do without you. But, once we find Cherish and bring her home to Gibson, you can come back and live with us, if you still want to. I have never had a little sister, but if I did, I couldn't love her any more than I do you."

Chapter 28

The weather was pretty, with a strong, crisp wind blowing. Jack helped the girls down onto the Gibson's train platform and waited for the men to bring them their luggage. As they waited for the livery owner to bring Jack their carriage and horse, the stationmaster waved to Jack.

"Step inside. I got something strange to tell you."

Jack hurried up the steps and waited patiently for the room to clear of other passengers.

"You remember how you questioned me about your wife leaving with that old Amish man weeks ago."

Jack nodded. "Well, that man got off the train a few days ago with a small child. He asked Johnny, my runner, if he would go into the dry goods store and have a list filled and bring it back before the next train pulled out. After they left I questioned the boy about what he wanted him to purchase at the store. He said it was baby things— bottles, canned milk, blankets, and lots of white material. He did say that Mrs. Mason kept asking him who wanted the things, but he didn't tell her anything about the man." Before Jack could comment, he said, "I believe it was the same man your wife left with to Kansas. I would almost swear to it."

Jack grabbed the older man and hugged him so tight that his feet left the ground. "That old man took Faith's baby, and he's trying to sell her. We are heading to Montgomery and Orchard, near Mobile. This is great news. He still has the baby and he's on the run. Thanks so much."

The liveryman arrived just as Jack leaped off the platform and helped the girls into the carriage. "Great news!" he said. "Old man

Studerman rode the train here and picked up some supplies for the baby. He got back on the train and headed south. We are on his trail for sure."

Mrs. Mason was thrilled to see Jack, Faith and Sally. She peeked around them for the sweet baby that she had fallen in love with. "Where's Cherish?" She asked anxiously.

"Listen, Mrs. Mason. I need you to remember what day you filled an order for baby things for a man who came in on the train. He sent Johnny in here with a list."

"Of course, I remember. I wrote the sale in my register because he bought many items that I would have to replace. Here it is. October 22nd—that was three days ago. What's going on?" She asked just as Mr. Mason came in from the back room.

"Elder Studerman, the Amish man that Faith left with, was not her uncle. He only wanted Faith for himself and planned all along to sell Cherish. He's an evil man, and thanks to you and the stationmaster, we feel closer to catching up with him. Tomorrow Faith and I will be leaving on the train heading to Montgomery. My father is very sick, and Mother needs me to come home. I'll hire some men to help with the search."

"Mrs. Mason," Faith said, "My memory has returned. After we get settled back here, I'll tell you my story. I can't thank you enough for being such a good friend. We are leaving Sally here with her mama. Please see that they have everything that they need and a few things they want," she whispered the last part of her request.

Jack reached into his back pocket. "Please tally up my bill and let me settle my account while we are here. Also keep it open for whatever is needed at my place and Sally's little farm. I know Glenn has been a great help."

"That young man is a good worker. I told him when you get settled back here, that I wanted to hire him to work for me here at the store," Mr. Mason said.

Jack wrapped his arm around Mr. Mason's shoulder and walked him toward the back of the store. "Do you know if those two acres of land at the edge of town are still for sale?"

"Yep, they sure are. Are you interested in them?"

"When I return, I want to build a house closer into town and open myself a law office. This town is growing, and it is not too far away from other ones. People could use a good lawyer, and I am tired of trapping. Do I need to put a deposit down on the land today?"

"Why don't you bring in a contract tomorrow before you board the train, and I will post a

'sold' sign on it."

"Do you think the owner will take my bid?"

"I believe I just did," he said patting Jack on the shoulder. "I'm the owner of those lots."

Jack laughed for the first time in weeks and shook Mr. Mason's hand. "Thank you, sir."

***

As Jack drove into Sally's yard, she leaped from the back of the carriage before it stopped.

"Lordy, that child is going to kill herself one day. She runs and jumps everywhere she goes, "Faith said, as they watched her run into the house.

In a few minutes, Sally came out of the house with her arms wrapped around her small mama. They both looked so happy.

"Oh, Mr. Mills, thank you for bringing my gal back safe. I know you must have wanted to skin her alive when she got on that train instead of Glenn."

"I have to admit I was surprised, but I forgave her when she presented that big basket of food you prepared for us," Jack said, scanning the yard. "Your place looks nice."

"That Glenn works here and heads to your place every day. I knew he worked hard for that sorry pa of his, but I had no idea he was so handy. He can fix near anything, and the boys are crazy about him." Mrs. Parker watched as her daughter retrieved her small carpet bag.

"Sally," Faith reached for her hand. "We are going to see Jack's family in Montgomery, Alabama, and then head down to my home in Orchard. As soon as we can, we will be returning here to Gibson after we find Cherish." Tears streamed down Faith's face. "We're going to miss you, but its best you stay here with your mama."

"You're sure you don't need me to go with you? Ma will understand, won't you, Ma?" Sally didn't even glance over her shoulder at her mother.

"We will always need you and want you near, but you should stay and help your mama with the boys. I know they need you here for a while." Faith had seen how frail and unhealthy Mrs. Parker appeared. She knew the older woman was plain tuckered out from cooking and washing for three boys and herself day in and day out.

"You sure you're coming back? I already miss you, and you ain't even left. I love you, Miss Faith, and you too, Mr. Jack. I will be here when you get back." She turned and raced into the house.

"Mrs. Parker, my account at the store is open to you for whatever is needed. Mr. Mason will give Glenn whatever he needs at your place and mine. Glenn and Sally both have earned it. If we aren't back before Christmas, you make sure you buy the youngsters presents to go under the tree."

"Gosh, I hope you'll be back sooner than that. I'll say a prayer for your parents and Cherish." She waved at Jack and Faith as they drove down the lonesome trail to his cabin.

Glenn came out of the barn when Jack drove up close to the house to help Faith down. Bear was already jumping up and down in front of the carriage. Bear placed his front paws on Faith's chest when she stepped to the ground. He barked, whined, and attempted to lick her face. Laughing, she rubbed Bear's head and gave him a slight push down so she could walk.

"Welcome home," Glenn said with a big grin on his face.

"Howdy, young man. So glad to see you looking so well. I believe you've grown several inches and put on some pounds."

"Yes, sir. Mrs. Parker's three square meals a day hasn't hurt me none," he commented with a broad smile. "Let me help with the horse and carriage."

"Thanks, son. I appreciate it. Come in the house when you're finished." Jack grabbed their bags from the back of the carriage. "It looks like I have lost my dog's affection. He cares more for Faith than he does me," he said as he strolled up to the front porch.

Faith had already put on a fresh pot of coffee to boil. The fireplace was lit and was removing the chill from the cabin.

"You've been busy." Jack said, glancing around at the very tidy cabin.

"Glenn had fresh water here, and the fire all laid and ready. He's a jewel for sure." Faith took her bag and went behind the curtain into the bedroom to change into some comfortable clothes.

During a light dinner, Jack told Faith about his childhood. "I always had a comfortable life. My father had a good job and sent me and my sisters to the finest schools. We never really wanted for anything, but we weren't spoiled. We each had chores to do, and if we didn't, we got punished. Oh, Father never mistreated us, but we didn't receive our allowance, or we had to do extra jobs around the house. I always loved being outside with animals, but Father wanted me to be a lawyer. Being the only son, he wanted me to follow in his footsteps. So, I finished school, became a lawyer, and worked in his law office until he started the job at the capital, working for the government."

"How did you get from Montgomery to Gibson?"

"Love. I fell head over heels in love with a beautiful girl. She lived in Nashville, the Capital of Tennessee. Her father also worked for the government. I was ready to spend time with her after lengthy letters between us. She proclaimed her love for me, so I saddled up and rode hundreds of miles on horseback to see her."

"I bet she was happy to see you." Faith was enjoying their first heart-to-heart talk about his life.

"The butler told me that Miss Lorraine was out in the garden. I rushed through the open double doors onto the terrace, and I saw her standing in the arms of a Yankee soldier. I froze in place, staring at her and then at the young man. Suddenly, the silence was broken with laughter coming from Lorraine, the love of my life. She started laughing and couldn't seem to control herself. I glanced at the young soldier, and he looked at me as he grabbed his hat and hurried away around the back of the house. Lorraine's laughter grew louder and more hysterical.

"'Run, you scared rabbit,' she screamed at the back of the soldier. Finally, Lorraine stopped laughing, noticed me, and sneered, 'What are you doing here? You weren't invited.'

"I didn't realize I had to have a formal invitation to see the woman I love. It would appear that I did need one. Goodbye, Lorraine. Give my regards to your parents."

"Mercy. So, you just walked away, and you never saw this girl again?" Faith asked.

"That's right. I never saw her again, and I didn't want to either. She didn't love me, and I learned it the hard way. Believe me, riding horseback for days and nights was not an easy trip. I bought a ticket for myself and my horse home on the train." He peered up from his soup and grinned at Faith. "My backside ached for days, and every time I felt pain, I wanted to kick her." They both laughed.

***

Later, Faith repacked their clothes and personal items for the trip to Montgomery. She fought back tears as she packed some new things for Cherish. "Please, God, please keep my baby safe." Faith looked up to see Jack at the door staring at her. She sniffed back tears, stood, and walked into his arms.

Hugging her tight, he kissed her on the temple. "I will find our baby, I promise. Goodnight."

***

Jack stood in the barn, surveying the whole interior of the building. He'd had a long talk with Glenn, and he was pleased with everything the young man had done to keep his place in good condition. His piglets were about ready to sell, and Betsy looked better than ever. Glenn admitted that he gave her a bath about once a week.

The chicken yard had flourished with many more chicks. Glenn said that he sold six dozen eggs three times a week to Mr. Mason's store and a few neighbors. Jack confessed to Glenn that he missed this place, but he wanted to live in town so he could open his law office. He still hadn't discussed this with Faith.

Chapter 29

The train whistle blew over and over, and the train slowed, alerting the passengers that they had arrived in Montgomery. Faith stood and tried to see out the windows. She had never been in a big city before. Lawrence, Kansas, was a big town but nothing like a large city. Her hometown was a small country village with only a train depot, a few stores, and a church doubling as a schoolhouse.

Jack hailed a hack and gave him the address to his father's home. Faith pulled the curtains back to look at the busy streets, but the wind was too cold to allow the air inside. "We'll tour the city before we go home, Pet. I promise. "He winked at Faith when she agreed.

"I guess you can tell that I'm a country gal."

"You should have seen me learning how to trap and skin animals. The older man who taught me had many good laughs at my expense. So, believe me, I do understand how you feel."

The big circle drive appeared, and the driver stopped in front of a large white mansion. "I thought we were going to your parents' house, not the capital building."

"Sweetheart, this is my parents' home. I lived here most of my life." Jack grinned at Faith's expression. He tried to take her hand and help her down, but she sat back inside the hack.

"I can't go in there. I'm not dressed properly."

Jack laughed. "Tell me, Pet. How are you supposed to be attired?"

"Well, I'm sure calicos or gingham aren't the proper dresses." She lifted her chin and faced the front.

"Come, Faith. My parents will love you. They won't even notice how you are dressed. Besides, I think you look beautiful."

Without warning, the large front door opened wide and a beautiful older woman rushed down the stone steps. "Oh Jack, my son. I was waiting for you to arrive. Why are you sitting out here in the cold?"

Realizing she looked silly, Faith stuck her head out of the hack and smiled into pretty blue eyes that sparkled with happiness.

"Please let's go inside before we freeze. This wind is blowing like its hurricane weather."

Jack practically carried Faith up the stone steps into the front door. Faith slid down the front of Jack's hard body. She gasped at the foyer, which was the lovely room she had ever seen much less stood in. Brass angels decorated the huge wall mirror that held two large stem lit candles. Half-naked people fluttered around in blue clouds on the ceiling. She couldn't seem to lower her eyes and look forward.

"Jack, take Faith to your room. I have redecorated it a little, but I think you both will like it. If you disapprove, please don't tell me. I worked hard."

"Mother, I'm sure it will be fine. May I request a small snack be sent up to our room? I want to see Father after I wash up, but my stomach is growling."

"Of course. Mattie will bring you a tray. Dinner will be at six, as usual. Hopefully, the girls will be home in time to join us."

Faith turned to Jack as they strolled up the large staircase to their room. "We're going to share your room?"

"Yes, and please don't make a fuss. I haven't told my parents about our forced marriage or our living arrangement. It is not their business."

The bedroom was like a something Faith had read about in a book whenever her pa was out of town. She was never allowed to sit and read, but she did love reading about knights and castles. Her pa only read the Bible, often quoting the verses in his own made-up version.

Jack grinned as he went into the water closet, leaving Faith looking starry-eyed at the bedroom.

The pillows and bedcovers were perfectly matched along with the drapes. Two chairs clustered in front of a fireplace with small foot stools placed in front of each one. Lovely Oriental rugs covered the beautiful, shiny wood floors. She'd glanced in the water closet in the corner before Jack entered it—large enough for a person to have a private tub bath and change clothes. This house bespoke volumes of money. Jack never hinted that his parents were rich.

Walking out of the water closet, Jack asked if she was happy with the room.

"You never told me that your parents were as rich as kings and queens. Are you rich, too?"

"Would you like for me to be?" Jack rubbed his hair dry.

"I never thought about money. I wondered how you always had enough money to pay for whatever we needed, but as far as being rich, I don't know anyone who has a lot of money, except maybe the banker in Orchard."

Jack laughed. "The banker usually has some money, but most of them aren't rich. They only handle other people's money."

"I want to find my baby. That's really all I can think about. Do you think your father will be able to help us?" Faith sighed.

"I am going now to see him. If he is feeling well, I will come get you to meet him. For now, you freshen up and rest before dinner. I hope my sisters will be able to dine with us."

***

Jack slipped quietly into his father's room in case he was sleeping. He saw that Father was wide awake and watching him.

"I wondered if you were ever going to speak to me," his father said.

"I didn't want to disturb you, but I am glad you're awake. I've missed you, old man." Jack grinned as he called his father by his nickname.

"You scalawag, you'd best come closer and hug me. I might appear to be on my deathbed, but I still have a lot of living to do. I just get a lot more attention from that lovely woman I'm married to if she thinks I am dying."

"Father, that's awful," Jack whispered as he leaned over and hugged his father.

"I know, but don't judge me. Just wait until your wife has a thorn in her backside, and you can't make her forgive you. When you get sick or hurt, well, things can change back to normal. They can't love you enough." The old man chuckled and looked over Jack's shoulder.

Jack pulled up a straight chair and spilled out the whole story about Faith, the loss of her memory, the baby and the kidnapping. He omitted the part about the ladies of Gibson, forcing him to marry Faith, and that he didn't know how Elder Studerman convinced Faith to leave with him to go to Lawrence, Kansas. *I want her to tell me in her own time*, he thought.

"Father, I have to find the Amish man who took our baby because he's trying to sell her. Studerman is a wicked man. He's hurt his own wife many times, and he was attempting to make Faith his mistress, right there in the Amish Community. The sheriff and the bishop of the community did try to help me hunt for Studerman."

"Jack, you said *our baby*. Is that little baby girl yours?"

"I was standing right beside Faith when she gave birth in my small cabin. The doctor handed me the baby, and she was smaller than the palm of my hands. I bathed her and pinned on her first diaper. And I married her mother. Yes, she is my child. I couldn't love her anymore if she had come from my loins." Jack sniffed and swiped at his eyes. He knew his father pretended not to notice how upset his son had become speaking about the baby.

"We have no time to lose, my boy. I can't get out of this bed, but I want you to pull that cord." When he did so, a big strapping bodyguard named Jude came barging into the room. He looked from his employee to Jack.

"How may I be of service, sir?"

"Jack, this is my number one man. You never know he's around until you need him. Jude, my son, Jack." Both men nodded at each other but said nothing.

"Jude, get Detective James and the chief of police here now. Tell them it is of most importance, and don't dally."

In less than an hour, the two law enforcement men were standing over Mr. Mills' bed. He was propped up against his headboard as Jack told the men the situation about Elder Studerman and his baby, Cherish. "He has about three days' lead on us, but with this being a large city, I feel he will hang around here and try to find a customer to sell the baby to."

"Rest assured, sir," the detective spoke loud and firm, "if this man is in our city, we will discover his whereabouts. With his description, I am sure he will be easy to find. We don't have many of these people in our city, especially a lone man with a baby. I'll be in contact with you as soon as possible, most likely first thing in the morning."

Jack watched the men take their leave and his father lie back down.

"Now son, we will soon have some news. You need to go tell your sweet wife that we have good people looking for this awful man. I will meet with your wife after dinner, but for now I'm going to take a nap before your mother comes charging in here." He smiled while closing his eyes.

***

A few hours later, Jack and Faith walked down the staircase to the dining room. They were greeted by Jack's youngest sister, Maria, who was attending an all-girls college to become a schoolteacher. She was tall, slim, and very blonde. Her blue eyes had a sweet sparkle just like her mother's.

"Welcome, Faith. Now I have another sister, and that means one more woman to gang up against our big brother. Jack has always said that he didn't have a chance to get a word in at the table." She smiled at Faith, took her hand, and led her to the table. "I don't know about you, but I'm starved. I haven't had time to eat today."

"Mattie was nice enough to bring Jack and me a snack after we arrived. I have to admit I ate more of it than Jack, and I had a nice long nap."

"I hope your room is fine. If you need anything, please ring the bell cord in your room, and someone down in the kitchen will bring it to you." His mother's eyes darted from Jack to Faith.

Faith smiled and said, "Our room is lovely, and so far, we have everything we need. The aroma from the kitchen smells wonderful."

After dinner, Jack escorted Faith into his father's bedroom. The old man wore an evening dressing coat, and his gray hair was smoothed back. He immediately reached out to take Faith's delicate hand. "My dear, it is so nice to meet you. I feel as if I already know you because Jack has told me so many wonderful things about you and the babe."

Faith glanced at Jack and smiled. "Thank you, sir. I am afraid that I don't know much about you as Jack has been very quiet about his personal life. It is so nice to meet you, and I must say you have a beautiful home. Jack and I could put our whole cabin in this bedroom," she commented as she glanced around the beautifully decorated room.

"I'm sure my son will soon furnish you with a proper home once his law business is off the ground," Jack's father said.

Faith turned to Jack, giving him a questioning look.

"My dear, I want you to know how concerned we are about your baby. I hope Jack told you that we have every available man in Montgomery searching for that Amish devil. I am sure it won't take the police department long in discovering his whereabouts."

"Thank you so much for your help, and yes, Jack assured me that the men will find my baby."

The old man covered his mouth with a yawn and tried to appear alert. Jack hugged his father and told him that they needed to get some rest because they'd had a long day, and they would be very busy tomorrow. "Good night, Father."

Faith went into the water closet and changed into her thin night dress and wrapper. She hurried over to the bed and found all the decorated pillows removed and the covers turned back. What luxury, she thought.

She climbed into the large four-posted bed and relaxed until Jack sat down in a chair and started removing his boots, shirt, belt, and pants. "Wait," she whispered.

He looked at her and waited for her to say what was on her mind.

"You don't plan on sleeping in this bed...with me?"

"Where else would I be sleeping if not in this bed? You'll never know that I am next to you."

"Yes, I would. You can sleep in another room. This house has many more bedrooms, I'm sure."

"It does, but don't you think my parents would think it is strange that I'm not sleeping with my beautiful wife and consoling her?"

"You can sleep in this room but not in the bed with me. Make yourself a pallet in front of the fireplace, like you do every night in the cabin."

Jack marched barefoot in his white long johns to a storage chest at the foot of the bed. He pulled out two large quilts and spread them onto the floor, then strode to the bed and snatched a pillow from behind her back and tossed it on the quilts. "Satisfied now?"

Adjusting another pillow behind her back, she smiled. "Perfect."

Jack stretched out on his pallet and fell immediately asleep, but Faith had taken a long nap so it took her longer to fall into a deep slumber. In her sleep, she heard someone calling Jack's name and knocking on the door. She sat up and it wasn't a dream. Jack's mother was at the door. Tossing a pillow down on the floor and hitting Jack in the head, he sat up like lightening had struck him.

"Your Mother is at the door," she whispered.

As fast as he could, he grabbed the pallet and opened the storage chest and crammed the covers into it. Then he leaped under the covers in the bed next to Faith. He wrapped his arms around Faith and pulled her up close.

She felt his hard body part pressing up against her side, and she gasped.

"Sorry, he whispered, "I can't help that I have to pee," he said. "Come in, Mother. Sorry, we didn't hear you knocking at first." Jack smiled and nuzzled Faith's neck to show her that he couldn't keep his hands off his wife.

"Good morning, lovebirds. I hope you slept well," she said and pulled on a cord allowing sunlight into the big room. Faith and Jack both covered their eyes from the bright light.

"What time is it?" Jack asked his mother.

"Way past the time for you two to be up. Mattie is holding a delicious breakfast in the breakfast room. Now hurry and get dressed. Your father said he had some news for you both, but breakfast first. I don't want to upset our Mattie."

After a big breakfast of ham, bacon, eggs, biscuits, toasts, grits, oatmeal, and all types of jams and jellies, Faith wanted to lay back down, but she was more interested in hearing the news.

***

Jack hurried up the stairs to his father's room. His father held a tray of bacon, eggs and several buttered biscuits on his lap. He held a coffee cup in his right hand and waved for Jack to take a chair.

"Good morning, my boy," he said. "Received some good news about that old Amish man. He was spotted sitting on a park bench late last night with a baby. The patrolman didn't know about him until this morning. Several officers went back to the area, but he was gone."

His father took another sip of his coffee and said, "A patrolman was going to hang around the park this morning."

Jack hung his head.

"Now, son, this is good news. We know that he is still in Montgomery and he has the baby. He hasn't sold her."

Chapter 30

Later that morning, Faith asked if she could use some of Jack's mother's stationery. She wanted to write a letter to her mama in Orchard, Alabama. Once they discovered the baby's whereabouts, Jack would take her to her home to see Mama. She also needed to confront her pa and let the preacher know that she didn't run off with a man. Her mother had suffered at her pa's hands and she was afraid that he was mean to her little brothers as well. Jack had said that her family could come and live with them in Gibson. The letter would let her mama know that Faith was still alive and well.

***

Jack had left the house in search of the Amish man. He hoped he could catch a glimpse of him walking the streets close to the park and the Baptist Church where people congregated. He climbed out of the hack and headed toward the coffee shop near the park. After ordering a coffee, he took a window seat so he could watch the comings and goings of people.

***

A young lady suddenly glanced up from the park bench she sat on with her husband. "Did you hear that, John?"

"What?" her husband said, barely lifting his head from his paper.

"I overheard a man shout, 'shut up.'" The girl glanced around and saw an older man dressed in black talking to a baby who couldn't be more than six months old. When the baby cried, the man picked her up and shook her. He then flopped the baby down on the bench and placed his elbows on his knees, clenching his fists. "Shut up, or I will toss you in the river," the man seethed.

"John, that old man is being mean to that baby. Go to the entrance and tell that policeman to come into the park. I'm afraid for that infant's life."

"Now, we don't need to intrude into anyone's business. Don't listen to him," John said.

"If you don't go and get the policeman, then I will. Nobody should be mean to a baby. I wonder where the baby's mother is."

"Shut up!" the man screamed again, and this time John looked up.

He jumped up, raced to the entrance, and brought back the patrolman. Immediately, the policeman walked over to the Amish man, and words were exchanged. The couple couldn't hear the two men, but the policeman turned and waved for them to come over.

"Now, you've got us into trouble," John said to his wife.

"Miss, I need your help. Will you hold the baby while I handcuff this man? I'm sure that he has abducted this child and is wanted for kidnapping." The policeman waited for the young lady to pick up the baby.

"Lord have mercy," the young lady said as she took the baby in her arms. The sweet baby calmed down after crying so much that she had the hiccups.

The policeman handcuffed the man in black and hooked the handcuffs to the park bench. The policeman walked a distance away and blew his whistle three long times.

* * *

Jack placed his cup down and listened. Something was happening in the park. He tossed coins on the table and rushed outside. Several policemen raced toward the park entrance, so he followed as fast as he could.

A miracle was appearing in front of his eyes. There sitting on the park bench was the old Amish man, and a young lady was holding Cherish, his baby. Rushing up to a policeman, using his educated lawyer's voice, he spoke to the officer. "Sir, this is the man my father and I called about. The chief of police is heading up this search along with several detectives."

Jack rocked on the soles of his shoes and pointed at the young lady. "The baby that woman is cuddling is my child, and that man kidnapped her." Jack walked over to the young woman and smiled. "Thank you for helping with the capture of this man. He kidnapped my baby, Cherish, in Lawrence, Kansas, and has been trying to sell her to anyone that would give him money." Clapping his palms together, he pleaded with the young lady, "Please, may I have my child?"

The lady smiled and caught her husband's arm. "I knew something wasn't right. That is a very bad man." She frowned in his direction.

"I will never question your instincts again. You did save this beautiful baby," the woman's companion said touching Cherish's foot.

"Please give your name and address to the policeman. I want to make sure you receive a reward." He juggled Cherish in his arms and walked over to the policeman. "May I take my baby back to my father's home where her mother is waiting?"

"Yes, I am sure that will be fine, but you will have to come down to the station and file formal charges against the man. You, being a lawyer, know about all the paperwork that has to be filled out."

***

Faith sat with Mr. Mills, telling him about her past and how she came to be with the old couple who was murdered and then found herself at Jack's cabin. She could tell he found her story fascinating, but she was careful not to reveal too much about how she and Jack became married. Being a smart man he probably figured that they needed to marry to protect her name.

After lunch, the doctor dropped in to give Mr. Mills a checkup. Faith hurried out of the room and headed down to a cozy chair in the comfortable parlor. She wondered what Jack was doing. Just as she was falling asleep, a carriage clattered up the drive. Faith stood and craned her neck out the window to see it, her heart pounding in her throat.

Jack reached inside the carriage and held a bundle in his long arms. When he turned toward the house, Faith saw her baby. "Cherish is home!" she screamed and ran down the stone steps. She rushed to Jack and reached for her baby. Chubby arms lifted toward Faith's tear-filled face.

***

Mrs. Mills held her breath as she watched Jack and Faith circle their arms around each other. Everyone was talking, laughing, crying, and hugging. A knot formed in her throat, and she squeezed her younger daughter's shoulders. The house was in chaos for the next hour as the chief of police told how Elder Studerman was arrested.

"The old man told us at the station house that he was plumb tuckered out. Taking care of a baby was harder than he'd thought. He was ready to give her away, but no one would take her." The chief paused, wiping his mouth with his handkerchief. "Thank goodness, there was this young lady who noticed his actions. She said he was screaming at the baby and attempting to get her to sit up on the bench, so she knew something was wrong. The older man said he was too tired to run and hide anymore. He didn't even put up a fuss when I told him he was going to jail for a very long time."

Faith stood and shook her head. "I'm glad that he will be put away for a long time. While in jail, he can preach to the other inmates. I will feel so much better knowing that he cannot hurt his wife, my dear friend every again." Hanging her head, she said softly, "There's been enough misery in my life. Cherish is home, and that's all I care about. Please, Jack, I don't want to have to go to court. Please take care of this for me."

Everyone sat as still as the night. The big mantel clock chimed three times, but not a sound came from anyone or the police chief.

Cherish whimpered, so Jack hurried to Faith and took the baby, then said, I will be down at headquarters to file charges against this man. "

Jack smiled at the older officer as he walked over to stand next to his beautiful wife. "Go ahead and visit with Father and tell him that the old Amish man won't hurt anyone else for a long time."

Early the next morning, after a lengthy goodbye, Jack and Faith promised to stop by Montgomery on their way home, back from Orchard, heading to their home in Gibson.

***

Faith sat next to the window on the train, gazing out at the passing scenery. When she left Orchard with Cornelius and Mary Jansen, she was forced into the back of their covered wagon and couldn't see anything but the sights after they'd passed. Her wrists were tied so tight to the wall of the canvas that she could hardly move around. After a few days, her skin was rubbed raw and bleeding. Old man Jansen didn't seem to care, but Mary placed soft rags under the rope. In the evenings, she was allowed out of the wagon to relieve herself and sit around the fire to eat.

After a week of travel, she convinced the old man that she wouldn't run away, so he allowed her to help his wife. Many times, Mr. Jansen would leave and go into the forest and shoot a rabbit or squirrels, but he always tied her to a tree. After returning with the critters, Mrs. Jansen taught her how to skin and prepare them for the stew pot.

During her travel with the old couple, she learned that Mr. Jansen's cousin had found a small farm to purchase when they arrived in Lawrence, Kansas. His cousin had assured the owner that they would be arriving in a couple of months.

Faith remembered the weather was hot with only a cool breeze blowing at night, and she felt like she would melt during the day. The Jansen's forced her to dress like the Amish. Over her shift, she had to wear a long, heavy dress that buttoned on each side and had long sleeves. The dress front was covered with a long apron that covered her chest and flowed to the hem. She also wore long stockings with her heavy brown boots. No wonder the fabric stuck to her damp skin.

At night she was forced to sleep under the wagon, which was so much cooler than lying in the covered wagon which was like a sweatbox. After hearing the old man snoring, with her free hand, she would slip off her boots and take off her stockings. The next morning while the old man was off in the woods taking care of his private business, she would hurry and put them back on.

Many nights she would pray that they would camp by a creek so she could take a bath and wash her hair. Since she could smell the old couple when they were near her, she knew she smelled just as bad. She never saw Mary wash her face or arms, but she tried to clean herself as best as she could with the little water that she was allowed.

They would pass different travelers several times on the trip, but Mr. Jansen would just tip his hat and keep moving, even when the other men attempted to stop and talk. One morning after breakfast, she pleaded with the old man to stop the wagon. Faith was having pains in her stomach and need to have a minute of privacy. Later, after coming from the woods, she told the old couple she was going to have a baby. She was not just fat like they thought.

The old man had thrown a tantrum when he heard that he would have another mouth to feed. He was ready to drop her off at the nearest town, but his wife refused to allow him to do that. She seemed very happy with the idea of having a new baby to raise.

"What's so interesting out the window, Pet? Do you see horses and cows?" Jack questioned his sweet wife. "Are you getting nervous about seeing your father again?" Before she could answer, he told her she had nothing to fear from him. "I am here, and I will never allow anyone to harm you or our baby again."

Reaching to take Jack's hand, she smiled into his blue eyes. "I know. You are the best thing that ever came into my life. God guided me to your small cabin, and I will always be grateful."

"You just seem so far away," he commented.

"Guess I was. I was remembering the trip in the covered wagon to Gibson. I didn't get to see anything but the inside of the wagon for weeks." She smiled and turned to face Jack. "I am excited about seeing Mama and my little brothers." She sighed. "I want Mama and the boys to come home with us. I haven't mentioned this before now, but I feel it in my heart—they need to be with us. Please think about it."

Chapter 31

The train began to slow, and Faith could feel her heart starting to race. She didn't realize how nervous she was until the porter's announcement. "Orchard, next stop. Gather your belongings and prepare to depart in a few minutes."

Jack stood and reached for Cherish, who was now six months old and a bundle of joy to carry. Faith stepped behind him and followed him to the exit door. He leaped from the train onto the platform and turned to take Faith's hand. "We're here, Pet. Let me speak to the man standing in the depot and see about some transportation into town."

"Orchard has only a few buildings, and they are over there, all in one row. This track runs down the center of town." She watched Jack frown at the run-down buildings.

"My folk's home is over behind the dry goods store. We can walk." She whirled around and said, "Maybe you can get one of those young men to carry our bags."

"Stand here, and I will ask one of them." In only a few minutes, two young boys, who appeared about twelve, were eager to help.

After walking a few minutes, Jack noticed a boardinghouse. He told Faith that he would go in and get them two rooms. "If you want, you can walk over to your folks' place and see if they're home. I know you are eager to see your mother."

Faith stood still and only stared forward. "Listen, I'll carry the baby, and the boys will tote our luggage. We will meet you in a little while. Cherish needs a fresh nappy."

Once Jack and the boys had entered the boardinghouse, she stepped off the boardwalk and headed to her folks' house, which really wasn't more than a shack. As she neared the gate to the front yard, she noticed that the shack had been whitewashed and the front porch repaired. She opened the gate and approached the door. Something was cooking.

"Mama," she called while sticking her head inside the room. The place appeared dark because she had been walking in the sunshine.

"Who are you?" a shrill came from the dark room. A young woman dressed in a lovely calico-patterned dress with a dishtowel wrapped around the front.

"My name is Precious Millstone, or it was until I married. I am looking for my folks who lived here before I left." Faith felt funny calling herself Precious and seeing this shack practically restored.

"Who are your kin? My man and I have been here for several months. We moved in, but the place was empty." The young lady smiled at Precious.

"My mama's name is Louise Millstone. My pa calls himself a preacher and walks around Orchard speaking the Word of God to anyone who will listen to him. You probably have seen or heard him."

"Yes," the young lady said. "Your mama is a sweet lady who works as a cook in the only eatery that Orchard has. She is most likely there, being close to lunchtime."

"Oh, thank you so much. I will go there now." Faith hurried down the path to the gate. She looked toward the boardinghouse, but she didn't see Jack coming down the boardwalk to meet her.

Entering the eatery, she saw several people she recognized, but she didn't stop to speak to them. A few men jumped up and stood with their mouths open. Faith walked straight to the kitchen. When she opened the door, the heat in the room hit her with a blast. The four burners each held a boiling pot. At once, she saw her mama standing at the kitchen counter rolling out pie dough. She appeared so small and frail. Faith eased over to the counter and said softly, "Mama."

Mrs. Millstone turned to her two boys who were washing dishes. "Now, don't bother me. I have dough all over my hands."

"Mama, it's me. Look up."

Her mama slowly lifted her head and nearly fainted. "My heavens. My baby." She cried as she hurried around the counter and took Faith into her arms. Tears were streaming down both of their faces, and the two boys circled them with their small arms. It was a glorious reunion.

"Mama, what are doing working in this hellhole? A person can hardly breathe in this heat, and the boys are here, too. Why aren't they in school?"

"First, where did you come from?" She wiped the dough off Faith's shoulders and attempted to clean her own hands. "How did you get away from that old couple? Did you make it all the way to Kansas?"

"What in the blazes is going on here?" Sam Jimmerson, the owner of the eatery, bellowed. "People are lining up for lunch already, and you haven't gotten it ready."

"No, she hasn't and she's not going to be cooking for you another minute. My little brothers won't be washing and cleaning for you either. I'm taking them out of here right now." Faith's blazing eyes burnt a hole at the man. She lowered her voice and said," Mama, get your things, and come, boys, we're leaving."

"Over my dead body! No one is leaving this kitchen until lunch is cooked. Get back to work before I make you all sorry," The giant bellowed at Mrs. Millstone.

Faith's ten-year-old brother stepped in front of Faith, his voice nervous and croaking, "You'd better leave my sister alone."

Suddenly, Faith grabbed her brother's arm and moved him behind her shaking body. Before giving it a thought, she picked up a large meat cleaver and held it high in front of her. "Now, Mr. Sam, back off, or you'll be the one sorry. I'm tired of men bullying me, pushing and slapping me around, and giving me orders. Now I'm the one who is calling the shots. Get out of our way, now!" Faith waved the cleaver in the air, and the loud-mouthed ogre backed away.

***

Sheriff Roundtree and Jack stood in the kitchen's doorway with their mouths wide open. Jack had never seen his sweet wife demonstrate such an angry temper. If he had been the target of her anger, he would have run for the woods.

Jack was holding a sleeping Cherish on his shoulder and watched his wife, her mother, and two little brothers file out of the kitchen like soldiers who had just fought a war and won.

He smiled at the sheriff and asked him if he would follow them to the boardinghouse. "Faith needs to hear about her pa from you."

The sheriff fell in line behind Jack to the tune of Sam slamming pots and pans around in his kitchen. "I feel sorry for Sam after that tongue-lashing."

Faith stopped on the boardwalk and hugged her mother and her little brothers. "Oh, Mama, I went to our home, but there was a strange young woman living there. She told me where I could find you, and I am thankful that you were still here in Orchard. Where in the world is Pa and where are you living now?"

Jack stepped beside Faith and smiled down at Faith's mother. "Faith, let's get off this boardwalk. We're drawing a crowd. So many people are surprised to see you," he leaned down and whispered.

Jack led Faith and her family up the staircase to the two rooms that he had let for the night. One room for him and one for Faith and the baby was his plan. The sheriff followed the group into the front room and waited for Mrs. Millstone to take a seat in the rocker by the window.

"Boys, make yourself comfortable on the bed, and I will be back in a moment." Jack rushed down the stairs and went into the parlor. "Mrs. Whitehead, will you make a tray of sandwiches for the little boys and a pot of hot tea for the ladies? You may add this to my bill."

"Be happy to, Mr. Mills. I will be serving dinner at six this evening. Will your family be joining my other boarders for the meal?" She smiled with expectant eyes.

"Yes, that would be nice, and if you're serving breakfast, we would like to eat in your dining room in the morning."

She smiled and nodded. "I will have the tray of sandwiches up to your room in ten minutes."

Jack entered the bedroom room and found Faith's mother rocking Cherish. "Oh, Mr. Mills, I can't tell you how thankful I am that you have cared for my Precious. She looks so good and healthy. I was so afraid for her when she was made to leave here."

"Please call me Jack, Madam," Jack said as he opened the door and found Mrs. Whitehead's servant girl holding a tray of sandwiches. The boys jumped off the bed and eagerly took them from her. Jack motioned for her to put the hot tea and cups on the table. He gave her a quarter, and she bobbed up and down and left the room.

"Golly, did you see that shiny quarter he gave the girl? He must be rich," Faith's youngest brother, Georgie, whispered to his brother, Billy. Jack heard them, but he pretended to be too busy serving the tea to their sister and mother.

"Come on, boys, and get yourselves something to eat. I know that you must be hungry. Afterward, you can go outside and play, if you stay close. We have some things we want to tell your sister and make plans for the future."

"If you are going to tell her about pa, well, Georgie and me already heard that he left town. We're glad he ain't here anymore." He took a big bite of his ham and cheese sandwich.

***

Mama laid Cherish on the bed and walked with the boys down the stairs to the back yard with instructions for them to stay nearby. "Precious is going to take you both to the dry goods store to buy you some new clothes."

"What about you, Mama? You need something new, too." Billy said.

"I'm fine, son, just fine now that my Precious is home."

***

The sheriff paced in the bedroom before he stopped. "Miss Precious or Faith, whatever name you are going by now, I know you are anxious to hear about your father. After you left, without anyone having any knowledge why or with whom you left, your pa started acting stranger than usual. He paraded up and down the streets almost all day long. Sometimes he would walk up and down the train tracks in front of the depot. Train whistles would blow and blow, warning him to get off. He'd step away from the tracks continuing to preach fire and brimstone. Your pa terrified the children, and the ladies had to walk across the street to avoid him. He was making a pest of himself until I finally had to threaten to lock him up if he didn't stop. Finally, he listened and stayed away from town for days on end, and then he would reappear for a few hours. One day, he didn't come home for several days, so your mama asked me to look for him."

The sheriff walked over to the window and looked down on the street. "One day I traveled by the farms where the freed slaves lived. I saw Willie Wilson sitting by a creek bank. His clothes were bloody and the whites in his black eyes were red. I asked him if had he been drinking, and he said, "no.'"

"I asked him why his clothes were bloody," the sheriff said.

"Well, it's like this. I was prayin' and tryin' to decide what I should do or where I should run to." He squatted down on one knee and started drawing in the dirt with a small stick. "You see," he said quietly, "I've been working at my cousin's farm for several weeks, day and night. My woman pushed me away at night and didn't want me to touch her after we went to bed. I didn't make her do her duty 'cause I was dead tired. Yesterday, my cousin said we all could go home' cause he had something he had to do. I rode my mule in the barn and after I rubbed him down and fed him, I walked inside the house. Heard voices, and the springs on the bed squeaked like an old tire. I peeked into the room and there was my woman lying under that crazy preacher man. He was having his way with her, and she wasn't fighting him neither. I just went out of my head. Reached over the fireplace for my shotgun, and I rushed into the room. The door slammed up against the wall, and they both sat straight up. My woman screamed for me to get out. I fired the full load. Body parts flew all over. I looked down, and shore enough, blood spattered on me, but I didn't care. I walked away from that their house, and I have been sitting here ever since."

"I asked him what he had done with the bodies, and he just shook his head. He didn't even look at me."

"They're still there?" he said.

"I took Willie, and we walked to the house. Lordy, the place was an awful mess."

"What is going to happen to Willie now that he murdered two people?" Jack used his lawyer tone of voice.

"I tell you the truth, Mr. Mills, I haven't decided what to do with him." The sheriff rubbed his chin and sat down in the rocking chair.

***

Faith didn't want to hear any more, so she left the room and stormed down the stairs to check on her mama. She had heard enough about how her pa had died. She was surprised, but then again, she wasn't really.

***

Sheriff and Jack watched Faith leave, and Jack noticed that she had not said a word or shed a tear.

"Sheriff," Jack said, "You know if you arrest this old man for murder, the men will convict him, and he will hang. If I were you, I'd turn him loose and let him go on his way. He would be sentenced to hang because he is a black man that killed a white man. Faith would be crushed if she knew someone else was hurt because of her pa's actions. Her father was a mean man who beat her just because she smiled at her little brothers. He was crazy mad and hid behind the Good Word. Later, he sold her to an old Amish couple. He gave them money to take her to Kansas and they held her prisoner for months. If I had my way, her father was going to be sent to prison for a long time anyway."

"I know all about how mean that man was. I figured he probably forced Willie's wife to be his woman. Guess that's why I brought Willie into town and locked him up, but I haven't told another soul about what happened at his farm. Still, I was pondering as to what I should do because I'd heard rumors that a white man was fooling around with women—black and white," Sheriff Roundtree said. "The men have been standing guard at night around town and at their farms. If caught, they've threatened to string him up for sure."

"If you don't say anything about Willie and the bad thing he did, the men will give up and get back to normal. You won't have to worry about a lynching taking place in your little town." Jack walked across the room and looked down on the street front. How was Faith taking all this?

"I believe you have saved me from a big headache. Before I release Willie, I am going to ride out to his shack and burn it to the ground. The bodies will never be found, and if they are, no one will know who they are." The sheriff stood, straightened his pants down into his boots, and headed to the door. "I'm going to the jail and have a long talk with Willie and send him on his way tomorrow. He said he had a brother in Meridian, Mississippi. Maybe he will go and live near him."

"You have made a wise decision. Look," Jack reached into his vest pocket and pulled out several large greenbacks. "Give this to him. I'm sure he can use it to get out of town."

Sheriff Roundtree took the money and smiled. "This will help the old fellow, for sure." He turned and walked down the staircase and met Faith coming up.

"Good day to you, Mrs. Mills. I never said it, but I'm glad that you're home safe and sound." The sheriff touched the rim of his hat.

"Thank you, but we will be leaving soon. We'll be headed back to Gibson, Tennessee."

The sheriff leaned against the staircase and looked down. "You would have had no way of knowing, but I did look everywhere for you. I never believed your father's story about you running off with a man. Everyone knew that your father wouldn't allow a man near you. I was sure your mama knew something, but she was terrified of your father and wouldn't say." He doffed his hat and disappeared out the front door.

Faith sighed, looked up the staircase, and saw Jack standing in the doorway. He stepped out on the balcony, reached out his hand, and pulled her into the bedroom. She immediately took a place on the side of the bed and peered up and him.

***

His body stirred as he watched her get comfortable. He would love to pull her into his arms and press a scorching kiss on her rosy lips. Jack loved this sweet girl, and he was ready to become her real husband, but he wanted her to make the first move. "Sweetheart, how do you feel about your father's death?"

"Surprised somewhat, but he was a mean man who hid behind the Word of God. When he wasn't working, he was terrorizing Mama, the boys, and me. We couldn't do anything right. Poor Mama. She stood between me and him many times. I begged him over and over to leave us alone, but he only stormed out the door. I should be sad, but I'm not. Mostly relieved, I guess."

"That is understandable," Jack said, sitting beside her on the bed. "We need to get ready for dinner. Mrs. Whitehead is expecting us to eat with the other boarders. Afterward, we, the three of us, need to make plans for our trip to Montgomery and then back to Gibson." He smiled and squeezed her hand. You know, I miss our gal, Sally. I wish we had time to send her a note and tell her that we'll be home soon."

In the hour before dinner, Jack and Faith took her mother and the boys to the dry goods store and purchased them new clothes— from the skin out, her mama would have said. The boys were thrilled with their new cowboy boots and hats. They paraded around in the store while Faith forced a new wardrobe on her mother. She had gone into the storeroom and put on a new dress and a sturdy pair of ankle boots. Faith had picked out several colorful ribbons for her mother's hair while waiting for her to come out.

A loud whistle came from the front of the store, and Faith turned to see her mama standing by the front counter, looking so pretty.

"Mrs. Millstone, you are lovely," Jack said.

"Oh my, I feel like a new person," she said to Faith.

"Good. Let's pick out several more dresses and nightgowns, now that we know your size." Faith selected five more colorful calico and gingham dresses.

"Please don't spend all your money on me," Mama said. When she saw her boys, tears sprang to her eyes. "My, don't you two look fine."

After a fine home cooked meal back at the boardinghouse, the boys were exhausted and went to sleep as soon as their heads hit their clean pillows. Mama and the boys would share one room, while Jack, Faith, and Cherish would have the other room next door.

Mama knocked on Faith's bedroom door and entered for their meeting. "Take a seat in the rocker, Mrs. Millstone," Jack said, as he motioned for Faith to sit on the end of the bed.

"Son, you must call me Mama or Louise," she said as she smoothed her new dress, making her look like a fairy godmother.

Chapter 32

"Louise," Jack smiled, remembering to call his mother-in-law by her first name, "we want to be on our way home, if at all possible, tomorrow. Faith, or Precious, and I would like you and the boys to come to Gibson, Tennessee, and live with us. We'll have plenty of room later, but at first we will be a little crowded in my cabin. I'll take care of that problem once we arrive home. But, if you have some things you wish to take, we'll go and pack them tonight and carry them on the train with us."

Jack waited for her to think about her items. "I have a rocker that my pa made me and my Bible, of course. The boys don't have anything but maybe a bag of marbles. All the clothes they have, besides the new ones you purchased today, are on their backs. Sad." Louise sat quietly for a spell. Jack didn't rush her. "I never thought I would live anywhere else. I was born in this place, married, and had my children. Now, my man is—" She wiped her mouth, "heaven knows where. Life has a way of changing."

Mama covered her clouded eyes. "After your pa disappeared, we ran out of money." She glanced up at Precious and shook her head. "That fool had borrowed money on our house and never paid a dime back, so the banker made us move out. We had no place to go, and your pa wasn't nowhere to be found. We wandered around for a few days and slept in the alleyways at night until I found a job.

"Mrs. Coatsworth, the preacher's wife, discovered us sleeping in the livery and took pity on us. Reverend Coatsworth took us to a back room in the church and said if we kept quiet, we could stay there. He put my things in a box, and he let me sleep on a cot, and he made the boys a pallet. During the day, we were working at the eatery. Sam let us eat three meals a day, but he took it out of my wage."

"Mama, I'm so sorry you had such a bad time. You'll never have to live like that again, I promise you," Faith said. "I would like to speak with the reverend and his wife before we leave. We can go and pick up your rocker and box of things."

"After breakfast, I'll buy our tickets to Montgomery. We'll stop there and visit for a day or two with my folks. They will welcome you with open arms."

**

The train ride was an adventure for Georgie and Billy. Mama tried not to show her excitement as the train drove into the big city of Montgomery. In all of her life, she had never been more than ten miles away from Orchard, and now she was riding a train and viewing another world.

Jack hailed a large hack that took them up a stone driveway to the biggest house she and her boys had ever seen.

Faith patted the boys on their knees, giving them a warning. "Boys, this is Jack's folks' beautiful home, and it's not a playground. You must be on your best behavior or else." She glared at them and said, "If you misbehave, Jack will skin you alive. Understand?"

Both boys' eyes widened at Faith's strong, tall husband and they gave fearful nods.

**

As Jack lifted the boys and his mother-in-law to the ground, he took Faith in his arms and gave her a little shake. "You and I need to have a talk," he said, his face red.

What in the world had caused Jack's wrath to turn on her? Was he going to change, now that she had her memory back and he was married to her?

**

The big double door opened, and Mrs. Mills stood at the entrance. "Hurry inside, son, and bring your lovely family with you. Your father is in the parlor this time."

Jack took Cherish out of Louise's arms and raced up the stone steps. When his mother saw the baby, tears sprang to her eyes. "Oh my, what a beautiful child. She looks just like her mother."

"Yes, she does, but I'm afraid this little one needs changing before I can pass her off to anyone."

"Of course, come inside, everyone." Mrs. Mills smiled at Mrs. Parker, Billy, and Georgie. "Welcome to our home. I hope you will be comfortable while you are here. Dinner will be ready in about a half-hour. I know you all must be hungry."

Jack left the others in the hallway with his mother while he went into the parlor. "Father, it's so good to see you up and out of the bed. You look like your old self now."

"Come, son, and hug me, and let me get a good look at this child. She looks like she has grown since you were here," he said, smiling at Cherish.

"Now, Father, we haven't been gone a week. I will say that she is feeling better and happy to be back with Faith." He adjusted her onto his shoulder. "Faith's mother and her little brothers are here with us. Mrs. Millstone and the boys are going to live with us or nearby. I have to make living arrangements for everyone when we return to my cabin."

"I know you will get everyone settled as soon as you can. I had my staff bring your law books, files, and office supplies from the cellar. We can have everything shipped on the train to Gibson. I have a big surprise for you. It will arrive in about a week. You'll get a notice from the conductor of the train when it arrives."

"Father, I don't know what to say. We'll talk after dinner, but for now I need to get this little one taken care of and back to her mother." Jack hurried up the staircase to the room that he shared with Faith when they'd visited before.

Faith was sitting at the dressing table, brushing out her lovely red curls. She leaped up and immediately took Cherish and laid her on the bed. Jack reached down in their carpet bag and gave her a dry diaper.

"What in the world do you want to talk to me about, and why were you so riled up about?" Before he could answer, she said, "Are you displeased with me as your wife, now that you feel responsible for my family, too?"

"Don't be silly, Faith," he growled. "I am happy to have your mother and the boys with us. Believe me if I didn't want them with us, I could have made arrangements for them to remain in Orchard."

"I should have stayed with them," she snapped.

"Over my dead body, but we'll discuss our future later, but for now, I want to give you a warning." He gently pushed her down on the edge of the bed, bent low, and placed both hands down beside her. "If you ever threaten the boys about misbehaving and then tell them that I will punish them if they do, you'll be sorry. Your mother is responsible for her two sons. I may be responsible for their livelihood, but I will never lay a hand upon their small frames. I am their brother-in-law, a friend, someone that they can count on. I am not a man for them to fear. Do you understand me?"

"Of course," she said, hanging her head low. "I'm sorry, Jack, really, I am. I was so afraid the boys would run up and down the staircase and act up, since they have been restrained so much on the train."

"We will forget it this time, but I want you to explain to them that I am their friend, and I will never raise my hand to them in harm. Now you, young lady, had better toe the line, or I might forget you only want me to be your husband in name only." He smiled, pulled her up off the bed, and kissed her forehead. "I'm starved. Finish your toiletry so we can go downstairs for dinner." He turned around and stripped his shirt off and replaced it with another.

***

She couldn't take her eyes off his lean waist, and the firm muscles across his wide shoulders. *Lord help me*, she thought.

After Faith, Mama, and Mrs. Mills had a long discussion about their plans to settle in Gibson with Jack, they rounded up the boys and went upstairs to bed. It had been a long day and they were tired from the train trip.

***

Jack and his Father chatted about business for several hours. Once all the talk about starting his own law office was finished, his father stooped down and opened his wall safe. Giving the dial a good spin, he closed the door.

"My boy, I have been keeping this for you. I know you'll be surprised, but you were an active partner with me for several years, and I never sent you any money. I still have several lawyers working for me—really us—because I never took you off the business partnership. After you get settled and your law business is off the ground, then I may dissolve our partnership. Until then, I will send you quarterly payments." He looked at Jack who appeared dumbfounded. "Now, don't say anything. This is your money;

besides you have an office to build and many other expenses. I know you will want to build your wife and baby girl a lovely home, and all that takes money. There's more in First Bank of Montgomery if you need it."

Jack thumbed through the white padded envelope. "Father, this is so much. I don't know what to say."

"Don't say anything, my boy. Enjoy your new life with that beautiful wife you have upstairs and give your mother and me many grandchildren. Your sisters are too busy to start a family."

Jack walked over to his father and hugged him. "I will make you proud of me."

"I'm already proud of you, son. Just be happy." They took one step at a time up the staircase.

After a lengthy goodbye and promises to come back soon, Jack and his new family left on the eleven o'clock train to the outskirts of Gibson, Tennessee. After the long trip, the train began to slow and the whistle blew over and over. The steam bellowed all around the front of the big black engine, and a crowd of people gathered on the platform.

Jack was the first to leap off the train onto the heavy-shelled ground. He gathered each boy and set them down with a warning for them to stay close. Then he reached for Louise, and then Faith, who was holding tight to a pouting Cherish. She did not like the sound of the train whistle.

"Come to Papa, sweetheart," Jack said, surprised that he referred to himself as papa. Faith laughed at him as he blushed bright red.

"The name fits you perfectly, Papa," Faith said.

"Don't cry, darling. We'll be home in a little while and we will see Sally soon." Cherish laid her lovely head on Jack's shoulder as they made their way to the platform and the stairs to the depot.

"Welcome home, Jack!" The station manager yelled after the conductor called for all the new passengers to board. "As soon as I saw you step off the train, I sent my nephew to get your carriage. With this many people, you're gonna need a big wagon. Would you like for him to drive some of these folks to town?"

"Great, I would appreciate the help very much. You know I will pay."

"I'm sure he'd like the money, but he's a good kid. He would help you for nothing." The stationmaster said as he eyed the attractive older woman with Jack.

Grinning, Jack didn't say anything as they waited for the young man to bring the carriage. He was eager to take Faith to see Mr. and Mrs. Mason at the dry goods store.

Jack drove slowly down the main street of Gibson. He pointed out to Faith and her mother the two lots at the end of the road that he'd purchased to build the new home. The two horses moved on and Jack pointed out the old building that would be his law office. Next door was the boardinghouse with a For Sale sign nailed to the front door. Immediately, Faith's mother sat straighter at the sight of the sign. Jack noticed a smile cross her face. "What is it, ma'am?"

"I have an idea. Let me mull it around first."

***

The Masons were standing on the boardwalk in front of their store. They had heard that Jack had found Faith and Cherish, and he would be on the first train of the day. Mildred stepped down into the street as Jack pulled the two horses to a stop.

"Oh Jack, you found our girl and baby. Hurry, bring them down so I can get me some kisses from that precious baby. Golly, look how big she's become."

Mr. Mason offered his hand to Faith's mother and helped her to the ground. The boys leaped off the back of the carriage and ran around to join her. Faith hugged Mildred so close tears flowed down the ladies' cheeks.

"I was so afraid I would never see you again," Mildred said as she used her apron to wipe away the tears. "You are going to have to come in and tell me all about your trip and Lawrence, Kansas, but I know you're ready to go to your cabin."

"I will, I promise, but you're right. We need to stop at the Parker's place. I missed Sally so much. Jack hasn't really worried about his property because Glenn took care of the dog and the other animals."

"He has been doing a good job, too, bringing me dozens of eggs every week. Mrs. Parker looks so much better since she has had the supplies to cook three decent meals a day for them all."

"Mildred, my real name is Precious, but Jack and I both like Faith better, so I'm going by Faith. Mama still calls me by my real name, but that is understandable." She smiled and hugged her friend again. "I will see you soon—tomorrow maybe."

Everyone loaded back in the carriage and headed to the Parkers' place. As they drew near, they could hear Bear barking. Jack gave a loud whistle, and Bear tugged hard and broke the rope loose. He leaped up on the carriage. Jack stopped and climbed out and hugged his dog. Bear fell onto the ground with his all fours in the air. Jack rubbed his stomach and talked to him.

Sally and Glenn came running from the barn when they heard the loud whistle. The young girl rushed to the carriage with tears streaming down her rosy cheeks. "Oh, Miss Faith, Miss Faith, you're home!"

Faith couldn't jump down fast enough. She circled her arms around Sally's waist and pulled her into her arms. "My girl, I have missed you so much. Look here at Cherish. Can you believe how big she has grown since we left?"

Mrs. Parker and her two boys came out of the house. She smoothed her hair back and ran her hands down the front of her apron tidying herself for company. "Ma," Sally pulled her forward, "Jack has brought Mrs. Faith and the baby home. Isn't it wonderful?"

"My, oh my, this is a grand day," she said softly. "I wish we knew you would be here today. I would have cooked a celebration dinner."

"Mrs. Parker, Sally, I want you to meet my mama and two brothers, Billy and Georgie. They are going to live with Jack and me."

"Where are those boys gonna sleep in that small cabin? Hardly enough room for two people much less all of you." Bobby started counting heads.

"Now that's the truth of the matter," laughed Jack. "We are going to move into the boardinghouse in town until I can build another room or two. Sally, would you like to go into town with us for a few days? I know we could sure use your help with the baby."

"The boardinghouse had a for sale sign on the door," said Mrs. Millstone. "I sure would love to run a boardinghouse," she mumbled low, but Jack and Faith didn't miss her comment.

"If your boys would like, they could lay their heads at our place tonight. Wendell and Bobby are going fishing this afternoon. They'll let your boys tag along. I'm sure Glenn could fix them a pole to use."

"Can we, Mama? Can we? We'll be good and mind Mrs. Parker." Louise looked at Jack and Faith for their consent. They both smiled at the boys and nodded.

"Oh, Mama, this young man is Glenn Mudd," Faith said. He smiled sheepishly and peered at the ground. "He's Mrs. Parker's handyman, and he lives here now that Mr. Parker passed away." Faith smiled at Glenn and watched his neck turn red.

Sally came from the house carrying a basket that contained two quart jars of homemade soup and fresh baked bread. "This should help with your evening meal since you haven't stocked up on supplies. Don't worry about your brothers, Miss Faith. I'll take good care of them."

"Sounds like a good plan," Jack said. "We'll bring them clean clothes to wear into town in the morning." Jack glanced at the boys. "Now mind your manners and catch a lot of fish."

"Can I, Ma? Can I go into town with them?" Sally could hardly contain her joy.

'Sure, child. I may tag along for the day and come home with the boys." Mrs. Parker smiled while she watched everyone load up and head to the little house.

Louise, Jack, and Faith, with the baby in her arms, drove to the cabin. Bear rode in the back seat and barked with excitement. Cherish clapped her little hands and tried to reach for the furry animal.

***

As they drove into the yard of the cabin, Jack sat still for a moment. The beauty of his home and its surroundings always made him feel good. "This is home for now, Louise. Like I said in town, I am going to build a nice house big enough for all of us just as soon as I get my law business started." He helped the ladies down and rushed to open the front door of the cabin. Glenn had opened several windows to allow fresh air in and lay a fire in the fireplace. The two-room cabin was neat and clean.

***

Faith sighed as she strolled into the kitchen. She whirled around and walked into the bedroom, running her hand across the bed. Noticing the drawers in the chest, she knew that Cherish was too big to sleep in the makeshift bed. Smiling, she headed back into the kitchen, feeling like she was home. This little cabin was her safe haven.

Louise entered with Bear directly behind her. The dog raced to the bedroom and back into the kitchen and out the front door. "That is one big dog, daughter," Louise commented. She walked over to the table, placed her small bag down, and glanced around the cabin. "This is a cozy little place but not big enough for our big family."

"I know. Jack is moving us into town tomorrow to live in the boardinghouse. He will be near his law office and the boys will be able to go to school." Faith took her mama's hands in hers. "Everything will be just fine."

"I was just thinking about the boys. They haven't been going to school, and I'm afraid that they have gotten behind. Georgie won't like being bunched up with smaller kids."

"I'll work with both boys to see where they should be placed in school. If they can read well enough and cipher numbers, then I will tell the teacher. I'm sure they will be just fine and happy to go to school, instead of having to wash dishes."

"You're right. Let me warm the jars of soup that Sally gave us for supper. I can mash some of the vegetables for Cherish to eat. This loaf of fresh bread smells so good." Louise washed her hands and placed Faith's apron around her waist. "Let get this meal on the table because I'm hungry and tired."

As the sun set behind the tall trees and a nice cool breeze was blowing, Jack stood with his hands in his pockets. "Faith?"

"Yes?" Whenever he stood like that, he had something big to tell her—sometimes things she didn't want to hear.

"After you put Cherish in bed, would you walk with me to the barn?"

"Of course. Let me just talk to Mama first." Faith told her mama that she would sleep in the bed along with Faith and the baby. "Jack will sleep on a pallet in front of the fireplace, like always."

"Like always?" her mama sounded confused.

"Jack and I are married, and we live together, but not as husband and wife," She stated matter-of-factly.

"Why?" Mama's brows furrowed.

"Because, I lost my memory and didn't know if I already had a husband, where I came from, and really, Mama, it was complicated. Better to be safe than sorry and wait until I could remember my past."

"Your memory has returned, and you have spent many nights with your man. Why haven't you started sharing the marriage bed?"

"We had a lot of things to take care of with Cherish being kidnapped and me being hurt. Jack and I need to get to know each other." Faith walked to the window to look outside at the bright stars in the sky. "Besides, after I stumbled up to this cabin, Jack had to take care of me and my baby. Later, our marriage was forced upon us by the ladies in Gibson. Some things have to be straightened out between us."

"Well, you have shared a bit here and there about what happened after you were sold to that old couple. One day, maybe you will open up to me and fill in the other bits and pieces of your life after you left." She approached her daughter and actually hugged her, something she was never allowed to do in the presence of her pa. "Night, daughter," Louise said. "Now I'm going in that bedroom and climb into the most comfortable bed I've ever seen."

Chapter 33

Faith walked onto the porch to find Jack sitting in the rocker with Bear at his feet.

"Come, Pet," he said, using his nickname for his sweet wife. "Let's walk out to the barn where we can talk." He took her hand and led her down the path.

"Before you say anything, I want you to know how happy I am to have my mama and my little brothers here with us. Thank you for giving us all a new temporary home."

Temporary? Jack heard the word come out of his wife's mouth. "Faith, I want to know the reason you left with Elder Studerman. How did he convince you that you were his niece? And most important to me, why didn't you wait until I came home to talk to me about leaving?" He waited for her to answer these few questions. When she didn't respond, he asked, "Didn't you know that I would be scared out of my mind with worry over you and the baby?"

Still no response came forth from Faith.

"You were...are my wife, and that baby in that cabin is my baby. I couldn't love her any more than I do. I was frantic with worry that I might never find you." Jack sat down on a barrel and watched his beautiful wife wipe tears from her eyes.

"Jack, I know that you were forced to take care of me and Cherish. I didn't even know my name, much less realize that I was with child. You couldn't put me out. Later those women came and made you marry me, a total stranger who might have already had a husband, or could have been a barmaid that entertained many men." Faith walked around in the barn where the goat and piglets were. "Besides, I overheard you talking to Sally. You told her that you wanted me gone, and you wanted your cabin and privacy back to yourself. I couldn't believe what I was overhearing. I had fallen in love with you, and I was sure you had feelings for me. So I ran back to the cabin and cried myself to sleep."

"Sweetheart—" Jack tried to take her in his arms, but she held him at bay.

"The next day, I went into town and met my new uncle. I told him that I would go and live with him and his wife in Lawrence, Kansas. I told Mrs. Mason goodbye, and we left on the afternoon train. After we arrived at his small farmhouse, it didn't take me but a day or so to know that I had made the biggest mistake of my life. Even without my memory, I was sure this man who claimed to be my uncle was no good. Now, Mary, his wife was good to me, but he was no better than my own pa. He beat her and pretended to be a Christian man." Faith visibly shuddered. "I will always be grateful that you rescued me and brought me back here to your home, even for a little while."

"Have you finished? May I speak?" Jack turned Faith to face him. He gently pushed her down on a barrel as he towered over her. "The afternoon you came out to the barn and overheard my conversation with Sally, she had asked me how I felt about you. I laughed and asked her if she meant now or when I came home and discovered a beautiful red-curly haired vixen in my bed." Jack laughed and shook his head.

"Sally wanted to hear the whole story from the beginning, so I told her about how you had lost your memory and the doctor came to deliver the cutest baby in the whole world. I went on to tell her how much I loved you and Cherish, and I would die if we discovered you had a husband. Someone who could claim you and take you away from me."

"You told her all that?" Faith whispered.

"And probably more, and I meant every word," he said with a knot in his throat. Before Jack's wits got the best of his passion for his wife, he pulled her into his arms and gave her a soft and sweet kiss on her lips.

***

"Faith, I need your help," Louise called from the doorway of the barn.

Jack and Faith broke apart and rushed to the entrance of the barn.

"What's wrong? Why is Cherish crying?" Faith took her baby into her arms. She nearly stumbled holding her baby because her body was so weak from the passion she had just felt coming from the man she prayed would love her.

"I wish I knew," Louise said frowning and went to sit on the barrel that Faith had occupied earlier. "She woke up crying, and nothing I did for her smoothed away the tears. She fought me when I tried to hold her while in the rocker, and she wouldn't take her bottle."

Faith strolled the baby around in the barn, and Cherish's loud wails and tears finally disappeared. Cuddling her close, Faith felt her baby's head on her shoulder. She had developed the hiccups.

"Let's all go back inside, and, Mama, go back to bed. I will take care of Cherish."

"I'm sorry to interrupt your privacy." Mama gave Jack a sheepish smile.

***

Jack ambled to the cabin and watched as Faith sat in the rocker in front of the fireplace. He prepared some water in a bottle and handed it to Faith. Cherish grabbed it and began sucking.

Faith rocked until Cherish fell into a deep slumber. She stood and said goodnight to Jack and disappeared into the bedroom. He watched until she laid the baby in the middle of the bed and closed the dark green curtain that divided the two rooms. He lifted his quilts from the corner and made his pallet on the floor.

Much later into the night, he heard the headboard thudding against the wall again and again. He knew that she was flipping from side to side to get settled. She would be more satisfied lying in his arms. "One night, sweet wife, you'll be mine," he said to the dancing flames in the fireplace.

Chapter 34

After the six-mile ride into Gibson and visiting with the Masons at the dry goods store, Jack herded his family, Sally, and Mrs. Parker, to the boardinghouse. Both of the older ladies stopped and reviewed the For Sale sign up close. With their heads together, Jack caught a few phrases of their conversation. It seemed to him that the women wanted to ask about the boardinghouse and the possibility of buying it. He was surprised that the two wanted to take on such a big responsibility. Caring for a large house with many boarders and cooking three meals a day would be an enormous undertaking.

"Welcome to my establishment," Mrs. Jenkins said. "How can I help you today?" She directed her question to Jack.

"My name is Jack Mills and my family, and I need a place to stay for a while." Reaching for Faith's hand, he introduced her and the rest of the family. "We would like to let three rooms if that is possible. I can pay you in advance for as many weeks as you like."

"My lands, son. You are my miracle!" Mrs. Jenkins smiled broadly. "I sure can use the money, but I have this place up for sale, and I need to go to my daughter's in Hickey Hollow as soon as possible."

Jack gave her a disgruntled look but asked, "How soon do you have to have a decision if someone is interested in buying your place?" He looked down at Faith's mother and Mrs. Parker, who were eagerly waiting for her response.

"Today, wouldn't be soon enough for me. You see, my daughter has three kids, and she's about ready to have another babe soon. The doc there says he hears two heartbeats, and he's worried about my daughter's health."

"After we get everyone settled in a room, may these two ladies have a look around?" Both women were holding each other's hands and smiling broadly. "We will need to know how much you want for your building and land too." Jack signed the register, then Mrs. Jenkins led them up the staircase to their adjoining rooms with the water closet down the hall.

The two older ladies were down the stairs before Jack and Faith could get Cherish settled. "I'd better follow the girls. I need to barter with Mrs. Jenkins if you agree with me about helping them purchase this place."

Faith smiled sweetly at her husband. "They want to have something to do and not feel underfoot. I'm so happy that Mama has found a friend. As far as I know, she's never had one." Faith rested her head on Jack's shoulder, and he gave her a squeeze.

"Louise," Mrs. Parker punched her. "Come, let's go check out the kitchen and dining area. Most of the men who'll stay here will want good meals and plenty of it. I hope it has a nice stovetop and oven. I like to cook four loaves of bread at one time."

After Jack had written a lengthy settlement contract with Mrs. Jenkins, he was thrilled to see the women's happy faces. Louise and Mrs. Parker were like two giggly, young girls.

"Mr. Mills, you have no idea how happy you have made us. I have been so lonely living on the farm by myself after Mr. Parker passed away. With Sally working for you, I have been just plain miserable. Now, I will sell my farm and give you the money to pay for my part of this place."

"Do you think that I could talk Glenn into living at my cabin and taking care of both places, or until your place sells? I need someone to look after my animals until I finish building our new home. I can pay him a small wage too," Jack said, pondering about Mrs. Parker's farm. "Now, Mrs. Parker, you may sell your farm, if that is want you want to do, and I suggest you use the money to help run this establishment. You'll need food supplies, feed for the animals out back, and fresh towels and linens for the rooms. I will let you and Louise make small payments to me each month for repayment of this place."

"Oh, Jack," Faith's mother said, "I was wondering how in the world I was going to pay you back. You know that I had nothing when you returned to Orchard with my Precious and Cherish. Now, I feel so good. I have never liked being dependent on a man. Had to take in washing and ironing because Mr. Millstone wasn't someone the kids and I could depend on for anything." She reached over and hugged Mrs. Parker. "Were going to make this a wonderful place that Jack and Faith are going to be so proud of."

A week later, Jack stood in the doorway of his new office. Mr. Smiley, a carpenter, was building shelves in the backroom to store items that he was going to need. The smell of strong glue was giving him a headache. He stepped out onto the boardwalk and glanced down the street. Faith held Cherish in her arms, but she slapped at the hand of a man who was standing too close to her.

"What the hell?" Jack yelled to Mr. Smiley that he would be back in a bit and hurried to where Faith was having a confrontation with a strange man.

***

"Get away from me and don't you dare touch my baby. I will make you a sorry man if you don't back off and let me pass." Faith's red-haired temper was exploding. Seeing a pistol in Ned's hand made her fear for her own life, but the hate she felt for this young man gave her courage.

Before Ned could respond in any way, Jack stepped between the couple. "What's going on here?" Jack took Cherish out of her arms and faced the young, citified man. Ned was dressed in a brown, three-piece suit with his hair slicked down with barber's tonic used on the businessmen.

Jack's eyes widened at the gun pointed at his wife. 'Why the gun, Mister? Are you planning on shooting or robbing someone?"

"I'm Ned. Faith's first lover. She may not have ever mentioned me, but I'm the baby's—"

"He's never been my lover, Jack. Ned's not going to shoot anyone; he's only trying to scare me. He knew me a long time ago, but he is nobody." She attempted to take Cherish from Jack, but he wasn't ready to give her up.

"Ned, this big man is my baby's papa."

"Papa," mumbled Cherish and reached to touch Jack's eyes.

"We both know that's not true." He waved the gun in the air. "My mother wants to help me raise my baby. We are leaving town today, and I am going to take her. Later, we are going to court and

218

have her declared legally mine." He reached for Cherish who turned her face away and hid behind Jack's neck.

***

Suddenly, everything changed. With Jack at her elbow, so composed, she knew that the young man had no idea what was to come next.

Jack passed Cherish to Faith and drove his right fist into the man's young face, causing two of his front teeth to go flying. Blood ran down Jack's hand, but he didn't seem to care. The man fell against the store front, but Jack straightened him up and landed another punch to his stomach.

Doubling over and falling to his knees, he held up his right palm. "I'm leaving. Don't hit me again." Blood was oozing down his chin. Jack had done some damage to the man, but at that moment, he didn't seem to care.

A crowd had gathered to see what all the excitement was about. Jack straightened and rubbed his knuckles. "This man has a carriage waiting for him behind this store. Will two of you see that he gets in it and leaves town?" Two men gladly placed an arm under each armpit and hurried Ned out of sight.

***

Faith practically fell into the capable hands of Sally, her mother, and Mrs. Parker who had rushed to the scene. They clasped their arms about each other "It's finally over," Faith said. "I will never fear that Ned or his mother will cross my path again."

Days later Jack was surprised that Faith recovered so well. There had been terrible days of grieving over what had taken place in her life—beaten by her father, raped by a young man, sold to an Amish couple, her memory lost, forced into a loveless marriage, and later her baby kidnapped. With all the misery in her life, she had not let any of these things turn her into a bitter, ugly person. She had the tenderness soul of anyone he knew. She was definitely a warrior at heart.

Epilogue

"Faith, you aren't ever going to guess what Father sent me," Jack said as he drove to the two lots at the end of town where he planned to build their new home.

"Have you seen the surprise?" She asked as she held Cherish on her lap.

"No, but we're going to meet the men who brought it in a minute."

Sure enough, as Jack leaped down from the carriage, a tall young man strolled over to him. "Howdy, Mister. My name is Butch Holliday, and I am your new foreman. These other men are some of the finest carpenters in the south, and they are going to frame the outside of your new house. When we're completed, another crew of men will do all the finishing work on the inside. When all is said and done, you and your missus will have a fine southern mansion—one you will be very proud of."

Jack had no idea what to say to this young foreman. "Thank you. I can hardly wait to see the design that my Father chose for you to build."

"You and your missus will have three different designs to pick from. The lumber, special sand, hardware, and glass windows are being shipped as we stand here. After supper one evening, I will bring the designs and you can look them over."

"Speaking of dinner, where will you and your men be staying while you are here?"

"Well, we have a big wagon and some tents. Most places don't have enough space to board us. There are six men, total."

"My mother-in-law owes the boardinghouse in town, and I

believe she has some extra rooms to let. I know that your company is paying your expenses. Why don't you follow us back into town and you can look the boardinghouse over. They serve meals and will pack each man a lunch, if they desire one."

***

After dinner, Jack and Faith sat in the small parlor alone. "Pet, I was wondering if you would like to marry me again."

"What? Remarry, have a big wedding?" Faith stopped rocking and sat up straight. "Why would you want to do that?"

"For several months and many weeks, we have been courting, dancing around each other, touching, but not touching—" He watched the surprised look on her face. "I think it is time that we made our relationship real. We could have a big party. Your mama, the boys, the Parkers, the Masons...well, heck, the whole town could come." Jack smiled and his eyes were sparkling.

"Mercy." Faith sat for a quiet moment. "Couldn't the party be like a grand opening for the boardinghouse and then later . . . we could celebrate our wedding night?" Her face turned as red as her hair, but she softly said, "You know, Jack, when I said my wedding vows to you, I meant every word." With tears brimming behind her eyelids, she said, "I already loved you."

Jack lowered his tall frame next to the rocking chair. "I had no idea, my pet. I felt the same way about you, too." Jack bent over and kissed her soft lips. "The grand opening is a wonderful idea, especially following our own party." He kissed her lips softly. "Until our wedding night."

***

Excitement was in the air with the cooking for the big party. Sally had cleaned the largest room in the boardinghouse and placed clean linens and fresh flowers on the table. Tonight would be special for her two best friends. With the shy glances and hand holding, she knew things had changed between the two. She would keep Cherish with her and Ma and give the lovebirds some privacy.

After the party was over, Jack helped pack away the extra table and chairs. He walked Faith to the staircase and told her that he would be up in about thirty minutes. Sally smiled, and all the others ladies in the room smiled broadly, too. One would have thought the two old widows were going to have their first wedding night. Sally hurried to her room to check on Cherish and dressed for bed. She didn't want anything to disturb the sweet couple.

***

In due time, Jack came into the lovely bedroom and found the bed empty. He waited for a while and decided to get into the bed. In reality, his wife was like a virgin, since she didn't have a romantic night her first time with a man.

Slowly, the door opened, and Faith stood across the room in a lovely white silk night gown, made especially for tonight. He watched her for a moment and then patted the bed.

She lifted the covers, slipping in beside him. She didn't want him to jump on her like her first time with a man. Pulling the covers up to her chin, she rolled over on her side and faced her husband.

She felt his hand move toward her body. "Jack, have you made love with many other women?"

He appeared surprised by the question. "Certainly, hundreds," he finally answered.

"Oh you, be serious," she said punching him on the shoulder.

***

Jack pressed a strand of her curly red hair to his lips and tried to tickle his shaking wife under her nose with it. "A true gentleman never kisses and tells, my pet. You are the only woman in my bed now." He raised his eyebrows like a wicked man in the opera. "Faith, tell me. I want to hear you say the words. Please," he whispered, as he snuggled closer to her.

He had been with this beautiful young woman for months, and he had fallen in love with her the moment he held Cherish in his rough hands. Every time he was near her, he had to fight the desire to pull her into his arms and whisper his love for her. Jack longed to hear her repeat the same words back to him.

"I love you with all my heart," she said softly.

He covered her lips with his, but it wasn't a soft gentle kiss. Faith came to him with a demanding desire for more to come.

The End.

The Importance of Reviews

Reviews are the foundation of a good book. Please share your experience of meeting my beloved characters with others by placing a short review on Amazon or Facebook. Readers like to know that it's worth their time to read my book. Your opinion is the *voice* of my writing—good or bad. I appreciate your help with this. Just one line is enough. "Something like: Great story. I enjoyed this book, etc. You don't have to write a book. You can just read mine.

Linda Sealy Knowles is an historical-romance-western writer that brings her love stories and characters to life. She gives God the glory for her talent that has given her much joy and happiness. Since 2012, she has written ten novels. Linda is from Satsuma, Alabama but resides in Niceville, Florida, near her daughter, Kelli, and son, Pete, II. She has three lovely teenage granddaughters.

Other books by Linda Sealy Knowles

The Maxwell Saga (five books)
Journey to Heaven Knows Where
Hannah's Way
The Secret
Bud's Journey Home
Always Jess
***

Kathleen Sweetwater of Texas
Abbey's New Life
Sunflower Brides
Joy's Cowboy
Trapped by Love
The Gamble